The King in Darkness

Evan May

Renaissance

Cover art and design by Caroline Fréchette. Interior design by Caroline Fréchette. Edited by L.P. Vallée, Evelyn Cimesa, and Caroline Fréchette. Author photo by Rohit Saxena.

Legal deposit, Library and Archives Canada, October 2015.

Paperback ISBN 978-0-9936575-9-7
Ebook ISBN 978-1-987963-00-7

Renaissance Press
http://renaissancebookpress.com
info@renaissancebookpress.com

This book is dedicated to every friend, teacher, and family member who believed that I could be a writer of fiction and has been behind me in the pursuit of this dream. I am forever grateful for your support and apologize that it took quite this long to prove you right.

Chapter 1

It began with a book. In and of itself this would have been no surprise to Adam Godwinson. On that particular morning he arrived early at the premises of W.M. Howard, Bookseller, which was near enough to the eclectic merchant district of the ByWard market to benefit from tourist foot traffic but also near enough to suffer from deposits of things such as used hypodermic needles or pub-inspired vomit on the front step.

That morning, Adam discovered nothing more unpleasant than a cardboard yam box, now overflowing with an assortment of paperback books whose condition could most generously be described as 'well loved'. Someone had written 'Donation - Free!' on the box in black marker, along with a smiley face. Adam was not smiling as he unlocked the door to the shop and nudged the box over the threshold with his foot.

He had encountered many such boxes during his time at W.M. Howard, first as a part-time employee following a rather abrupt change of career, then full-time, then effectively running the store as the owner eased gradually towards retirement, and by now Walter (please, call me Walt) Howard had not been to the shop that was still notionally his in over a year. The subject of changing the name had never come up. Adam didn't feel like the store was his and certainly didn't feel like explaining a name change to its fairly modest pool of repeat customers.

However, in all that time Adam had never found any reason to smile about the 'donations' people insisted on leaving outside the shop, or, even more awkwardly, delivering in person. At best, the creased, faded, and broken-backed books delivered in this manner would make it onto the three books for $1 table that sat out on the sidewalk when weather permitted, though there was rarely any shortage of potential stock there. Most of them would end up in the recycling.

Adam switched on the lights by the door and briefly stooped over the box to determine whether it smelled strongly of cat pee or mildew, in which case it would go straight out the back door to the alley. Fortunately, this discarded collection was not offensive in that particular manner, anyway, and so he gave it a left-footed shove against the counter for now. Sorting through the yam box would be an alternative to playing FreeCell or answering email if customers declined to present themselves.

The door chimes gave a brassy jangle as the door shut, and Adam left the sign flipped to the 'Sorry: Closed, please call again' side as he went through the morning opening routine. The shop was not expansive: there was one large room at the front which contained about as many bookshelves as it was possible to pack into the place, as well as a short counter to the left for customer service. This was where the store did the bulk of its business: buying and, more ideally, selling used books in good condition for reasonable prices. Adam tried to keep the selection here restricted to recent fiction that had sold well, genuine classics, and non-fiction works on consistently popular subjects like World War II, gardening, and self-help. Usually, he found the multicoloured spines of the books on their wooden shelves, for Walt Howard had always insisted upon wood, gave the store a warm atmosphere, though Adam conceded that it might be necessary to like books to appreciate it.

A door opened to the left, behind which was a tiny office containing an ancient computer, several filing cabinets, and, most vitally, a coffee maker. Adam set about brewing the first of what would be many pots of coffee and considered the day ahead. It was too early yet for mail, and for once there were no bills demanding attention upon the battered desk which, along with a minuscule employee washroom, completed the behind the scenes world of W.M Howard, Bookseller.

In the rear wall of the main room, a second door led to a smaller back room which contained the rarer and more esoteric books that were much beloved by the store's founder and occasionally the subject of interest by collectors in search of biblio-treasures. These quests usually ended in disappointment, since neither Howard nor Adam had either a great deal of money or the connections necessary to get their hands on truly coveted volumes, but the old historical publications, travel books, near-forgotten novels and obscure poetry collections had their own charm for a certain kind of customer. Since it was sometimes this kind of customer who was likely to spend relatively significant amounts of money on books, the back library was worth maintaining. Another door to the left led down to a small, damp, basement, home to a somewhat reliable furnace, cleaning supplies, and shelves requiring repair.

A final door led from the back room to the alley, and it was this door that Adam now opened and stepped through, emerging next to a pair of metal garbage cans that had seen better days and a capacious plastic bin for paper recycling. There was no trash that needed throwing out — this having been done the previous evening — but Adam still liked to check the alleyway each morning. It had become a tradition after one occasion, when towards the end of the working day, he had gone to the recycling and discovered a modest-sized pool of blood and shards of glass on the store's back step. As he spent the next several hours in conversation with police officers, Adam had resolved to determine as early as possible exactly what kind of day he was going to be dealing with, and get such discoveries out of the way immediately.

This morning he found nothing especially horrible in the alley and returned to the front of the shop, now enhanced by the smell of fresh coffee and sunlight streaming through the front window. Adam turned on the rest of the shop's lights, activated the cash register, and flipped the sign to 'Open: Please come in!' before settling down behind the counter with an armload of books from the yam box.

He quickly set aside three Patricia Cornwells and a pair of Danielle Steeles for the three books for a dollar table; people did insist on buying them. A *7 Habits of Highly Effective People* was arguably sellable but there were three copies on the shelf already, so this went into a milk crate under the counter that served as one of the many overstock containers secreted in various nooks and crannies around the shop. Adam grimaced as the rest of the pile turned out to be novels based in the universes of a variety of video games which he doubted would leave an immortal mark in the literary canon, and at best might make a meaty thud when hurled into the recycling bin.

Adam polished his glasses on the bottom of his shirt and decided that cleaning the shop was a better option while waiting for the coffee to finish brewing than sorting the dubious donations from the yam box. He retrieved the broom from the back room to sweep and await the day's first customer. He had progressed to sweeping the back library when he heard the door chimes.

As usual, it seemed he recognized the smile before the rest of his visitor's face. It was a brilliant infectious grin that conveyed not only happiness and warmth, but a genuine delight at the happiness he engendered in others. So Adam found himself grinning back at his visitor, Napoleon Kale, who Adam had known since the young man was a six-year-old incapable of sitting still and who found the whole world amusing.

Once Napoleon and his friends had learned some history, he had soon attracted the nickname 'Bonaparte', and then 'Boney', 'Boneman', 'Bonesaw', and most recently just 'Bones'. He was dressed, as usual, in clothing that appeared to be wearing out, falling apart, or both, but had probably cost a lot to achieve the look.

Today the ensemble included a Montreal Expos t-shirt which, Adam was fairly sure, was younger than the team's move to Washington. Expos wear in general spiked in popularity following the demise of the actual baseball team, and although Adam was generally left bemused by fashion, this particular phenomenon was especially strange. He couldn't decide if it was, in some way, an act of mourning, a rebellious gesture, or if all those people in Expos hats and shirts just missed what they could no longer have. On some days he wondered whether a similar conscious affection for something whose day had passed was what brought people to places like W.M. Howard, Bookseller, instead of a website. It was best not to dwell on that, he found, if you were well on your way to becoming the owner of a used bookstore.

"Well that's not a paying customer," said Adam. "Hello, Bones."

"Hi, Father," Bones answered. "What's up?"

Chapter 2

"I have told you, Mr. Kale, that you don't have to call me that anymore," said Adam, still cheerfully. This had been the enduring script of their meetings for many years, now.

"Sorry sir, sorry. I just got used to it, you know," his visitor replied, grinning even more widely. Bones was enjoying his half of the exchange as much as always.

Adam rolled his eyes at the 'sir', leaned the broom in a corner, and headed for the office. He had never asked Napoleon, or any of the children at his former parish, to call him anything other than by name. Bones had always seemed to delight himself by ignoring requests to be more casual. "You'd think it might have stuck sometime over the last ten years, but I know you have a lot on your mind. Coffee?"

"Sure, sir, sure. So, how you doing these days? You staying out of trouble?"

Adam returned with two mugs and put them down on the counter, sat on the stool and shook his head slightly. "I think I'm supposed to be asking you that, aren't I?"

Prior to what Adam's career change —as he still thought of it — a dozen years ago, Bones had been a somewhat reluctant parishioner at a small church dedicated to St. Michael in Lowertown where Adam Godwinson had been the celebrant. It had been the church his parents brought him to when they moved to the city; he had grown up there with Adam as a spectator.

"Didn't you just say you don't do the 'father' thing these days? You ain't worried about me, are you?" Bones' grin suggested that he found the idea entertaining, and indeed once he had left school, Bones had rarely been in any kind of trouble. Most people liked him almost on sight, and of those that didn't, many came around after a brief conversation or two. Bones always wanted to hear what his friends were up to, and if he didn't enjoy it directly, he genuinely seemed to enjoy that they enjoyed it.

"Worried? No. On the other hand, you being out of bed, let alone out and about, before noon is a minor miracle, unless things have changed since we last talked. How's the music?" As usual, Bones had his guitar case with him, looking as if he had just bought it, although he'd had it for years. When he'd finally been able to get his own guitar in high school, he had treated both it and the case like precious treasures, and both stayed in astonishing condition.

"Oh pretty good, pretty good." Bones had horrified his parents when he decided to go full time with his band instead of going to college, but apparently did all right playing shows at a selection of bars and clubs around the city. "You should come check us out some time, Father."

"Yes, I'm sure I'd fit right in," Adam replied dryly, then occupied himself with his coffee.

"Aw come on! If you came out it'd be sick, you know it." Bones' band played reggae and island music, and Adam doubted that the audience trended much towards white middle-aged ex-priests, but he thought the invitations, made as a matter of course every time the two conversed, were probably genuine. Bones liked to play for everyone.

"One day I will call your bluff, Bones, and hopefully we'll both survive it." Inwardly, Adam accused himself of putting off going for far too long. He hadn't darkened the door of a nightclub for many years, but he knew Bones would appreciate it. He hadn't been out for quite a while, though, and perhaps that also needed correction.

"You just let me know when, sir, you just let me know when." Bones toyed with his coffee mug and kept nudging his backpack with one foot, then the other. Usually, Adam recalled, he had an amazing ability to seem completely at ease. Adam decided to help him along.

"All right. Now, did you honestly get up and down to the store before ten in the morning to update me on your music career, Mr. Kale?"

"Nah, well, not only that. I brought you something, something I think you might like," Bones explained, opening the backpack. He brought out a plastic bag which proved to contain a relatively large leather-bound book. It was about the size of a good dictionary, or a Bible, Adam thought immediately. "I picked this up the other day, and I thought you'd want to have at it."

"Did you indeed," asked Adam absently, gently pulling the plastic bag it was now sitting on to bring the book towards him. Its sandy brown binding was wearing towards white at the corners and spine, suggesting years of touches and handling. It looked to be several hundred pages thick — folios, Adam corrected himself internally, given the book's apparent age. There was nothing printed on the cover he could see, nor on the spine. Only two white letters: KD16.

Using both hands, Adam picked up the book and lightly ran his fingers over the binding. "Where did you pick this up, Bones?" It certainly looked and felt old, and not like a novelty item or reproduction, although Adam always acknowledged his lack of formal training along those lines. He had picked up a bit working with Walt Howard and, before that, a little at university, but he was certainly no expert.

"I was at this estate sale my girlfriend took me too, you know? It looked like your kind of thing, so I figured I'd grab it, see what you thought about it, that's all." Bones seemed to be enjoying himself.

"I'm not sure how well your band is doing, exactly, but I hope you didn't spend your rent money. It's fairly old, as far as I can tell." Adam's concern was genuine. Last time he had visited Bones at home, it had been a one room apartment in a fairly run-down part of Lowertown. Then again, he hadn't visited in a while.

"Oh yeah?" The grin blazed back into life. "What do you know about that?" The question of cost went unanswered, and Adam knew better than to push the issue. Picking up the cheque when you went to lunch with Bones was usually an impossible mission, and although he would lend money without any questions he would rarely accept repayment.

"The binding is Victorian, I think, or a good reproduction. But the pages... well, they're paper, but it seems quite old. Older than the binding, certainly. What did they tell you this book was, Mr. Kale?"

"They didn't, Father. It was just a lot number that came up and I thought of you when I saw it. Actually I was kinda hoping you could tell me something about it."

"It's ... very strange," said Adam, leafing through the first few folios. "It's handwritten, and the ink makes it look very old too. However..." He paused, looking at page after page of spidery script. "It isn't English, obviously. It isn't French either, or Latin, or Greek, as far as I can tell. I honestly don't recognize the script at all."

"Seriously? Some kind of mystery then, Father?" Bones seemed pleased.

"Well, it is to me, right now. Probably not if a little research is done, though, or if we have some other people look at it."

"If that's what you think, Father," said Bones, smiling broadly. Adam watched the smile bloom and decided that the book might not have been entirely an impulse buy, and that Bones was enjoying seeing him interested in something other than sorting yam boxes of paperbacks. Bones had always been quietly unhappy with Adam's change of career, and especially the job he had ended up with.

"I'll need some time to work on it, though. Maybe a few days, if it isn't urgent." It was difficult to see how it could be urgent, but on the off chance Bones was hoping the book was valuable, and needed the money, it would be good to know that before starting. Knowing whether or not Bones was in need of money was the sort of thing Adam would once have known as a matter of course, and he chided himself inwardly for not being sure about it now.

"No, sir, you do what you need to do," Bones replied. "I'd like to know what you come up with though, when you've got something, you know." Adam considered for a few moments. The book was clearly unusual, and the writing was completely unfamiliar. It really would take a bit of work to even figure out where to start, although he did know who to visit with his unexpected problem first.

"It would also be useful to know what sort of estate sale you found this at," Adam observed, anticipating a question he knew he would inevitably be asked himself. "If I knew the owner was a Renaissance collector, or something like that, it might get things started."

Bones nodded agreeably. "Trouble is I don't really know, you know? It was some rich dude lived in Rockcliffe, I guess it was in the paper or something. Anyway Bella likes old furniture these days, so we went by, and I got to looking at stuff and thought this was maybe your thing," he explained. Bella was not the girlfriend Adam remembered, but he wasn't sure when they'd last discussed the subject. "You OK to look at it a bit?" Bones said this last perhaps a bit hopefully.

"Let's see ... it's Friday today, I'll have to watch the store tomorrow, but Sunday and Monday we're closed and I can see what I can find out for you. Unless you'd like to work on it as well, of course." Adam took a touch of pleasure in watching Bones squirm just a little. He had never been at home in the classroom and, although Adam was fairly sure he was pleased to have provided a puzzle to work on, he really wouldn't want to have to help solve it.

"Nah, sir, nah, not really my wheelhouse, you know? I'll come back by Tuesday and see what you got though?"

"All right. Is ten too early a start for you?"

"Sounds good, Father. Talk to you about it then."

"You have a good show tonight, Bones." As Napoleon left, Adam opened the book again, towards the middle, exposing more pages of odd, crabbed writing in ink that had long since faded to brown. There were no illustrations, no notes in the margins, just line after relentless line of characters that were almost, but not quite, letters he recognized, that could almost, but not quite, be made into words.

Even so, beneath his notice, the morning trickled away as he puzzled over the pages, leaving Adam tired, hungry, and thoroughly dissatisfied.

Chapter 3

Adam took the book home with him, deciding that, although W.M. Howard, Bookseller, did have a locking under-counter cabinet, it wasn't anything really secure and there was at least some chance that Bones' discovery had some value to it. It was certainly old, unless it was a reproduction of some kind, but old did not necessarily mean it was especially valuable. Piles of family Bibles, kept through the generations, yet worth essentially nothing to anyone who was not related to the names inscribed inside the front cover, were testimony to that. Adam occasionally had to send people away from the store with this disappointing verdict on what they were sure was a retirement package or cruise vacation unearthed from a relative's attic or bedside table.

Friday night, he went through the entire thing, cover to cover. There was nothing whatsoever to give it any context — not a drawing, table, or notation anywhere to break up the ranks of indecipherable text. There was not even numbering on the folios. Without having any way to know what had been written, the question of completeness was more or less irrelevant, but it would at least be useful to know that they were in the original order. The binding was certainly in good shape, though, which suggested the book had been kept with care, and that nothing had fallen out in the recent past.

He tried holding the text up to a mirror, and turning the book 'upside down', not really believing that the problem was likely to be that simple, but not to have checked might come back to haunt him later. None of this provided any revelations, and Adam ended the evening quite uncertain what the 'correct' orientation of the book even was.

On Saturday he brought it back to work with him, although originally he had planned to leave it at home rather than risking damaging it or losing it by carrying it around unnecessarily. In the end he decided that there might be time to look at it a bit during the day and it would be a pity not to take advantage. As it happened, the store was unusually busy, and by the end of it Adam had spent little time puzzling over the book.

On Sunday, he took Bones' discovery to the closest thing to an expert he knew. Along with training as a priest, Adam had studied theology. His thesis supervisor still lived in the city and was usually very pleased to have a former student drop by. Adam therefore took his strange treasure to the Sandy Hill home of Dr. Todd Marchale, still an active professor in religious studies despite a long-expressed longing for retirement.

Adam hadn't visited in a while, but Marchale had very little patience for small talk, so they focused on the book fairly quickly. "You got this where, again? One of your church kids brought it in to you?" Marchale asked this as though the whole idea was ridiculous, but Adam had learned early in their relationship that his supervisor virtually always seemed to think everything was an annoying waste of time. You could tell when he when he had really lost interest when he stopped paying any attention at all. Up until then, if it was difficult swimming against a tide of sarcasm, at least he was nearly as critical of his own ideas as he was of his students.

"That's right. He said he got it at an estate sale, and I think he was trying to give me something to do," Adam explained, scratching one of Marchale's platoon of cats behind the ears. They were a universally plump and spoiled bunch whose population had fluctuated significantly over the years, but Marchale's devotion to the beasts was constant.

Marchale was wearing what he virtually always did: a dress shirt — blue or grey, in this case blue — and black pants. Also, as usual, Adam briefly caught a strong unwashed odor from him. He had never been able to determine if Marchale simply forgot to bathe regularly, if it was part of some issue with saving water, or possibly deliberate disdain for social conventions. It didn't seem to be the sort of question it was possible to ask, so Adam simply prepared himself for Marchale's aroma whenever they had a conversation, and tried not to show any reaction to it.

Sometimes he wondered if that was the point of it all — how offensive could Marchale be and still have people pretend they didn't notice?

"Something to do? I thought you were quite busy selling romance novels?" Marchale glared accusingly at Adam and, receiving no contradiction, let out a disgusted noise. "Had I but known that what you really wanted in life was to hawk Tom Clancy books, I could have saved us both a great deal of time, booted you out without having to read that bloody thesis, and all the rest of it." This was an old issue and, in this case, Adam suspected his old professor's disapproval was probably genuine.

Adam started to deploy the opening of a well-rehearsed and well-practiced explanation. "When I decided to leave the church," he said, only to be cut off by another noise of annoyed disgust. Marchale was shaking his head dismissively.

"I don't care if you're not preaching, you fool," Marchale said derisively. "But why you aren't researching, I'll never understand. Could even be making yourself useful around here, stick you in front of a classroom. I seem to recall you're not a complete idiot." In fact he had offered Adam several research assistantships over the years, but Adam had always felt these should go to graduate students working on their studies, when the need for money was usually pretty acute. Ex-students abandoning their post-graduation careers should fend for themselves.

"Well, never mind, let's have a look at what you brought with you," Marchale relented, turning his attention back to the book. He set it on a wooden book stand, and, opening it apparently at random, weighted the pages with a long snaky length of fabric containing lead weights. He scowled at the text for several minutes before looking back in Adam's direction. "Weird bloody thing, isn't it?"

"That's exactly the kind of insight I was hoping you'd have for me, professor," Adam said with a smile, and was rewarded with a short bark of laughter. Marchale enjoyed being skewered almost as much as he enjoyed doing the skewering. He picked up a much-abused pipe, and started filling it with tobacco, then seemed to think better of it and discarded it among a pile of papers awaiting grading. Marchale's students often waited a while to get their work back, and then, in many cases, wished that they hadn't.

"Well it is bloody weird," he insisted. "Not in any flavour of English or French, as I assume you were able to realize. Not Latin, not German, Italian, or any other damned thing I've seen before. Not the original binding, of course, that looks Victorian, but the text itself is much older, late medieval from the look of it, unless it's all a damned fake and made last Wednesday. Which I don't think it is."

"All right, so what next?" When Adam had worked with Walt Howard on books in the back library, they had never had to deal with an unidentified volume. The question was always determining what printing a work was, whether it was in worthwhile condition and, very occasionally, if it was genuine. This was an entirely different sort of problem.

"What next? Not bloody much. Binding's no help, doubt it's got anything to do with British and Irish law somehow." Marchale looked up expectantly, lightly drumming his fingers on the edge of his desk.

"I'm sorry?" The professor's train of thought was prone to veering off in unexpected and unannounced directions, to the consternation of many of his students. For Adam, this had made for more than one difficult supervisory session and more than one evening spent puzzling over comments on a thesis draft.

"KD! On the spine, you fool. Library of Congress subject heading," Marchale cried. "Completely useless, of course. Probably some private kind of shelf mark that tells us nothing whatsoever." His tone now suggested deep scorn for the idea that anyone might have thought otherwise. "If we knew who owned the damned thing, prior to your parishioner of course, we might make some headway but of course you've no bloody idea."

"Do you have any idea about the writing, though?" Adam asked. "It looks almost like something I should be able to figure out."

"It does, doesn't it?" Marchale agreed, sounding reluctant to admit it. "There's a few books like this, of course, ones no one can read these days. That Voynich thing, a few others. Of course this is much less interesting, no drawings or what have you," he added darkly. "It could be in code. If it's just a substitution even you'd work it out in no time."

"Substitution?" Adam asked. "Codes have never really been my thing." Marchale shook his head as if amazed at his former student's ignorance.

"Z for A, Y for B, that sort of thing. Do it with numbers of course, pictures even. Haven't you read your 'Dancing Men'?" Marchale scowled at the text again. "Anyway it's almost certainly not that easy. Simplest code in the book, so to speak, and you know perfectly well that your writer here is probably a clever bloody fellow. Might get something if you gave it to one of those cryptography fellows," he observed, making a vague motion with one hand, "but who the hell knows. Like I said, some of these things have never been figured out."

"But what sort of book needs to be in code?" Adam asked. "This is, what, a book of 16th century classified files? In a library in Canada?"

"Could be any damned thing," Marchale explained. "Could just be some fool's diary, put in code so no one could read about his longing for the milkmaid and because it made him feel bloody clever. Could be research, I suppose, make sure no one steals it. Could be any damned thing someone thought had been difficult to find out and didn't want anyone else to make free with. Never know until you figure out how to read it."

"All right. So let's pretend for a moment that this was a problem you were interested in," said Adam. Marchale grinned widely — Adam knew perfectly well that if he wasn't interested, the conversation would have been over in about a minute and a half. "What would you do next?"

"Well, what I would do next is stop being so damned lazy and find out who owned the thing," Marchale declared. "You said the sale was in the paper? Well then, I hear there's a strange sort of place where they have newspapers, whole series of them, going back days and days. Library or something? If you knew who owned it, we might have a clue as to what they studied, what they collected, might have a hint as to what this," he tapped the book lightly, "is. Other than that, I suppose leave it with me a few days. I'll show it to a few people 'round the department, maybe someone will have a bright idea." Another dark expression showed that he very much doubted it. "That all right?"

"I'd be very grateful," Adam agreed. "I'll call you later in the week and see if we're any the wiser?" Marchale laughed with genuine delight.

"Oh, well, I doubt that, doubt it extremely," he said. "Known you what, seventeen years, you're still as thick as the day I met you. So am I, of course. Anyway, yes, at least a couple of people should have cast their eyes on it by then."

"I really do appreciate it, Professor," said Adam, getting up to leave. He supposed a lengthy bout with back issues of the Ottawa Citizen was inevitable now. "I know you're busy."

"Oh, well, I've been waiting for a time when I won't be busy for forty years," Marchale replied. "Never mind, never mind. If you bring by everything that confuses you I'll never see the back of you, but you could visit a bit more often, you know. You can occasionally make intelligent conversation and Lord knows I'm starved for it."

Chapter 4

By Tuesday afternoon, Adam was in a foul mood. He had spent a long day Monday, first with Ottawa newspapers, eventually discovering that the previous week, there had been an advertisement for a sale of the estate of Charles Hope Warrington, lately a resident of Cloverdale Road, which would be open to the public. The rest of the day had been spent trying to find out anything about Charles Hope Warrington that might shed some light on the book he had once, presumably, owned, and was now hopefully being examined by some of Professor Marchale's colleagues. By late that afternoon Adam hadn't learned a thing and, thoroughly tired of the library, had called it a day.

Still, there was a little bit to tell Bones about, and that was the real reason why Adam was annoyed, for ten o'clock had come and gone, in fact it was now going on for two, and there was no sign of Napoleon Kale. This had always been the problem with him, Adam fumed, dumping the last contents of the yam box into the recycling bin. He had no regard for schedules — other people's, or his own, — and would turn up for things whenever it suited him, or not at all, if something diverted him, which was not a difficult thing to do. Adam slammed down the lid of the bin (unfortunately it was made of plastic and did not make for a satisfying slamming experience) and then the back door of the shop (which was made of metal, and did) and tried to forget about it. But damn it anyway, he had spent both his days off running around after this book of Bones' and now he couldn't be bothered to turn up when he was supposed to talk about the damned thing.

Adam was startled out of his annoyed musings when the phone rang. He answered, and recognized the voice immediately, which did a lot to allay his mood, for it was another member of his former parish, who had been about Bones' age and part of a group of young people their priest had tried to cultivate. "Hello, Sophia, it's good to hear from you."

Sophia Beaudry, he realized, sounded anything but cheerful. "I'm afraid it's bad news, Father," she said. "I'm at the Civic Hospital. We think you should come down here."

Adam began to feel an unpleasant tingling sensation in his stomach. "Why, what's happened?"

"It's Napoleon, Father," said Sophia, and now he could hear the tears in her voice. "He was beat up last night, it's really bad."

"I..." Adam found his mouth suddenly very dry. "I'll be there as soon as I can."

It took the better part of half an hour to get to the hospital and get directions to where Bones was — still in the intensive care ward, although it was possible to visit. Adam hurried over, hoping to be able to speak to one of the doctors treating Bones. There were no doctors or nurses in the room, though — just four people, and a young man in hospital bed.

He was attached, it seemed, to far too many machines. From visiting parishioners in hospital, he knew that the setup was actually fairly standard, but it didn't seem that way when attached to someone he knew so well. Or was supposed to know well. What could Bones have possibly been doing that got him so badly injured?

Most of his body was covered by sheets, of course, and his face was partly covered by an oxygen mask and gauze but, even so, it was obvious Bones had taken a beating. The flesh around one eye was swollen and deeply bruised, and, judging from the bandage, there was a large cut across the bridge of his nose. Bones was not awake, and Adam did not know whether this meant he was sedated or simply unconscious. Either option was worrying.

Gradually, Adam took stock of the other people in the room. Sophia was there, of course, along with Jane and Fred, two other members of that little circle of friends and former members of the Fridays Guild. They would be there, of course. The last person was a middle-aged man with a close-cropped dark haircut and a grey suit that Adam didn't recognize. It was entirely possible, he supposed, that this was an acquaintance of Bones that he hadn't met, but it seemed unlikely that a worried friend would be writing steadily in a black leather notebook. Adam supposed his arrival might have interrupted an interview.

"I'm sorry, but I don't think we've been introduced," Adam began, mentally arranging some arguments in case the man turned out to be a reporter. Surely he could satisfy himself and the demands of his story with the details available from the police, and leave the patient's friends in peace. The man finished the sentence he was writing, flipped his notebook shut with a quick motion of one wrist, and transferred his attention to Adam.

"Inspector John Kolb," he said, flicking a tight little smile on and off for a heartbeat. "Major Crimes Unit. I was just getting some background from Mr. Kale's friends here. They mentioned you might be dropping by. Perhaps we could have a word?" He nodded towards the hallway. An interview then, but not the kind Adam had imagined.

"You'll forgive me, but I'm a little surprised to have someone as high up the food chain as you here," said Adam, leaning back against the wall. The smile flicked back on and off, and the notebook flipped back open. A pen, either silver or steel, was clicked into readiness.

"Contrary to popular belief, we do take armed assaults on citizens quite seriously, Mr. Godwinson," Kolb replied firmly. "It's also a possibility that this will be investigated as a hate crime, so if you prefer to be cynical you can think of me as getting ahead of the game regarding that contingency." Another momentary smile punctuated this last.

"A hate crime?" The idea of someone hating Bones Kale seemed thoroughly ridiculous, but of course that wasn't what was meant by a hate crime. We like to think that we don't have those kinds of problems here in Canada, in a city like Ottawa, Adam mused, but that was a comforting fiction. Perhaps it was one those people who don't have to worry about being the victim of hatred told themselves.

"Potentially. Young black male, isolated victim, perpetrators who had clearly prepared in advance of the offense," Kolb was consulting his notebook as he spoke. "As of yet we have nothing to indicate a motive specific to the victim. Robbery seems unlikely from the manner of the attack. Racial motivation is certainly plausible."

"I've just arrived, as you saw, and I don't know any details, Inspector — what do you mean by manner of the attack?" Adam wasn't sure he really wanted to know, but knowing the particulars of problems afflicting parishioners had once been his responsibility, and even many years later it was easy to fall back into the well-worn habit.

Kolb seemed to consider for a few moments. "That information is likely to be on the news by this evening, if not earlier, so I suppose you may as well get it from me. The victim — Mr. Kale — was walking alone on Frank St. when a white van pulled up beside him. Three suspects exited the van — we believe the driver remained inside — and then attacked the victim with blunt instruments — at this stage we hypothesize either bats or pipes. They took his wallet and a guitar in a black case, and then fled the scene in the vehicle. We have one witness who was across the street and several blocks away, who called 911."

"But you don't think it was a robbery?" Bones had never been in trouble, not serious trouble, for as long as Adam had known him. Music and his friends occupied the lion's share of his attention, and although it was, with effort, possible to make him angry, Bones had always been a natural peacemaker, smoothing things over between children at the church, and never a fighter.

"In my experience, Father, muggers don't operate out of vehicles and tend not to use this level of violence. I regard it as an unlikely explanation, although we believe Mr. Kale was probably carrying a fairly large amount of cash at the time," Kolb explained. The cash, of course, would have been from the gig Bones had just finished. Bands were usually paid in cash and he would have been on his way home with his share. Why couldn't he have gotten a lift with someone?

"You don't need to call me Father," said Adam absently. "He'll be heartbroken about the guitar." The story of the young person scrupulously saving money from a variety of odd jobs was something of a cliché, but it was also true in Bones' case. Adam remembered him putting money away for at least a year, always refusing to take assistance and turning down loans, until Bones was finally able to get the one he had his eye on.

"I'm very sorry, sir. Now, since I've shared my information, perhaps you could answer a few questions for me?" Kolb's bright eyes were now fixed on Adam, apparently ready to gauge reactions and analyze responses.

"Yes, fine, although I'm not sure," Adam began. He had really spent so little time with Bones lately; he hadn't even known he was seeing a different girl. So much for keeping touch.

"It won't take long," Kolb assured him smoothly. "Now, you're no longer religious?" When Adam didn't immediately reply, he went on. "You said not to call you 'Father'." The smile flickered back for a moment, perhaps a little apologetically, as he revealed the deduction.

"Yes, well, I left the church some time ago," Adam answered. "I suppose these days I'm sort of non-denominational, but I haven't been a priest in a long time." Neither Bones, nor any of the other Guild members, had been very happy with that, but some things can't be helped, Adam had reassured himself. Things like being attacked on the street.

"But you knew the victim, and his friends, through the church?" The manner of the questioning gave nothing away — whether they were background information, if he was establishing a baseline to evaluate Adam's answers to later questions, or if he thought the church was somehow relevant. Adam reflected that Inspector Kolb must be a good card player.

"Yes, yes, they were all members of my parish when they were young."

"You've kept in touch since then?" Kolb's pen was moving quickly, it seemed to Adam that he must be writing a great deal more than the answers he was getting. What could he possibly be concluding from this?

"Intermittently. Not as much as I should, I suppose. I didn't want to impose myself." Would keeping in closer touch have made any difference last night? Adam supposed not, and yet somehow guilt was a lead weight in his gut.

Kolb nodded, perhaps a little impatiently. "I see. So prior to this, when had you last spoken with the victim?" The writing had been paused, but the gleaming nib of the pen was poised and ready.

"Friday, as it happens. He visited me at work, unexpectedly." Again, that seemed impossibly long ago. Everything had receded into the background after Sophia's phone call and the sight of Bones intubated and electronically monitored in the hospital bed.

"Was there a problem? Something he wanted advice about, possibly?" Kolb's writing paused again as he offered an explanation. "If there was anyone giving him a hard time, or if he was in money trouble, that would be potentially useful information to have."

"No, nothing like that," Adam replied, fretting with his watch band. "If anything, I think he was worried about me. Keeping to myself too much, getting in a rut, that sort of thing. He wanted me to come to one of his shows, you see."

"And before that?" The policeman was now, it seemed, running through an almost automatic list of questions. Adam had done it himself occasionally, when he wanted time to decide what he thought about someone and needed to keep them talking more than he needed information. Couples who wanted to get married at the church, in particular — were they serious, or frivolous, were they in it together, or was one pulling the chain.

"I'm sorry?" Adam was still trying, inwardly, to convince himself that there was no reason to think last night would have gone differently if he had been at Bones' show. Perhaps they would have left together, and perhaps Bones would not have been alone when the van pulled up. Perhaps that wouldn't have made any difference at all.

"Before last Friday, when was the last time you had seen the victim?" Kolb elaborated patiently, most likely a well-practiced skill for extracting information from the distracted and the confused. Adam recognized that he was only devoting part of his attention to the inspector's questions; the rest was scouring his memory to see if there had been any indication from Bones that he might have been in some sort of trouble.

"Oh, more than a month at least. Maybe longer." Possibly considerably longer, Adam reflected. In fact, he wasn't completely sure when he had seen Bones before last Friday, which was certainly not the way things had worked in the past.

"I see." The pen hurried across the pages of the notepad. Again, what he was finding to fill the pages from these responses was a bit of a puzzle. Adam wondered now if he was taking notes at all, or just using the time to write down his own thoughts about the case.

"Is there something I should know, Inspector?" Adam inquired. The policeman certainly appeared to have plenty on his mind, and it didn't make sense that it had anything to do with Adam.

"I have nothing I can share with you at this time, Mr. Godwinson," Kolb said. The smile flicked back on and off. "The case will get my full attention, and you'll be informed of developments when it's possible to do so." The notebook flicked shut again.

"Thank you, Inspector," Adam replied. "I'm sorry if I offended you, earlier."

"Not at all. I know these are difficult situations. Thank you for your time, Mr. Godwinson," Kolb said smoothly, "and I am sorry about your friend."

Adam nodded in acknowledgement and returned to the hospital room. Sophia, Fred, and Jane had all been children at his old church. They had all been around the same age and just old enough to want adults to take them a little seriously. As they got older, to the point where young people start developing their own interests, Adam had tried to make the church a more comfortable fit into young peoples' lives and so he had started a youth group, the Fridays Guild, of which they, Bones, and a few others had been the core members.

The Fridays Guild would meet for pizza or chicken wings or a barbeque at least once a month, and Adam was always very careful not to preach at these gatherings. Instead they would spend time talking about whatever the kids had on their mind that day, share a meal, and occasionally, he would offer some general advice. The club was justified in the parish budget by the little pieces of work that would also be done at meetings: rolling change from donation boxes, sorting through the clothes dropped off at the church for the homeless shelter, arranging materials for the annual garage sale. Accomplishing these tasks was always just an excuse in Adam's mind, though — the real point had been for the children to be in each other's company, to talk, and to enjoy being a part of a church community.

With some of the parish children the Fridays Guild had never worked, or they had joined for a while and then dropped away. Adam was also very careful never to make an issue of this when it happened, although he tried to make it clear that anyone was always welcome back. A few of them, though, had made the meetings very much a part of their lives and kept attending Fridays Guild gatherings right up until Adam's change of career.

Adam thanked Sophia for calling him and took a moment to greet the other two children, or young people, he supposed he should think of them. Jane Moore was one of Sophia's closest friends, all through school and afterwards. Adam had been at her graduation from journalism school at Concordia University in Montreal, after which she had moved back to Ottawa and found work at one of the local papers. Adam was surprised, and a little disappointed, that he couldn't remember which one, but perhaps she had changed recently, or possibly she even freelanced?

Fred Wallace was, at least occasionally, a computer science student at Carleton University, although he kept taking time away from his studies to pursue a hobby that verged on becoming a career — stage magic. Adam and Fred's parents had, at first, been amused to see the smallish, shy boy blossom into 'Alfred the Astounding', who delighted in being in center of attention as long as he was making things disappear or reading minds. Eventually, they did become concerned at how much of his attention sleight of hand and escapology was taking. Several years ago, Adam and Fred's parents had agreed that he would probably grow out of it. Since then, though, Fred had switched from full to part-time at the university, a decision motivated by wanting to take on bookings for performances and study more tricks. The issue, Adam knew, remained unresolved.

All three of them were visibly upset, and just as visibly had been at the hospital for some time. Adam asked what they had heard about Bones' condition, so far. "His doctor was in a little while ago, talking to that detective," Sophia explained. "He said Napoleon has a hematoma on his brain, skull fractures, broken ribs — who would do this?"

"The inspector told me he thinks it might be a hate crime," said Adam quietly. "I suppose that might explain the violence."

"We would have called you sooner, but no one could find the number for the store," said Sophia tearfully. "I'm sorry."

"It's all right," Adam assured her. "I'm here now, and that's the important part." It seemed hard to believe that they hadn't known which number to call, but he supposed they hadn't needed to use it very often. "When did you hear?"

"Bella called as soon as they brought him here," Jane explained. "She was here all night, we just convinced her to go home and get some rest. You know how she is." Adam decided not to mention that he had, in fact, never met Bones' current girlfriend.

"And you've been here all day?" he asked instead. "Someone needs to give you a break as well."

"When Bones wakes up, we all want to be sure someone is with him," Sophia explained. "Bella will be back soon but for now this is where we all want to be."

"He'll appreciate it, you know that," said Adam. "On the other hand now that I'm here as well perhaps you could give yourselves a break? Have you eaten?"

"It's all right, Father," Fred assured him, "I made a run to the cafeteria a while ago and they have something like food there. Actually, it's been useful having a bunch of us here, sort of keeps it all on an even keel, you know?"

"My word, Fred," said Adam with apparent astonishment, "Someone taught you well."

"Yeah, I'll introduce you sometime," replied Fred with a little smile.

"Now that we are all here," Sophia announced, "I'll go and get some coffee and things — that cafeteria food was a while ago. We might be here a long time before the doctor comes back."

"Or a nurse," Fred suggested, with a mischievous little smile.

"Can you be serious?" Sophia demanded.

"It's all right," Adam said calmly. "There's nothing wrong with a sense of humour at times like this, as long as it's in the right taste." He offered this last comment looking steadily at Fred.

"Well, in that case, Freddie is going to have to be very quiet," Jane suggested sweetly.

Fred was clearly about to offer some rejoinder, so Adam headed him off. "I was going to go and help Sophia with the coffee, but perhaps you two can't be left alone," he said firmly.

"No, it's cool, Father," Fred replied in a somewhat chastened tone. "Sorry, I'm just trying to lighten the mood, you know." One thing that had always been a comfort about the members of the Guild was that their good intentions were never in question, and although they bickered occasionally, all of them understood that.

"Never mind," Adam answered. "What does everyone take in their coffee?" In fact he was looking forward to a moment to catch up with Sophia. She had sounded very upset on the phone, but now seemed much more composed. Perhaps having the whole group together was a sufficient comfort, but Adam was also hoping for her insight into how the others were handling the situation. She had clearly been in closer touch with them than he had.

Sophia had been the Guild member who came to Adam for advice the most; whether it was because she genuinely needed it or just appreciated another point of view was something he had been unable to decide. She had never been very interested in a lot of subjects at school, and he had worked hard to keep her from giving it up entirely. It wasn't a question of ability; Sophia was bright and had a particular gift for figuring out how things worked.

Adam had given her several clocks and old radios leftover from church garage sales to take apart, but had had to disappoint her by preventing her from disassembling the organ. At the time he had been pleased that he had suggested enough ways for her to find applications for those interests in her courses that she had gotten through high school and applied to university.

Advice about school had been the easy part. Adam vividly remembered the day Sophia had come to his little office at St. Michael's to tell him she had a girlfriend. She was 17 and just finding herself in the world and he had been genuinely touched that she sought his advice. He knew what he was supposed to say, there in the church office, but in the end he had said what he wanted to instead.

Adam had told her that everyone who loved her would want her to find love herself in whatever way suited her. He had told her that she was brave and that he was glad she had discovered her way to be happy. He had told her that God is love, embraced her fondly, and told her not to be late for choir practice.

Looking back, he wondered if that had been the beginning of his change of career, and certainly there had been a few members of the parish who had started to have a slightly different tone in their voices when they spoke to him, and have a little different set to their face when they thought he wasn't looking, but perhaps he had imagined it after all. Sophia had stopped coming to church not long afterwards and, although she had never talked with him about it, Adam was fairly sure he understood why. So many parishioners mentioned to him that they missed her, and so did he, but he also knew that a few of them who sat in the pews every Sunday felt they had done something good in pushing her out, and he had never really been able to forgive them for that, or feel the same way about the church community afterwards.

Fortunately, Sophia had kept coming to Fridays Guild meetings, when they were at Adam's house or a restaurant, and she still sought his advice from time to time, a gift of trust for which he was profoundly grateful. Even after he left the church, she had phoned him from Montreal to ask what he thought about her dropping out of university, and Adam had listened and known that what she really needed was someone to tell her it was ok to leave if it wasn't working out for her, and that it wasn't quitting as much as it was changing direction.

The next thing he had heard was that she was joining the army, which had been a surprise because Sophia had always seemed to have a peaceful soul. She had always been another peacemaker among the children at St. Michael's, eager for arguments to be over and fissures in the group repaired. As she had grown up in this role, Adam sometimes didn't find out about problems between young people at the parish at all until they had already been solved.

"Sometimes people out there need someone to help them," she had explained. "This is the best way I can think of to be that someone." As it turned out, the decision had been good; Sophia had loved the physical challenges of the military, and the structure seemed to give her confidence and certainty of purpose. There had also been an outlet for her love of building and fixing things. Adam had received a very proud letter from her when she was accepted for training as a combat engineer. He still kept it in his desk at home.

It wasn't a surprise, then, that it had been Sophia who had tracked him down and let him know that Bones was in hospital, and started organizing the other Guild members into shifts that would stay with their friend for as long as he needed it.

Adam and Sophia bought everyone's orders and a little food to go with them. When they arrived, there was a slightly awkward silence in the room, and Adam thought it looked like Jane was trying very hard not to cry. "Did something happen," he asked. "Was the doctor here?"

"No," Jane replied, her voice thick with emotion, "It's nothing." Fred gave Adam a helpless look from his chair by the bedside.

"It isn't nothing," Adam objected softly, "and there's no reason to pretend that it is. Our friend is seriously hurt, and it would be very strange if we weren't upset by that." Sophia moved quietly around the room, distributing coffee and muffins.

"It's not helping anything to be crying like an idiot," Jane said forcefully.

"Hey, if that's what you need to do, then that's what you need to do," Fred spoke up. "No point in feeling bad about it."

Adam smiled and put his hand on Jane's shoulder. "Mr. Wallace is right, on this occasion at least," he said. "No need to punish ourselves for our reactions. However, it's also not a bad idea to try to focus our attention on something other than worrying." Or feeling guilty, he added to himself. "I haven't seen as much of Bones recently as I would have liked. Why don't you all tell me how he's been keeping busy?"

After a little hesitation, Adam heard the story of Bones' search for a new apartment, and second hand accounts of apartment horror stories, and his new tactics for getting better bookings for his band. Before long, they were all trading favorite Napoleon Kale stories, and probably because he was such an upbeat person, most of the stories were that way as well, and the mood in the room lightened quickly.

Eventually a nurse arrived to check on Bones' vital signs. She had no new information for them, and emphasized that his condition was very serious, but also explained that he didn't appear to be in immediate danger. Recovery was expected to take some time, however.

They thanked her for the update and sat quietly watching their friend for a while. Eventually Adam checked his watch and discovered that it was getting late in the afternoon. Bringing everyone together and making sure they were all aware of the situation had been the right thing to do, and it was undeniably comforting, but he also knew that it wasn't sustainable. The bedside of a seriously ill or injured person was a difficult place to be and it was easy to exhaust oneself under the weight of concern and foreboding.

"You're all handling this very well, I think," observed Adam. "But you won't be able to continue to do that if you don't take care of yourselves as well. We don't all need to be here all the time. Take some time away, make sure you eat properly — more than coffee and hospital food, please. Go to work so you don't get fired. Make sure you're taking care of your own stuff or you can't take care of anyone else." It was a little surprising how easily the old discourse came back into action, Adam reflected.

"Father, I know it's a strange time to ask, but there was something," Jane began, and then trailed off.

"You can ask me anything you want if you promise to stop calling me 'Father', Jane," said Adam mildly. "That was a long time ago."

"Not that long ago," she smiled, "and if you're just another of my friends then I'm going to ask you to do something for me like I ask all of them."

"Oh no," said Fred with mock alarm, "I know what this is and you should've started running thirty seconds ago."

"You have no idea what this is, Alfred," Jane shot back.

"Oh, but I do," he grinned. "She's going to drag you to some horrible speech she's supposed to cover." It was good to see them joking with each other, Adam thought, and Jane doing her work would probably help keep her mind off of Napoleon.

Adam regarded Jane with assumed severity. "Are you planning on dragging me somewhere horrible, Jane?"

"No, of course not," she insisted. "Freddie always exaggerates, you know that! I do have something tonight that I'm supposed to do a story on and I just don't like going alone. Some people," she added with a sharp look at Fred, "said they didn't mind keeping me company but I guess they didn't really mean it."

"I'm always happy to keep you company," said Adam. It had been a long enough, he reflected, since he had really done that for Jane, or any of the other Guild members. Whatever it was would probably distract him as well. "Where are we going, exactly?"

"Louis Flambard is giving a speech at the Shaw Centre tonight. If I'm lucky I might be able to get a quick interview as well!" Jane said, excitedly now. Obviously this was something she relished rather than something she was merely obliged to do. It was good sign, Adam thought, if she was getting assignments she wanted. Wasn't it?

"You'll have to forgive me," said Adam, "but who is Louis Flambard?" Jane, Fred and Sophia all looked amused at his ignorance.

"Louis Flambard, seriously, do you never turn on a television?" Fred asked.

"He's an environmentalist, a writer, some people think he might go into politics," Sophia explained. "He's on the news all the time talking about global warming or the oil sands, you must have seen him."

"Anyway," Jane broke in, "he's speaking tonight on environmentalism, activism, and mobilization in social media, which should be fascinating, and I got the assignment. Come on, Father, we haven't talked in ages, it'll be fun, I promise."

"All right, you've convinced me, Miss Moore," said Adam. "Let me know when it starts and I'll be happy to accompany you."

Chapter 5

The speech Jane was covering didn't start until 7, which left Adam with several hours to spend, even allowing for dinner. Perhaps because he had seen all the other children, he decided to see if he could find Alex Sloan, and talk for a while. At least it seemed, somehow, like he should try.

Alex had been part of the Guild with Bones, Sophia, and the others. He had always been hard for the other children to deal with — he was erratic, difficult to understand when he spoke, with a tendency to mumble and to choose strange ways of expressing himself. After a brief conversation with Alex, many people were usually left wondering if he had been speaking to them at all. Alex also tended to wander, both literally and in terms of his attention. Eventually there was an explanation; Alex was assessed by a school-appointed psychiatrist and the diagnosis had been a blow. Alex heard voices, probably had other delusions, and generally struggled in telling what was real apart from what wasn't.

Adam remembered, with painful clarity, the doctor explaining that most of the symptoms were treatable with medication, but that the success rate for patients like Alex depended very much on strong support from families, to keep them taking the meds and to notice changes in behaviour that meant dosages needed adjustment. They also needed people who would keep reminding them of why the medicine had to be taken, since many patients would decide they were better and didn't need the pills any more, especially if they became tired of the side effects.

This need for support at home was not good news, because Alex had never had that. His mother was a single parent who often used drugs and disappeared with various boyfriends of the moment. His father had never, to Adam's knowledge, even seen his son. Because of this, and because many people didn't have the patience for a boy who was frequently paying more attention to things that weren't there than ones that were, Alex had seemed to need the church community more than the other children. He was always grateful to be included, and if he didn't always seem to understand or care about whatever activities were being done, he did enjoy just being part of the group.

For a while, they had all tried to keep Alex taking his pills and seeing his doctors but this had quickly threatened to become a full-time occupation. Whenever Alex wasn't supervised, he tended to vanish, and by the time he was tracked down, he would be off his medication and the whole process of persuading him to start taking the pills had to be started again. Eventually school, girlfriends and boyfriends, and jobs had demanded too much attention and Alex's supervision had been impossible for the children to maintain. Adam had tried as well, even after his change of career, but clearly not hard enough, he told himself.

The most important thing to remember in trying to locate Alex was that he liked places with trees, birds, and ideally some water, any of which he would spend hours watching. Today Alex was down by the river, where the canal locks were. Adam was glad to see he was wearing a fairly new looking coat, presumably from a charity, although sometimes one of Alex's friends could convince him to accept some clothes or a meal. His response was never consistent, except that he would never take medication, no matter how it was suggested. He would often accept the offer of somewhere to sleep, from a friend or a shelter, but would inevitably wander off before long.

"Hi Father, hello Father," Alex said quickly. He had seen Adam approaching from some way off and seemed almost impatient for him to get within talking distance. "Hard times, tricky times." He rocked back and forth as he talked, rubbing his hands together. Still, he had smiled when he saw Adam and seemed happy enough to be talking. Underneath the coat he looked rail-thin, but then he had always been skinny. Built like a stick insect, Bones used to say.

"You heard about Napoleon, then." Adam was a little surprised, but the attack had probably been on radio or TV that

Alex could have overheard, and had probably been the subject of a lot of rumours. It was even possible that one of the other children had visited him today. In truth, Adam admitted, he had no idea how often they might currently be checking in on Alex's well-being, except that it was probably more frequent than his own visits had been. "Why don't we sit and watch the river, eh?"

"She tells me things, tells me things all the time, Father," Alex explained calmly enough. Probably Sophia, then. She had often tried to get Alex into shelters or under medical supervision, which never worked for long. He had never been disruptive or difficult, as far as Adam knew. He had just left them all fairly quickly, and most of these places had neither the time nor the resources to try to track down the wayward or the reluctant. Short of locking Alex up, there seemed no way of keeping him off the streets, and Adam didn't think he would react very well to that at all. For now, getting Alex seated on a park bench instead of pacing in tiny little circles was a minor victory.

"That's good, Alex," said Adam. "Maybe you'd like to visit Bones? I'm sure he'd like that, once he's feeling a bit better. I could help you get ready, if you wanted." Perhaps this could be used as an excuse to get Alex some food today, or at least a shower. Even from a few feet away, he clearly needed one.

"Too busy, too much going on," Alex shook his head vigorously. He tapped the palms of his hands against the park bench rapidly, as if he was hardly able to sit still. He had never, as far as Adam and the Guild members had been able to tell, used drugs, but something had him very keyed-up today. He had what looked like a bottle cap and a pair of eyeglasses that were missing one lens, with what looked to be a shoelace threaded through the space. Alex had always been a collector of odds and ends.

"It's all right, Alex," Adam reassured him. "It was just an idea. I think you might make Bones' day, though." Alex and Napoleon had always entertained each other, before Alex's condition had gotten too serious. The odd, skinny boy had a vivid imagination and Bones enjoyed good stories and outlandish ideas.

"It's an infection! Once you get it, you give to other people — that's what they want!" Alex spat out the words sharply, and glared at Adam intensely. Alex's bony fingers clutched at the hem of his coat.

"Now, Alex, hospitals aren't like that." Reassuring Alex about authority figures and doctors was a long standing objective, but it never really seemed to take. On the other hand, he didn't usually dislike them, exactly; he just couldn't seem to pay attention to them. Five minutes after a conversation with his doctor or a social worker, Alex usually didn't remember it at all, although he could give you remarkable detail about birds or insects he had seen weeks or months ago.

"It's what they want, you know. They want you to quit, they want you rolling over, and over, roll over forever. Just leave it!" Alex sounded genuinely upset now. This had not been the point of visiting, but it wasn't a surprise if the news about Napoleon had disturbed him.

"None of your friends are going away, Alex. You know that. And we'll always try to help you, if you'll let us." Adam tried to reassure him.

"Don't you do it! That's what they want, you see it? Never let 'em tell you it can't be done! Don't get it in you, in your mind." Alex stood up abruptly and started to walk away, down the bike path, away from the locks. Adam had learned, quickly enough, that Alex did not want to be followed when he decided to move away. As always, he wanted his space, and sometimes the amount of space required seemed to increase quite suddenly.

"All right, Alex. We'll ... we'll talk again soon." Adam promised himself that this would, in fact, be the case. Alex was at least as bad, in terms of his state of mind, as he had ever been. There was no reason not to keep closer tabs on him, and perhaps in time he might become a bit more persuadable. Convincing people to accept help was meant to be part of a priest's skill set, after all.

"I know, Father. She tells me." Alex smiled an off-centre, brittle little grin. "Just remember, you don't need that book. You don't need it at all." Then, he skipped off along the asphalt, apparently happily enough. Adam watched him go for a long time.

Chapter 6

Fortunately, Flambard's speech was not a formal occasion, at least not in terms of clothing. Many of the people attending were in denim, cotton, and clothing they would proudly explain was made out of hemp. There was a smattering of suits among the crowd but, for the most part, the standard of dress was fairly relaxed. This was just as well, Adam decided, since it had been quite a while since he had needed to get dressed up, and most of what he wore was probably no longer appropriate.

Jane was smartly put together in a pantsuit, since she was ostensibly there for work rather than her own interest. Adam was fairly sure she would have been here in any case, though, whether she had gotten the assignment from her paper or not. "I take it, Miss Moore," he said as they found their seats, "that you're an admirer of tonight's speaker?"

"It is kind of important," Jane replied a little tartly. "Environmentalists aren't just tree-huggers, Father, they want to save the planet." Adam sometimes wondered whether or not the things he did in his day to day life really made much of a difference. Recycling, using reusable bags for shopping, composting, and having a home garden had all become habits, but did they accomplish anything, or were they just ways for us to comfort ourselves while still living essentially the same lifestyle?

"Yes, but I gather there's something special about this particular environmentalist, am I right?" There were not many environmental activists who would get booked into the national capital's main convention centre, or who would attract such a diverse crowd. Clearly Flambard had found a wide audience.

"He's just made such a point of connecting with young people, Father," Jane explained. "He's all about what everyone can do now rather than waiting for solutions to be provided by traditional authorities. They can be so out of touch, it's like we don't even speak the same language. No offense!"

"Jane, unless you include used booksellers as a traditional authority then I hardly count as one anymore," said Adam dryly. It was remarkable, and at times a little disheartening, how difficult it was for people to separate him from the church he had once been a part of, even after all this time. On the other hand, he supposed, he hadn't exactly been busy establishing a replacement persona. Most people he knew had assumed that work at the book store was a temporary arrangement, as had Adam. It was strange how the temporary could become permanent if you didn't pay attention.

"Oh, you know what I mean," Jane replied. "Now hush, it's about to start." Indeed, the house lights were dimming and a man walked up to the podium. Adam expected an introduction of some sort but instead it appeared they would go straight to the main event.

"Good evening mesdames et messieurs," he began in a deep, smooth voice, the voice of a radio announcer or a film narrator. "Good evening ladies and gentlemen, I should say." Louis Flambard was tall, with slightly thinning dark hair, a close-cropped beard and an affable smile. He looked as though he might have come directly from a canoe trip. "It is my very great pleasure to be here with you tonight and to share some of my ideas with you. You will have to forgive me if sometimes I don't find my words precisely, but I think the most important thing is not the exact words, but that we understand each other." Flambard had a light Quebecois accent but despite his self-deprecation, he seemed completely at ease dealing with this audience in English.

The first part of his address was mostly concerned with the problems he saw as most pressing, and there was nothing on the list that was especially surprising to Adam. Flambard mentioned global warming and resource depletion, but emphasized that the continuing loss of biodiversity was just as important. "Even if we look at the question in a selfish way," he explained, "We must consider that each time a species is lost — it's not important whether it is a plant, an animal, a bacterium — each time, we could be losing a resource vital to our future. We know some species are lost even before we discover them. That's a resource we have lost without ever knowing that we had it in our hands."

The content of what Flambard was saying wasn't anything Adam hadn't read or heard before. David Suzuki had covered many of these issues for years. What was remarkable about Flambard was both his evident passion for his subject, and also that even while addressing an audience of several hundred, he spoke as if he was having a casual conversation with good friends.

"What I would like to end my time with you tonight with is some encouragement to think in some different ways," Flambard smiled broadly. "All of us who have had the condition of the planet as one of our concerns know by now that it is not good enough to depend on old ways of getting things done. I want to encourage all of you to be open to bold new directions that we may have to go in, together, if we are to find a better circumstance than the one we are in." The friendly expression was gone and this was the most intense he had sounded throughout the whole address. "We must all have the willingness to consider solutions that we may never have thought possible. We must all be willing to pay a certain price to overturn the problems that confront us. I believe, and I know that more of you believe every day, that this is actually a price that we will pay gladly, because we know that to continue to do what we have done up until now is unacceptable." He paused, took a sip of water, and the smile returned. "Mesdames et messieurs, I thank you for the indulgence of your time this evening, I hope most of all that I have given you something tonight that you will think about as we all decide the directions we have to take, together."

"Wasn't he good?" asked Jane, raising her voice over the applause. "Aren't you glad you came?" He had spoken for nearly ninety minutes, as Adam discovered upon checking his watch.

"He's certainly very captivating," Adam replied. "I see why he's become such a phenomenon." Even if the message itself wasn't radically different from what he had heard before, sometimes a person who really knew how to deliver that message made all the difference. Flambard seemed an ideal standard-bearer for the green movement, from what Adam had seen tonight.

"Listen, Father, I need to see if I can get an interview," Jane said hurriedly as the ovation petered out. "Will you wait for me? I think there are still refreshments."

"Of course," Adam agreed. "There's no rush on my account. I'd like to hear what you made of all that afterwards. Come find me when you're done." Jane favoured him with a brief smile and began threading her way through the crowd towards the front of the room. Adam had no idea how likely she was to get some of Louis Flambard's time, but if determination was a key factor he liked her chances just fine. He ambled off in the opposite direction, seeking coffee.

There were indeed refreshments for audience members who wanted to spend a little more time viewing a photo-essay of Flambard's activist career through appearances at protests, debates, and youth camps. Adam was displeased to discover, though, that there was no coffee. A neatly printed sign explained that even fair trade coffee was an unsustainable industry and therefore, with M. Flambard's apologies, he could not agree to it being served. Mineral water and organic apple juice (from local growers) were offered and Adam decided to settle for water.

"Father Godwinson!" said a familiar voice. Adam turned around to find another former parishioner, and another who had grown up at St. Michael's during Adam's time there. Hugh Thomas had always been a big child and he had grown into a massive tree of a man, powerfully built and with the same huge hands Adam remembered. Hugh had been a prominent athlete in high school and Adam knew there had been some suggestion of a professional career for a while.

"It's not 'Father' anymore," Adam replied, "But it's good to see you, Mr. Thomas. You were here for the speech?"

"Yeah, I heard it might be worth checking out. Lots to think about, eh?" One of the things Adam had admired about Hugh was that even though he had never been the strongest student, he was always genuinely interested in lots of subjects.

"Very much so," Adam agreed. "It's been a long time, Hugh." He had seen even less of people like Hugh Thomas than he had the parishioners he had been particular close to, like the children from the Fridays Guild.

"I guess it has," Hugh grinned, "But it doesn't seem that way. I still think about some of the things you used to teach us, try to keep 'em in mind."

"That's ... that's very good to hear," Adam answered. He was a little surprised, to be honest. Hugh had not been part of the Fridays Guild for long — various team practices tended to interfere — and had drifted away from the church before Adam left. Still, he had known the community as well as anyone. "I imagine you've heard about Napoleon Kale?"

"No, don't think so," Hugh said. "What about him? Last I heard I guess he was playing in a band someplace."

"He was, or he is, I mean to say," Adam corrected himself. "It's just that he was attacked on the street last night, and he's still in hospital."

"Was he in trouble or something, Father?" Hugh looked concerned.

"No, nothing like that. The police aren't sure about a motive yet," Adam explained. "Anyway I think his friends would appreciate your stopping by, if you have the time. Once Bones is feeling better I'm sure he'd enjoy a visit, too."

"Oh yeah, sure, sure," Hugh nodded. "I'll figure out a time to do that."

"Thank you, Hugh. It's good of you. What are you doing with yourself these days, anyway?" Fortunately, Adam genuinely hadn't seen Hugh in long enough that he was comfortable asking the question instead of racking his brain trying to remember. He was sure he had heard, at some point, though.

Hugh Thomas offered a slightly sheepish little grin. "Well, you know, after the hockey thing didn't pan out," he explained, "I kind of got into teaching, a little counselling. People who have lost their way a bit, you know?"

"I do indeed," Adam answered. It was always amazing how people could go in very different directions than you expected them to — Hugh Thomas had been pretty singularly focused on sports and Adam would not have guessed that he would end up a counselor. Then again, perhaps working with a team and exposure to coaching of various kinds had taught him something about being there for teammates who needed it. In any case, it was good to hear. "That's a good thing you're doing, Mr. Thomas."

"Thanks, Father, I think so too," said Hugh, glancing at his watch. "Listen, I have to go, but it was good talking, you know?"

"It was," Adam smiled. "Have a good evening." Adam had to wait about another fifteen minutes for Jane to find him. Unfortunately despite her best efforts, Louis Flambard was resolute in not doing any interviews this evening. His agent had explained that Flambard was at the end of a long series of speaking engagements and unfortunately didn't have the energy to speak with the media. That sounded quite reasonable to Adam but Jane was visibly disappointed.

"Was the interview expected?" Adam enquired. Jane was paging through notes she had taken on a Blackberry during the presentation.

"No, not really," she admitted, "But it would have been so awesome to get it. No worries though, he gave a lot to work with already." She caught Adam's eye a little uncertainly. "Do you mind if I go straight home from here? I need to get this written up by deadline." Adam's face must have shown a little surprise at being dismissed after her request that he accompany her, because Jane continued almost instantly. "I sort of thought we'd go for coffee after and catch up, but that took longer than I thought and I want to get at this before I forget the angle I want on it. Is that OK?"

"Not a problem," Adam said, which was mostly true. The speech had been interesting, and he supposed that at least now he had enough familiarity with Louis Flambard to avoid appearing hopelessly out of touch in the future. "It's a fine night for a walk," he continued, "and I'll call Sophia for an update on Bones on my way. I'll look forward to reading your story tomorrow."

Chapter 7

In fact, he did not get to Jane's coverage of the Flambard speech right away the next morning because there was another box of donated books waiting on the front step of W.M. Howard, Bookseller. This time it was a banana box, and Adam's first reaction was to try to figure out if it was from the same person who had left the earlier pile of dubious-quality literature. This seemed to be a bit more of a mixed bag, though, and there was no smiley face, so he was inclined to think it was an entirely different person.

The phone was also ringing as he unlocked the door, so he dropped the box of books and hurried into the office. Perhaps it was new information about Bones' condition, which had not changed through the day yesterday. Instead, he picked up the receiver and was greeted by the harsh voice of Dr. Todd Marchale.

"Good lord, you take your damned time answering the phone," Marchale declared without preamble. "Third time I've called already, kept getting the voicemail, which is bloody worthless because I've no idea if you've gotten the message or not. I suppose you gave me your own number at some point but of course I lost the damned thing, probably immediately," he said with relish.

"No doubt," Adam said. "Good morning, Professor."

"Possibly, or it would be if I wasn't spending the whole thing on the damned phone," replied Marchale darkly. "However, I found something out about that book of yours, and thought I would share the fruits of my labours. Have a moment?"

"Of course," Adam said. "I was just opening the store."

"Well, I suspect the hordes of vampire lovers can wait five minutes, damn you," Marchale insisted. "I do have a class to teach this morning, assuming of course any of them can remember what room it's in. I could call back another time, you ingrate, but I was under the impression you were interested in the thing."

"No, Professor, I appreciate your call," said Adam. Marchale did not enjoy morning classes, or mornings in general, and probably a little mollification would go a long way. "I'm just a little surprised to hear from you already."

"Don't get excited, you might not appreciate it much," Marchale began. "You left a message about the previous owner of the book, this Charles Hope Warrington, yes? Well, I found out a bit about the fellow but it's not much bloody help."

"In that case, I can see why you felt you had to call right away," observed Adam, smiling to himself. He had forgotten how enjoyable sparring with Marchale had become, once he had figured out the rules of the game, about two years into his degree.

"Since I knew you had precisely nothing to go on," Marchale said gravely, "I took pity on you, my boy. In any event, the sad story is this — I did show your book to some colleagues in the History Department, who were none the wiser, and none of the misbegotten rabble had heard of Warrington either." This was disappointing news — Adam and Marchale were both hoping Warrington had had a reputation in a particular field of study that might throw some light on the content of the book. "However, as I have told many a wayward soul, most of whom ignored the advice entirely, sometimes genius is creating the situation that allows a happy accident to take place."

"Sounds familiar," Adam allowed. Marchale was honestly full of advice; it was just that much of it was offered in an abrasive and backhanded manner. "Have you been a genius today?"

"Not yet, not yet, but the day is young," Marchale replied. "However yesterday I was undoubtedly in fine form, for I left my notes about this wretched tome out on my desk when someone from the Department of English Literature happened by, lost no doubt, but he happened to cast his eye over what I'd written and recognized the name."

"That's interesting," Adam said, "Where did he know it from?"

"This, I fear, is where the outlook becomes bleak," Marchale admitted. "It seems Warrington was a writer, some travel documentary nonsense but mostly rather dire fiction, I am told. Mummy's Curse and all that rubbish, I'm sure you would be doing a thriving trade in it if it hadn't all been out of print since Methuselah was young."

"Well what was he doing with a medieval book in code, then?" Adam demanded. "It's not a showpiece, you said yourself, and if there's no reason to think he could read it why would he have bought it, or kept it?"

"Oh, I doubt he could read the damned thing," Marchale agreed, "Or at least my friend does. Warrington was not a linguist, or at least never gave any signs of it. But, you see, if he was a writer, he could have bought the thing for inspiration or a prop or God knows what, or even had it made. Makes the idea of a forgery much more plausible, you see."

"I suppose it does," Adam concurred, glumly. "Dead end, I suppose."

"Well, don't give up yet," Marchale scolded him. "I remember you weren't a complete layabout, after all."

"What, then, would you recommend as our next step, Professor?" asked Adam. It had been too long since he had tackled a research project and his instincts felt impossibly rusty.

"If you're determined to plumb this problem to the depths," Marchale suggested, "Use some of your very ample free time and have a read through Warrington's corpus of horrible writing. My literary friend gave me a stack of references as high as your knee. It may be he mentions the book in some turgid tale, or writes of its discovery during his travels on the River Wear. Thankless task of course, but I recall you're ideally suited to those."

Adam considered it. "Thank you, Professor," he replied after a moment. Continuing to work on the problem would be a distraction, and it seemed the least he could do for Bones. "I'll be by this afternoon to pick up those references, if that's all right."

"Delighted, delighted," agreed Marchale. "I'll put away the good china and get out some stale cookies."

Chapter 8

Adam's first plan was to go to the university on an extended lunch break, but this was thwarted by the jangle of the door chime announcing someone's arrival to the store, just as Adam was in the office polishing off a sandwich from the Italian bakery nearby. Had this person turned out to be a customer, the delay would have been slightly annoying, but the potential for making a sale would have been ample compensation. As it was, though, Adam immediately concluded this visitor was not interested in buying a book.

The man was of middling height but with a heavy build that had probably been stout muscle in his younger days. It was now well along the transformation into 'pudgy' on its way to corpulence. He had a thick, bristly beard to go with a rapidly receding hairline, and a face Adam knew very well. His name was Reverend Stephen Smiles, founder and guiding force behind the Hand of God Church.

"Good day, Father!" Smiles' voice was a cheerful boom. "I'm pleased to meet you, indeed I am, and I believe we may have much to discuss." Smiles had, at one point, been an Anglican minister but had left over twenty years ago to start the Hand of God Church, first in Ottawa but now boasting branches across five provinces.

"Hello, Reverend Smiles," Adam replied, shaking the offered hand. "You of course I know from television and the papers, but I can't think how you'll have heard of me." Smiles' church, or ministry as he sometimes had it, was doctrinally fundamentalist, zealously conservative in policy, and active politically along both lines. The Reverend Smiles was a frequent subject for interviews on social issues, always good for a meaty quote and never shy of letting fly with his opinions. There had been some momentum behind the idea of him running in the last municipal election, but Smiles had pled the necessity of frequent travel to his various churches that would prevent him paying proper attention to a council seat.

"You do yourself an injustice, Father," Smiles declared, brandishing a stern finger. "You're well-known enough. Your flock, your former flock I should say, speaks very highly of you." Smiles clapped Adam on the shoulder in companionable fashion. News that the parishioners of his old church still had good memories of him was a pleasing surprise, if indeed it was true. Adam recalled that the Reverend had been found liable to embellish histories in service to his cause, both his own and those of others. Members of the Hand of God Church who came from perfectly ordinary backgrounds were described to the media as 'souls plucked from the gutters of crime and despair', and Smiles often exaggerated the number of protest marches, rallies, and fundraisers that he had actually been a part of.

"That's kind of you to say, Reverend Smiles," Adam replied, thumping the banana box full of books down on the counter, and pulling the first several volumes out. "In that case, you'll have heard that I'm not a priest any longer, so there's no need to call me Father."

"Nonsense, nonsense!" insisted Smiles. "The service of the Almighty is a calling for life, not a job from which we are hired and fired like moneychangers." That had the sound of a practiced line, Adam reflected, probably part of a speech or a sermon he had used. "Why, I myself chose to walk my own path, much as you have done."

"I'm flattered by the comparison of course," said Adam blandly, regarding a hardcover copy of *Weaveworld* with a colourful, but lamentably faded dust jacket. He weighed the merits of selling the book with or without it. "However, when I make my choices, I live with what comes of them, and to be frank, I don't approve of using a title to which I no longer have any claim. Am I clear?"

"Quite, quite, and I commend your honesty," Smiles answered, apparently unoffended. "All too rare a commodity in these latter days, indeed it is. To be just as honest, I had hoped to talk over some matters with you, and I wonder if I might impose on you both for some of your time and a chair, if you'd be so kind." He gave an embarrassed-looking grin, and spread his hands. "God sends infirmities to us all, I fear."

"Of course, just let me fetch one from the back," Adam replied, cursing inwardly both for what was evidently going to be a significant delay and for his lack of hospitality. He didn't agree with Smiles' spirituality or his politics, but he had no reason to think the man was anything but well-meaning, and there was no need to be unkind. Adam returned with the least rickety of the chairs from the office and set it down near the counter. "I'm sorry I can't offer you anything more comfortable, but you'll understand that seating isn't usually something we're asked to provide."

"Perhaps something to think about for the future," said Smiles, settling himself down. "A comfortable chair in which to peruse your wares might appeal, might appeal greatly. If, indeed, your future is in the selling of books, of course." He made this last comment with a shrewd glance at Adam, who had laid *Weaveworld* aside and was now determining exactly how many pages were missing from a much abused book of two-minute mysteries.

"Possibly, possibly," Adam allowed. In fact, he and Walter had occasionally talked about setting up a small seating area but, for some reason, it was annoying to have the idea offered up by Stephen Smiles. The primary objection had always been losing access to bookshelf space, an anathema to the proper order of things in Walter Howard's world. "But please, don't let me distract you from the reason for your visit." He tossed the mystery book into a milk crate for a trip to the recycling bin later.

"I was wondering why you left your church, Father Godwinson?" asked Reverend Smiles. Adam gave him a sharp glance, and the Reverend leaned forward in his chair and went on softly, "Did they cast you out, son?"

"No, no," Adam replied mildly, running his fingers over a worthless hardback mystery novel. "It was a personal choice, that's all." He was rapidly losing his charitable attitude towards

Smiles, although he wasn't sure why. Perhaps it was because he was so very tired of having conversations on this subject.

"Something between you and your God, of course, of course," Smiles nodded deeply, approvingly. "I quite understand, indeed I do. I believe we understand each other very well. I fear many of our ... more traditional churches are no place for a godly man, Father." He gave a sharp little nod, as though he had just made a particularly salient point.

"I'm not sure what you mean, Reverend, but I know I asked you not to call me that," Adam said, laying down the hardback and taking another book from the box without looking at it. He had imagined a variety of reasons why Smiles might have been here to visit him — some concern over the attack on Bones, or over Alex Sloan, had seemed possible — but a recruitment attempt hadn't occurred to him.

"I think you know what I mean, Father — excuse me, perhaps I can call you Dr. Godwinson?" Without waiting for an answer, Smiles ground on. "You do know what I mean, indeed you do. These churches, hardly worthy of the name, so filled with people of venality, of narrowness, of every kind of sin. How can anyone be surprised when the godly man turns away from that?"

"Is that what happened to you, Reverend Smiles?" Adam was trying to resist the assumption that Smiles' founding of the Hand of God had been motivated by the desire for a higher profile, and indeed for more money. The church was reported to make a tidy sum from donations, from fees to attend lectures and classes given by Smiles, and from the considerable line of publications put out by the church press. Some of these had made their way to W.M. Howard, Bookseller, although their resale value had proved be basically nil. Members of Smiles' flock got their products direct.

"Oh, I flatter myself that I have always seen clearly, Father. I knew the well-worn path was not for me from a young age, indeed I did." Smiles had a somewhat challenging look on his face now; probably this line of conversation was as familiar to him as the issue of why Adam had left his church was to him. To that extent at least, Adam empathized.

"Well, you've certainly gone in a unique direction, Reverend," Adam observed, tossing a book missing its back cover into the milk crate as well. "But what did you want with me, this afternoon?" This was clearly not a sympathy call, nor one regarding outreach to Alex. Adam was no longer sure he really wanted to know what the reason for Smiles' visit was.

"Well now, I had hoped that you might be willing, happy even, to join my work, in the work of bringing the good news to those who hunger for it," said Smiles, clasping his hands in front of him. "There is such a lack of clarity, indeed of guidance, in our world today, and a man like you, a man of learning, a man of God, a man not beholden to corruption — well, I believe you have much you could offer our cause, Father."

"That's ..." Adam paused to write a price onto the flyleaf of a collection of Poe stories with a pencil before continuing, "that's flattering, I suppose, but you can't really be reduced to recruiting in bookstores and coffee shops for your evangelists, can you, Reverend?"

"Reduced? Indeed not, indeed not. You were, how shall I put it, high on my list of candidates, and have been for some time." Smiles looked surprised that Adam would have made the suggestion, and perhaps the clench of his jaw suggested he was slightly offended as well. Well, it was no secret that Smiles was intensely proud of his creation, and believed strongly in the quality of its work.

"Have I? Where would you have heard of me, Reverend? Even before my -" another price carefully written into a volume on the archeology of Viking settlements in Yorkshire, "change in career I had a small parish, was never in the news, never involved in politics." Adam had always seen faith as an essentially private matter; for those who wanted guidance or instruction he had been there, those who were content with themselves he saw as none of his business. He made a mental note to put the archaeology book in the back library.

"Perhaps for that very reason, if you would be so kind, Father," said Smiles with an earnest look. "I don't think of myself as being involved in politics, not at all, I don't. I believe my organization serves a higher cause." The defiant, challenging look was back, as if Smiles anticipated the contradiction.

"No doubt you do," Adam answered, setting down a Penguin edition of *Captain Blood*, and his pencil. "I'm sure you do believe that." He knew he was probably rising to Smiles' bait, but couldn't quite leave it alone. "It's hard for me agree, though, not when you've told people to vote for this candidate, or not to vote for this party, and been so public with your condemnation and praise of government policies at every level. Wasn't it just last week you had that piece in the paper against high schools providing contraception?"

Smiles flushed slightly and rapped his fingers on the arm of the chair with irritated energy. "I had not realized, Mr. Godwinson," he said curtly, "That you were one of those who held that I am somehow disqualified from having my own opinions, simply because I happen to lead a church, or from explaining those opinions to interested parties." He looked away, out the window, at the street. "It would be a great injustice if men of faith were muzzled simply because of their belief, indeed it would."

"I'm sorry if I offend you," Adam said mildly, "It's not my intention. But as you say, you use your church, and your position as its head, as a way to promote your views. I'm not sure whether that's right or if it's wrong, but I do know that it's sophistry to pretend that it isn't being political when you're telling people who deserves to be in government." He paused and tapped the pencil against the edge of the counter. "If that surprises you, then I guess you hadn't heard all that much about me after all."

Smiles took a deep breath and sighed, visibly making an effort to damp down his annoyance at the turn the conversation had taken. "What I had heard, Father," he eventually said, "was that you were a person who was not unduly bound by convention, by dogma, by hidebound tradition. A man perhaps open to new directions for the faith, and the faithful. God knows there has never been a greater crisis for faith in this country, and around the world, and we cannot shrink from the task of saving it."

Adam waited and wondered what could have led Smiles to think he would be likely to be attracted by this offer. Had everyone ascribed his decision to leave the church to extreme spiritual views? Perhaps he should have made some public explanation, but at the time it had seemed both unnecessary and a bit presumptuous to enact what was a personal decision in front of a wide audience.

"Will you help me do this, Father Godwinson?" Smiles went on. "Will you be with us in the struggles that lie ahead?" He looked so genuinely hopeful that Adam slightly regretted having to disappoint him. It was easy to see how he had been so successful in gaining supporters and recruiting followers.

"I'm sorry, Reverend," he replied. "I'm afraid I wouldn't be the kind of ally you're looking for." In fact, he could think of few things that appealed to him less that becoming part of Smiles' church, but he also saw no need to be confrontational. It was probably also true, he reflected, that making someone with the public weight of Stephen Smiles into an enemy was probably best avoided if possible. "I'm sure the offer is a great opportunity, but I'm just as sure that I'm not really who you want for whatever the position is. Now, if you'll excuse me, I have some other matters to attend to this afternoon, and I was planning on closing the shop early."

Smiles gave no sign of reaction to Adam's refusal, one way or another. "Ah yes," he said, "I heard a boy from your church was in hospital. Some kind of attack, the news said. Do convey my blessing, if you don't object, of course. These times we live in," he went on, shaking his head sadly, "are beset by so many dangers. We must all be on our guard, indeed we must. If you should think better of my offer, Father, do call my office. You'd always be welcome."

With that, Smiles departed, leaving behind a business card and a pamphlet explaining the mission of the Hand of God church, courses that were accepting enrollment now, and a variety of literature available for order. Adam consigned this to the paper recycling crate, and tried to refocus on sorting through the box of books. This was a far more mixed bag than the previous lot of 'donations' had been, and more of them were likely to be sellable, but he quickly abandoned the task and set about closing the shop. It was past time to pick up the references from Marchale, and then make his way the hospital to visit Bones.

Chapter 9

Adam walked to the university, stewing over the visit from Smiles the entire way. It was true that he hadn't done much to be active in the community since leaving the church. Obviously the Hand of God would not be a good fit, but there were probably any number of ways in which he could help people who needed it. On the other hand, he reflected, after leaving his parish he had found a kind of relief in not having so many problems laid at his door. That had been a long time ago, though, and there was a difference between taking a break from one's responsibilities and abdicating them entirely.

This train of thought took Adam all the way to Marchale's office in the Arts Building, on Laurier Avenue. Professor Marchale was out — teaching his seminar on Folk and Popular Religions, his schedule revealed. He was fond of explaining that, since he was strange in every other way, he may as well study strange religious things, but Adam knew that the real reason had more to do with Marchale's impatience with anything institutional. He wanted to know what ordinary people found meaning in, not what they were supposed to believe according to authority. It was sometimes a wonder that he managed to tolerate the often torturous bureaucracy of a university, but then there were not many other options that offered someone like Todd Marchale a chance to devote his life to his passion for the arcane and the odd in the theological world.

The schedule also revealed that Marchale would not be back for nearly an hour, but then Adam noticed a Post-It note stuck to the door. *Godwinson: See Dept. Sec. Call Later.* Adam duly called on the department secretary and found that Marchale had left a rather sizeable manila envelope full of documents for him, along with a longer note.

Behold a rich vein of knowledge on all things Charles Warrington — not everything but enough to get you started. Should keep you out of trouble awhile. Do not lose any of this or flog it in your roadside stand or I will never hear the end of it. Got class all afternoon and supervision afterward so don't laze around waiting. Get to it. Compare notes later — T.

This was positively affectionate by Marchale's standards; Adam could tell once again that the professor's interest had been piqued. He shuffled through the papers in the envelope quickly and found a bibliography of Warrington's work, photocopies of several articles that seemed to be about Warrington, and a thin little book that was almost more of a pamphlet, with covers made of stiff cardboard and bound with two staples through the spine. On the front was a cheaply printed picture of the sun, with long wiggly rays coming out of it, along with the title *The Eater of the Sun*, and 'C.H. Warrington' underneath it. The bibliography appeared to have been produced on an old manual typewriter, and some time ago, judging from the yellowed and tattered state of the paper. All these documents had probably been borrowed from whoever it was Marchale knew in the English department, thus the warning against being careless with them.

Adam looked at his watch and decided that it was too late in the afternoon to go to the library now; he would just be getting into the research and it would be time to stop for dinner. Instead, he decided to visit the hospital, check in on Bones, and spend the evening taking a closer look at what Marchale had left him. He could probably spend some time on it during quiet times at the store tomorrow as well.

He took a bus to the hospital, and leafed through some of the documents from Marchale's envelope on the way. Marchale had clipped out a small obituary of Warrington among the rest of the papers. Adam supposed this was more of a reminder of work that he should have been doing than anything else. In any case, there were not many details in the few brief columns summing up the life of Charles Hope Warrington — he had been married, but his wife had died a decade ago. The couple had had a pair of daughters, but neither had apparently married, or at least they had not had any children. Adam supposed that explained the estate sale; Warrington's daughters would be old enough themselves to make dealing with their father's things more of a burden than they might be capable of handling, even assuming they still lived in the area.

When he arrived at the hospital, Adam found that little had changed. Bones had not yet awakened, and a nurse explained that he was still being kept sedated because of the danger of swelling of the brain. He was progressing well, if gradually, and his doctor was apparently hopeful that he might be taken off the sedatives in the next day or so.

Fred Wallace was in Bones' room, sitting in a chair by the bed and reading aloud from a fantasy novel when Adam arrived. He looked up, a little embarrassed. "Oh, hey Father," he said, "I was just ... well, you know they say sometimes they can hear you even when they're not conscious, and I thought Bones might be getting bored with the room being quiet and all."

"Makes perfect sense to me," Adam replied. "I'm not sure that's his kind of book though, is it?"

"Nah, or, well, I doubt it," Fred admitted. "It's just what I'm reading right now. I didn't think he'd mind though." Adam reflected that he probably wouldn't, either. "You ever read this one, Father? It's part of a series, but I guess you know that from the store and all."

Adam had seen this particular series come in (and sometimes out) of the stock at W.M. Howard's quite a bit over the past few months. Fantasy novels tended to be decent sellers so there were several shelves devoted to them. "I haven't read it," he admitted. It would probably be a good thing to do, at least so he could answer questions from customers. "Maybe I'll take your recommendation."

Fred grinned and then said, "That police inspector was here before. He said there wasn't much progress from yesterday. Looking for more witnesses, he said." Adam was a bit surprised that Kolb had been back again so soon, but he supposed that checking in with Bones' friends had not been his main purpose for the visit. It was more likely that he had been hoping that there might be a new visitor to interview, and that he was checking on the condition of the victim. Still, Adam was pleased that the inspector was evidently taking the case as seriously as he claimed he would.

"Why don't you finish your chapter, Mr. Wallace," he suggested, "And then I'll buy you dinner someplace."

"Hey cool, Father," Fred agreed eagerly. "There's this new Indian place I've been wanting to check out."

Chapter 10

Dinner with Fred was a welcome change from Adam's usual routine. The new restaurant on Elgin turned out to be rather mediocre, but it was good to spend some time with one of the young people from the Guild again. Fred also had a couple of new tricks he was trying to work into his act that he wanted to try out on Adam. One was a card trick where the card Adam picked turned out to be in Fred's shoe. The other was a little illusion where a spoon was supposed to magically pass through the side of a full glass of water, but Fred was still struggling with that one.

He explained that he was trying to increase the number of illusions he could do using objects that could be found anywhere. "Sometimes an audience wants to see a couple extra tricks at the end, or it turns out you don't have as much space to perform as you thought and you don't have anywhere to set up your gear," he went on. "Anyway, it's good to practice with someone right in your face. If I can fool you at like two feet, I can definitely do it if you're a regular distance away."

Adam was impressed with the amount of thought Fred seemed to be putting into his magic performances, and he really was a lot better than the last time Adam had seen his act. However, he wondered why more of that energy didn't go into finishing his degree. "What about class, Mr. Wallace," he asked. "Last we talked, programming was still your plan 'A'."

"We call it coding these days," Fred corrected him cheerily. "I still like it, but it's hard to do enough bookings to pay the rent and do class as well. Anyway, it's pretty rough trying to get into the kind of thing I'd like to do right now. I'll get there but, right now, this is working OK. You been talking to my parents, Father?" This last question was offered in a slightly peevish tone;

Adam imagined that they might be losing patience with Fred's protracted university career.

"No, not in some time," Adam replied, truthfully enough. He thought about reminding Fred about the importance of preparing for a career and not just getting by with a job, but decided that he was hardly in a position to offer criticism along those lines. Anyway, stage magic seemed to be making Fred genuinely happy, at least for now, and maybe that was all that really mattered.

They paid their bill and left; the night was warm and there were lots of people on the street. Fred needed to go a couple of blocks to get to a bus stop, and Adam went with him, considering a walk down by the canal after they parted ways. However, suddenly among the crowd of people outside a cheerily-lit pub, he recognized the tall, sturdy figure of Hugh Thomas again. He was alone, looking around with a slightly confused, searching expression as bar patrons flowed around him.

"Hello, Hugh," Adam called out to him. Seeing him on consecutive nights after so long was a strange coincidence, but not one Adam minded. Perhaps they could talk a bit about Hugh's outreach work after Fred caught his bus. Adam was even toying with the idea of asking if it was something he might get involved in, himself. "Good to see you again, and so soon. Are you all right?"

Hugh looked a little unsteady on his feet and his face shone with sweat. His hands were thrust into the pockets of his suit jacket, where they seemed to be clenched into fists. His eyes flicked around rapidly, but continually came back to fall on Adam. He took a couple of steps forward.

"Father," he said quietly, licking his lips. "I was looking for you. Hoping to see you." Under the streetlight his skin looked unusually pale, and he was blinking in a rapid, erratic pattern.

"Of course, Mr. Thomas," Adam said, holding out his hand. "What can I do for you?" Hugh was evidently upset or disturbed about something, so it didn't seem the time for Adam to do his usual correction.

"Do? Do?" Hugh spat. "You can't do anything for me; you're like a snake, full of poison, on everything you touch!" His voice was a snarl, tense with emotion. He took two more quick, unsteady steps towards Adam. "Poison! Poison, poison, it needs to be cut out!" With that, he reached inside his suit and pulled out a knife.

The knife looked like it was one of a kitchen set, Adam was surprised to find himself thinking. Strange how irrelevant details catch your attention at times of crisis. One of those sets of knives with the self-sharpening sheathes, he imagined. Hugh lurched forward a little more, perhaps a little shaky on his feet but still massive, and now, suddenly, armed.

"All right, Hugh," Adam said as steadily as possible. One of his hands was trembling and he pushed it into a pocket to keep it still. For some reason he didn't want to look any weaker than he probably already did. "You can hurt me really badly if you want to, and you don't need the knife to do it. Why don't you tell me instead — what have I done, to be so full of venom to you?"

Hugh's mouth twisted into a snarl. "You know! You old hypocrite," he spat. "Venomous. Spreading poison and thinking no-one knows. I know! And I know just what to do." He shifted his weight slightly, and seemed about to spring forward.

"Is that what happened to Napoleon, Hugh? Was he full of poison, too? Were you there? Do you know who was?" Bones had been beaten and not stabbed, of course, but two members of his old church touched by violence so close together seemed an unlikely coincidence. Adam was also hoping the questions might be a distraction from whatever Hugh was planning, and that making him think about answers might calm him down. Asking the questions gave Adam something to focus on aside from the knife, as well.

"I don't know anything about that," Hugh spat, "Stop trying to confuse me, stop trying to make it difficult! This is supposed to be so easy." He shook the knife at Adam, jabbing at the air. His teeth chattered suddenly, and it looked as though he had little quivers and twitches running throughout his body.

"I'm sure it could be, Hugh, but you need to think very carefully about everything you're doing. Don't do anything without being sure about everything that is going to happen." Adam tried to speak slowly and to keep his voice steady. Hugh seemed to be teetering on the edge of action and it was vital to do nothing that might push him over it. Adam tried to recall the mannerisms he had used with grief-stricken and despairing parishioners. The appearance of steadfastness had been invaluable then, as he thought it must be now. To his parishioners, it had been a comfort, but perhaps now it was keeping him alive. "Everything will be perfectly all right, as long as no one does anything they can't take back."

"You're toxic," Hugh insisted. "You're full of lies and you poison everybody!" His skin shone with sweat under the streetlights. Adam racked his brain trying to think of any occasion that might be at the root of all this. He had made his mistakes, especially as a young priest, but he could think of nothing that would have had such a strong effect on someone Hugh's age, who had been unaware of budget wrangles with the wardens and the politics of the church choir.

"Now, I wasn't perfect, at St. Michael's," Adam admitted, "But you know I wasn't like that. That's not who I was. I was always honest with you, Mr. Thomas." He had been, too, or thought he had. At one point Hugh had been convinced that he would play pro hockey and didn't need to pay attention to school. Adam had bluntly explained the statistics of the problem, the number of people who earned their whole livelihood just from sports. It hadn't been a pleasant conversation and Hugh had been upset with him, but he had also finished high school, and gone to college. At one point, Adam was sure he had heard that Hugh was a chef in training. Or had been, perhaps — there was this counseling work he had mentioned at the Flambard speech.

"No, but, it was," Hugh broke off and the hand holding the knife lowered. "You weren't, but I see how it is, now." There was a tremor in his voice now and he seemed to be losing a little of the manic edge that had been all too evident moments ago.

"Then tell me how it is," Adam encouraged. He felt a little flicker of hope amongst the knot of fear in his stomach. "We could always talk about things." Even when Hugh had basically stopped coming to church in his late teens, he still came by to look for advice every once in a while. It was unfortunate, Adam had often thought, that when people gave up religion they usually gave up a lot of other things that came with it.

"I don't need to talk," Hugh objected, "I need to ... I was supposed to, I mean ..." He seemed to be calming down, almost running out of energy. He definitely looked confused, and he was holding onto the knife very loosely. Finally it slipped from his fingers and he staggered into Adam, nearly collapsing against him. Adam thought he heard Hugh whisper for help as he started to slide towards the ground.

"All right, it's all right now," Adam soothed, easing Hugh down to the ground. "You're just fine, Hugh Thomas, you just need to rest yourself." He gently lay Hugh's head down and sat looking at him, lying on the sidewalk.

"I think someone called the cops, Father," Fred said, finally. "Well, I know they did. 'Cause it was me." He was standing exactly where he had been when Hugh had stepped out of the doorway, his phone clutched in one hand and his eyes very wide.

"Good, good," Adam answered, quietly. "Although I think he needs an ambulance more than he needs to be arrested, don't you?" Hugh's eyes were closed but moving rapidly behind his eyelids, as if he were dreaming. He was still extremely pale, and still perspiring as if he had finished a long run.

"I couldn't tell you," Fred replied, "It sure looked like he was planning to cut you up, though. That's about all I need to know." Fred had always tended to see things in fairly absolute terms, which had made his interest in magic a bit of a surprise to Adam when it had first appeared. Wasn't stage magic a series of unanswered questions and shades of grey? Finally he had asked Fred about it directly, and learned that, despite the Alfred the Astounding persona, Fred really saw magic tricks as a set of puzzles he was inviting his audience to try to solve. If he did it right, the puzzle went unsolved. It was as much of a science for him as computers were.

"I'm not sure what he meant to do," Adam said, wiping a sleeve over his forehead, "but I think he's out of his mind on something. I wouldn't have expected that of him." He stood up quickly and stepped away from the prone young man, suddenly wanting some distance between them.

"I haven't seen him in a while, Father," Fred answered. "People can change a lot." He was already half-turned away from Hugh and seemed on the verge of walking, or perhaps running, away. Adam understood the impulse and, on one level, shared it, but he also thought fleeing the scene of what would certainly appear to be a crime to the police was probably a bad idea.

"Sometimes, sometimes," Adam agreed. "Let me just satisfy my curiosity a moment." He stepped back and stooped down to have a quick look at the contents of Hugh's pockets. It was hard to believe that anyone who grew up in his church had become a violent drug addict, and in fact he found nothing but a wallet, a bus pass, a ring of keys, and a packet of pamphlets bound up with a rubber band.

The pamphlets were of the sort one left on information tables or, more probably for these particular ones, handed out on the street to passersby. Adam thought that because he had seen ones like them before, being pressed on commuters at bus stops and along Wellington, in front of the Parliament Buildings. The pamphlets were for the Hand of God Ministry, founded and led by Reverend Stephen Smiles.

Chapter 11

Adam and Fred stayed with Hugh until the police and ambulance arrived. The paramedics quickly had Hugh strapped to a stretcher and loaded up; they had not wanted to speculate about what might be wrong with him and had more questions than answers for Adam when he approached them: had Hugh been using anything? Was he a habitual drug user? Was he on any prescription medications? Had he been experiencing any mental issues prior to tonight? Did he strike his head when he collapsed? To this last question, at least, Adam was able to answer in the negative.

He also met a polite policeman who introduced himself as Officer Tessier, and took statements from Adam, Fred, and a few more forthcoming members of the crowd of bystanders. Tessier had a lot of questions for Adam, since he seemed to have been the focus of Hugh's hostility. Adam described his meeting Hugh at the Flambard lecture the previous night. He had seemed perfectly normal, friendly and relaxed. Their conversation had been brief, but he hadn't mentioned any anger towards Adam then. Adam admitted that before that, it had been a long time since he had seen Hugh, so he didn't know if he had been having problems of any kind or was under some kind of stress.

"I'm really not interested in pressing charges, officer," Adam said. "I'm not sure exactly what may have caused this but I don't believe Hugh was aware of what he was doing." He looked down at Hugh's body stretched out on the sidewalk, and even though the young man was either unconscious or asleep, periodically some of his muscles would convulse violently. A seizure? Or the continuing effects of some sort of drug? Adam had never worked closely with addicts or the groups that tried to help them, and he didn't recognize these symptoms at all.

"I understand, sir," Tessier replied politely, "and we'll take that into consideration, but it may not be completely up to you. Assault with a weapon is a serious thing and there are charges that can be brought without you registering a complaint, necessarily." He waved away a man who was stepping tentatively forward. Adam noticed as he hastily retreated that he was holding what looked like a microcassette or other type of sound recorder. The press, here already — they were remarkably quick.

"It's just that I think this boy needs help," Adam went on. Hugh was not the energetic child Adam remembered any longer, but it was hard not to think of him that way, unconscious and twitching on the ground. "He doesn't need to be in jail. He probably needs a hospital, for tonight at least."

"He'll get all necessary medical attention," Tessier replied automatically. "You don't seem very upset about him pulling a knife on you though — is there something you haven't said about all this?" It was subtle, but his soothing, understanding approach had instantly shifted into something more alert and probing.

"No, no," Adam said, "and believe me, this will probably stay with me for a while, but I'd prefer to try to understand what led a good person to this rather than punishing him. It's obvious he needs help from someone." The potential of an evening answering questions at a police station was beginning to loom and, more than anything, Adam wanted to go home. There was a great deal to think about and, once the adrenaline wore off, he knew he would need sleep urgently.

"It's a good attitude to have," Tessier replied. "But trust me, providing help is my main job. Your friend here will be looked after, after we make sure he's not causing anyone else to need help, you see what I mean?" He offered this explanation in a gentle and conciliatory tone, but there was enough firmness there for it to be clear that the policeman was not offering a negotiation.

"I do, officer," Adam agreed quietly. "Do try to be gentle with him." Whatever had affected Hugh so badly, it seemed likely that it would be a problem that he would struggle with for a long time. Adam added trying to be a part of that recovery to his list of things to keep track of.

Eventually, the officer took Adam's contact information, gave him a card with a number to call if he had further information, and said that he would be in touch if there were any developments. Adam reflected that, over the past two days, he had acquired two different police officers that he was awaiting 'developments' from, and decided that this was not a comforting direction for his life to be heading in. Still, being involved in the problems and crises of those around him had once been a significant part of his job, and one that he thought he had done reasonably well. Possibly he was just out of practice.

Fred jumped on a bus to go home, and Adam decided to walk. It was a pleasant evening once again, and he needed time to unwind before sleep would be even a remote possibility. There was the usual scattering of people on the street near the War Memorial, in front of the Chateau Laurier, and down through the market on his way home, but the encounter with Hugh gave it all a slightly different feel — Adam found himself looking at everyone walking towards him with suspicion or alarm, and himself walking more quickly than usual. Even after getting home, Adam was still full of adrenaline and sleep seemed very far away. He decided not to torment himself lying awake in bed and poured himself some red wine in a coffee mug. He did have wine glasses, somewhere, but he found them prone to spills and breakage and usually used more durable alternatives. At the moment his hands were not especially steady and so the coffee mug was definitely the better option. That it also held slightly more wine, he assured himself, was just incidental.

Adam did want something to occupy his mind, so that he didn't pick over the encounter with Hugh endlessly or allow his imagination to construct increasingly horrible scenarios out of it. It was probably too late to call Marchale and, in any case, he hadn't spent any time with the packet of papers the professor had left him — Adam had only ever showed up for a meeting once without having done the agreed upon readings and was not eager to repeat the experience. Instead, he would have a look at some of the material now and check in with Marchale in the morning.

Adam turned on the light above his back door and went out into the tiny yard behind his house. There was just enough room for a three-by-three arrangement of patio stones, two plastic chairs that had been outside for a few too many changes of seasons, a meager patch of grass, and a small vegetable garden. For a long time Adam had a little barbeque that he used for Fridays Guild meetings but, a few years ago, the bottom had finally rusted out of it and he had never replaced it.

Recently, the vegetable garden had been his main pastime. This spring he had his usual array of tomatoes, lettuce, and radishes already up, along with a first attempt at cultivating a pepper plant. The beans and peas were also just getting started, and would need to be tied to frames for them to climb in a few days. Adam almost always found it relaxing to weed the garden or thin out seedlings but tonight he sat in the pool of light cast over the little patio and leafed through the collection of documents on Warrington again. He drew out *The Eater of the Sun* and glanced at the title page. The little book had been published in 1946, which, according to the other information he had, meant that Warrington had been 28 when he wrote it. Adam wondered if Warrington had been involved in the war, and if he had been, if the experience was reflected in the story he wrote afterwards. He took a sip of wine and began to read.

After getting thirty minutes into the book, he understood why Warrington had not been a great success as a writer. *The Eater of the Sun* was a strange piece of writing indeed — it had no characters, and no particular plot that Adam could discern. It seemed to be a little report or descriptive essay, written in a completely factual, straight-forward manner. The problem with that was that the subject matter was completely fantastic; it described a being that somehow ate sunlight to give itself power, that grew in strength the longer it received the sun's rays, and would eventually 'burn the world to the ground and rule over the ashes', according to the book's dire prediction.

It reminded Adam a little of the material that came with role-playing games. Fred had tried to start a Dungeons and

Dragons club at the church and, although there had been a few sessions, most of the other children really only joined to spend time with their friends, and none of them were as enthusiastic as Fred. The club had fizzled out after only a few meetings. However, to help overcome parental suspicions about the game, Adam had read all the rulebooks and supplements. That was what Warrington's reminded him of, relating the 'facts' about strange creatures and magical realms in an almost clinical, matter-of-fact way.

He supposed it worked fine for roleplaying games but what Warrington had produced was something that seemed to have no real audience to appeal to: there was no story to engage fans of fiction, but only a lover of strange tales would have been interested in the subject. Some books tried to be everything to everyone, to their detriment, but *The Eater of the Sun* seemed to be on the other end of the spectrum. As far as he could see, it provided little insight except in that it confirmed that Warrington had been a mediocre writer, or writer of fiction, at least. Perhaps his travel writing was better.

Adam abandoned the little book, carefully returning it to the envelope, and finished his wine. He could feel the fatigue coming over him now like clouds rolling in from the horizon, and he couldn't face the dry academic prose of any of the articles on Warrington. There was a language expected of you in that kind of writing that seemed to damp down the passion he knew most scholars had for their subjects. In his more pessimistic moments as a student, Adam had wondered if this was a deliberate means of ensuring that only the most devoted would pursue their studies for very long, screening out dilettantes and dabblers through impenetrability and inaccessibility. That kind of thinking was usually a sign that he needed a study break, and had taught him that there was a point of no return for useful study while fatigued. There would be plenty of time to look at the articles tomorrow, perhaps after he spoke to Marchale. The professor's directive to call him seemed to indicate he had an idea, or had made a discovery. It would be worth knowing what that was before going any further.

There was a new problem to wrestle with now, in any case. Was it purely coincidence that Hugh Thomas worked for Smiles' church? Adam confessed to himself that he disliked Smiles fairly strongly, with his use of spirituality towards political ends and material gain, but surely even so it was a stretch to think that the church had somehow motivated Hugh's behavior tonight. It was more likely that Hugh had formed his connection to them because of a drug problem, and tonight he had simply been suffering from some kind of relapse.

As Adam went inside and locked his back door, he admitted to himself that there was something else that made him even more uneasy. What had Alex Sloan meant when he talked about "the book", down by the canal locks? Alex said lots of things that had no apparent connection to the world around him, and Adam knew it was a losing proposition to try to find meaning in most of it. He imagined it might only make sense if one had the same problems Alex did. And yet, Alex had seemed reasonably grounded, by his standards, and it was a strange coincidence, if that was all it was. Adam decided he was more rattled by the night's events than he had imagined, and assigning greater implications to Alex's comments was probably a similar symptom to feeling threatened by pedestrians all the way home — imagining threats and problems where none existed. There were enough problems ahead without inventing more, he told himself.

Adam undressed and checked that his alarm was still set for the same time it always was. He put the envelope of Warrington papers on the kitchen table, where he wouldn't be tempted to look at it until morning. Finally, he brushed his teeth, lay down, and tried to let the day go. It wasn't until the next day that he was surprised at how quickly sleep had come.

Chapter 12

Adam went to Marchale's office before opening the store. Morning business tended to be slow and, since he hadn't gotten in touch last night, it was probably important to show that he was still actively interested in the manuscript. Marchale's enthusiasms were always heartfelt, but could also be fleeting if some fresh distraction came along. He also had a high opinion of the value of his time, and if he thought Adam wasn't serious in his inquiries into the book, he would probably abandon it instantly.

Marchale looked more bedraggled than usual, nursing an immense cup of coffee and having apparently neglected to shave. Adam supposed he wasn't looking his best this morning either, though. Marchale went through life blithely unconcerned with, or unaware of, the impressions he made on the world around him, so the state of his appearance was no surprise. The tone of his voice when he curtly greeted Adam and told, rather than invited, him to sit down, was.

"Now, why in the hell didn't you call yesterday? No one buying books and got your phone cut off, that it?" Marchale demanded. Adam could tell he was genuinely annoyed, and remembered that one of the few things that he had no tolerance for was having his time wasted, as Adam had discovered by turning up 20 minutes late for a supervision. Marchale, as it turned out, had made a special trip in for the meeting that day and had excoriated his student for keeping him waiting, one of the few times his criticism had not had a playful or affectionate edge to it, and justifiably enough, Adam supposed. Now, he imagined, Marchale had been waiting for him to call and was very nearly as upset about it.

On the other hand, Adam felt as though he had a fairly good excuse for not making phone calls last evening. "You'll have to forgive me, Professor," he said. "I had an unexpectedly interesting evening. Someone tried to stab me in the street after dinner." He had listened to the morning news and heard no report of the incident. Probably attempted assaults were not quite newsworthy, even in a usually quiet city like Ottawa.

Marchale glared at him, apparently searching for any sign of a joke, and finding none, burst out in a brief laugh. "Well damn you, anyway," he declared, throwing up one hand, "A perfectly good fit of temper wasted! Stabbed, eh?" he went on, shifting seamlessly to a new subject as usual. "Bilk someone out of a first edition, or sell them a mystery with the last page missing, or what? Nothing in your wallet worth the trouble of carrying away, is there?"

Adam was still wondering why Hugh Thomas had tried to attack him himself, and didn't feel like explaining what little he did understand about the situation to Marchale, who would take wicked delight in the idea of Adam's attacker being a former parishioner. "It's still not very clear," he said instead. "The police said they would need to investigate." Adam hoped that they would indeed do that, and not just write Hugh off as a junkie. Whatever problems Hugh was having, he suspected they ran deeper than that.

"Investigate," replied Marchale with some venom. "That's if they know the meaning of the word, which I doubt. Mutter some platitudes to the press and get back to writing parking tickets, more like." Marchale was either unwilling or unable to understand the parking laws of every city he had ever lived in, and as a result got a steady stream of citations. He was often heard to declare that with the money he had paid out, he should be able to park wherever he wanted. "Anyway, an exciting night for you, must be the first in years," he grinned. "And you're here now, so what have you made of Charles Warrington, hmm? Enlighten me."

"Well," Adam began, "I really only made a start with the package you left for me. But I read part of his book, and I think I see why he wasn't very highly regarded as a writer." Thinking about it this morning, that led to another question, but Marchale pounced immediately.

"Book, hah," he said scornfully. "A mere pamphlet! But it really isn't good, is it? Can't think what fool would have published it, dreadful read, bad as these," he went on, jabbing a pile of essays with his unlit pipe. "Those articles I gave you will explain exactly why it's dreadful in proper academic form, but you got the essential point."

"There's a question, though," Adam said. "If Warrington wasn't a very good writer, where did his money come from? He was retired in Rockcliffe, after all." Marchale chuckled happily.

"You should know better than most," he answered, "That bad writing is no barrier to making a pile of money from it. Make most of your money selling it, don't you? Anyway, maybe his travel writing is better, he spent half his life wandering around the globe and possibly he was more readable about that." It was somewhat plausible, Adam considered, but did people get rich at travel writing? "Maybe his family was rich to begin with, but as usual you are distracted from the important point," Marchale declared.

"I'm sorry," Adam said blankly. "What was the important point, again?" He genuinely didn't know where the professor was trying to lead him, and felt as though his skills for this kind of thing, such as they were, were terribly rusty. Then again, perhaps he had an excuse in the other problems demanding his attention, as well as the earliness of the hour. It was also true that Marchale enjoyed little demonstrations of his own prowess, so perhaps this opportunity would put him into a better mood and was all for the best, Adam considered.

"No mention in the book or those articles about it of that weird thing you brought me the other day," Marchale said with a curious relish. Adam supposed he might have been disappointed to have a puzzle solved so easily. "No mention of it at all! And I doubt it's in his travel books either, unless he happens to wax poetic about his travels along the River Wear and stumbling over a delightful bookshop. No," he said, now in the tone with which he delivered most of his lectures, "We can discount his writing, I think, and will have to fall back on our own wits, God help us!"

Adam was somewhat inclined to think the same thing, although the problem of the book had lost some importance compared to other recent events. "Maybe it isn't worth the effort," he offered. "I mean there's no rush as far as I can see." With one friend recovering in the hospital, and another facing an array of problems that might include addiction and jail, the issue of an enigmatic old manuscript didn't seem terrifically pressing.

Marchale made a disgusted noise. "Good Christ, you'd never have gotten through that damned thesis without me dragging you, would you? Terrible attitude. I have ideas, my boy, and am not yet ready to admit defeat." He really was enjoying the problem, Adam realized. Adam also recalled that Marchale was loathe to abandon a project once he had gotten started with it, a trait that led him to have three or four different pieces of work underway at once on many occasions.

"What did you have in mind?" Adam asked with some trepidation. He expected Marchale to want a lot more time to be spent at the library, and Adam was hoping to give a lot of attention to Bones and Hugh Thomas over the next few days. He began rehearsing arguments for the upcoming negotiation as the professor began to explain his plan of attack.

"First thing, I want to take some images of the thing, send them to some people I know who are more manuscript specialists than I am," said Marchale. He was usually brutally honest about his own limitations, as well as those of his students. "Very possible some clever soul out there can read it, even if I can't. May even recognize the thing, I suppose." He made this last suggestion slightly wistfully; Adam knew Marchale would be disappointed if someone else simply handed him the answer.

"Sounds reasonable," Adam allowed. There was certainly no harm in asking the questions, and despite his prickly nature, Marchale did have a large number of close relationships with peers around the world. Academia did have a peculiar tolerance for social transgressions of various kinds.

"Next thing is for you to get back to the library, go through the rest of Warrington's writings with a fine comb, see if there's a reference to the book after all." Marchale waved his hand vaguely towards the window, which was more or less in the direction of the main university library. It was as though he was giving an indication that Adam should depart instantly.

"I thought you just said that we should discount his writing?" Adam demanded, slightly annoyed. Marchale did like to play devil's advocate, and then insist that an idea he had just spend twenty minutes demolishing was perfectly reasonable. It made figuring out which of his criticisms were heartfelt, which were demands for greater intellectual rigour, and which were entirely mischievous, a difficult and endless task. During his thesis supervision, Adam had vacillated between thinking that this was all a strategy to keep him from becoming too reliant on Marchale's opinions, and the equally likely prospect that the professor just enjoyed causing intellectual mayhem.

"Well, we probably can, but it's not worth taking the chance, and you have plenty of time on your hands. Probably a fool's errand, but you're oddly well-suited for those. Cross it off our list and we can move on to other avenues. Meantime I will exploit my vast web of admiring colleagues in search of a shortcut." Marchale offered these directions without any visible fear of contradiction. He and Adam had slipped back into their old roles of supervisor and student apparently unconsciously. It was remarkable, Adam thought, how indelible some patterns from the past turned out to be.

"And if that doesn't work?" Adam inquired. He was inwardly a little skeptical that the book would be recognized. If it was that well known, surely they should have found some records of it by now. It had occurred to him that Warrington's book might be a replica of a volume from a better-known collection, but again, were that true they should have found traces of it.

"Well, then we will have something interesting, won't we? I did make one minor discovery since we last spoke, which was the other reason I wanted you to call." Marchale opened a drawer of his desk and drew out the book Bones had bought at Warrington's auction. He had placed it in a box made of what Adam knew would be archival-quality cardboard; despite his somewhat flippant attitude about their research, Marchale clearly took the book itself seriously, at least.

"Ah. What did you find?" Here was the discovery Adam had expected, at last. Marchale did have a sense for the dramatic and often liked to save up 'the good bit', both of lectures and conversations, for the end.

"Nothing much, nothing earth-shattering, but worth noting in our quest. Here, what do you make of that?" he asked, opening the book to its last folio, and pointing to the bottom of the paper. This last folio, he remembered, had no writing on it, as though the book's author had finished with his subject on the recto side. In his own brief study of the manuscript, Adam had seen this as an indication that whatever other problems there were with the text, it was reasonably certain that all the pages were at least present for analysis.

Adam leaned forward and squinted at the paper, and where Marchale's stubby finger was indicating, he could just discern a few characters. The ink was a slightly darker brown than the especially age-discoloured bottom corner. 'mccccbxxxvii', he eventually decided they were. The string of characters only made sense as Roman numerals, but it was curious to see them in lowercase.

"Interesting," Adam said. "A date?" He parsed the numerals in his head and came up with 1487, which seemed to confirm what they had both thought about the age of the original manuscript. Significantly older than its 19th century binding. "I can't imagine how I missed it."

"Typical of you lot," Marchale growled, meaning his students, of course. "Never mind, you said you went through the whole thing straight, and it does make the eyes glaze over after a while. Happens to the best of us, but then the best of us are clever enough to come back and pay special attention to the parts we were glazed over for, which I did, and found that." He tapped out a little triumphant flourish on his desk. "Still, now that you've been led to it by your betters, any thoughts?"

Adam took a moment to consider, and offered the observation that it confirmed their ideas about dating to buy himself some time. "Roman numerals confirm, or strongly suggest anyway, that the book is from Europe, or the Mediterranean world, at least." There was something slightly odd about the numerals that was nagging at him. "It's a little odd that the rest of the book is in this mysterious script but the date is written in standard format." Standard format. Finally he remembered. "Shouldn't it be 'MCDL', and so on, not 'MCCCC'?"

"Are you asking me or telling me?" Marchale demanded. "Got me to write half your thesis that way." As Adam was talking, he had picked up his pipe again, looked in several desk drawers for tobacco that he was no longer allowed to smoke on campus, and now tossed it back down resignedly.

Adam sighed. "It has been a while since I've needed to do anything with Roman numerals," he said, "but I'm fairly sure 'MCD' would be the right way to write 1400, not 'MCCCC'."

Marchale nodded, apparently in satisfaction. "Right you are, right you are. And so?" He was quietly drumming his fingers on the desk again, anticipating the next point.

Adam sat back and thought it over for a few moments. Marchale included guesswork on his admittedly lengthy lists of pet peeves, so it was usually best to think through whatever conclusions you were planning on offering. "It's a mistake," Adam mused, "Someone who didn't know their numerals very well. I suppose that makes it more likely it's a forgery, possibly something Warrington made to go with one of his stories." Somehow, he found this vaguely disappointing.

"It could be so," Marchale allowed. "If I accepted that it was that sort of mistake, which I don't." He rubbed his hands together. "Now, you don't have my vast experience with these things, but in fact if you look at medieval documents, the real deal mind you, you find they made that exact type of 'mistake' all the time! Find 'MCCCC' for 1400 and 'xxxx' for 40 at least as much as you find the opposite. Maybe the fools were as bad in school as you are, maybe they thought the Romans were a bunch of has-beens, doesn't matter, for our purposes, why." He made a sharp cutting motion with his hand to indicate that this was not a point he was interested in discussing. "But the point is," he continued, "I think a forger would be paying so much attention to getting all the details right that they would have done it the 'correct' way. I think it would be a very subtle fellow indeed who would fake a book and risk deliberately getting it wrong like that. You'll also note the characters in the number are lowercase; medieval scribes did that, we think, because capital letters took up more space and parchment was worth a bloody mint, and took longer to write out besides. No, I think this is our best indication that this is the genuine article." He closed the book again with a happy little smile on his face.

Adam mulled that over. It was hardly conclusive, because a really professional imitator might have done their background research, learned the same thing from medieval documents that Marchale had, and included the irregular date by way of authenticity. However, it was hard to see what the profit would be in a forgery like this, and he was inclined to agree with Marchale's interpretation. "All right. Genuine article of what?" he asked finally.

"No idea!" said Marchale gleefully. "Still, finding out should be entertaining, much more entertaining than this damned stack of term papers." He was still scowling at the pile of essays after Adam had made his goodbyes and left, heading to the generally soluble puzzles of running a used book store.

Chapter 13

Adam arrived at the store and was relieved to find no donations this morning, nor anything that was alarming, unsanitary, or both, on either the front step nor in the back alley. As the morning promised to be sunny, he brought out the folding table from the basement and set it up on the sidewalk in front of the store, and placed several milk crates of books in poor condition or of dubious quality on it, along with the handwritten sign advertising the 'three books for a buck' deal. Mostly this helped clear otherwise useless stock, and attracted a certain amount of attention to the store that might then be redirected onto more lucrative targets. It was also true, Adam had to admit, that when the books had arrived via yam box there was a marginal benefit to the bottom line of W.M. Howard, Bookseller, as well. After going through the rest of his store-opening and coffee-producing ritual, he settled in to await the business of the day. This proved to be slow in coming, as was all too common for a weekday, and so once he was suitably fortified by caffeine he decided to further plumb the depths of the collection of Charles Warrington documents.

Warrington's writing, declared an academic article comparing him to several other fiction writers of the post World War II period, *evinces an almost clinical air and prioritizes broad ideas at the absolute expense of narrative or character. To this extent it can be said to reflect the post bellum emphasis on ideology as a preeminent driving force overriding all other concerns.*

Adam digested this briefly and decided the point made a degree of sense, although there wasn't much in *The Eater of the Sun* that fit into a political narrative or ideological argument. But then, it was always possible that the intention had been there, but the execution had simply been poor. Perhaps that had been the conclusion of the scholar who wrote the article, because she mentioned Warrington only in passing a few times for the rest of the piece. Ultimately his work was more of a buttress for her overarching thesis rather than a key part of it.

"Filler more than anything, hmmm?" Adam said to the pile of documents. Well, it was becoming abundantly clear that Charles Warrington had not been greatly regarded, during his life or after, as a writer of fiction, but that wasn't very useful, or even very relevant, towards the aim of figuring out what the book Napoleon had purchased was. Adam was increasingly inclined to think that if there was a clue to be found, it would be in Warrington's writing itself.

With some reluctance, then, he picked out *The Eater of the Sun* again and made an effort to plunge through a little more. *How the banishment or exile of the entity was accomplished, I have not yet been able to uncover, and while such methodology could, arguably, be of present utility, I do not regard this as a primary concern in writing here. How these past actors knew of a world without a sun to bind the thing on, and a way to send it there, is fascinating but of less relevance than what actions must be taken in the here and now.*

Adam shook his head slightly and finished his coffee. Surely it would not have been too much trouble to invent a suitably dramatic, arcane ritual, perhaps requiring the spilling of innocent blood or another painful sacrifice, to give the discussion a little bite. Instead the author had left that part of the story as 'unknown', which Adam supposed might fit with the conceit of a book resulting from 'research'. It seemed an unnecessary sacrifice in terms of appeal for the reader, though. Warrington had been so determined, apparently, to make it seem as though he was recounting actual facts that he hadn't thought about whether the result was very enjoyable to read. Adam wondered if he had some personal connection to the publisher.

He skimmed a little ahead and read on. *The present danger,* the book continued, *is that there will be those sufficiently depraved, foolhardy, or perhaps desperate, to attempt to undo what has been done before and effect a return of the exiled creature to our Earth, for while it is weakened in banishment there is no reason to suppose that it might perish. We can easily assume that just as there were those with the conviction to send the entity away, there will be those with equal determination to bring about its return, and they will inevitably have such tools as they believe necessary to accomplish their end.* Adam frowned and thought this over. Again there was a great deal of hand-waving of details, here, and details that might have been interesting to a reader. What were the 'tools'86? Why would they be 'inevitable'?

He had been reading for only a few minutes but already he was finding the book deeply frustrating to read, and wondered if this might be a job better delegated to Fred Wallace, who had rarely encountered a piece of fantastic fiction he couldn't squeeze some enjoyment out of. Well, why not, Adam thought. They had worked together on a lot of projects, when they had met as the Fridays Guild, and it might please Fred to help solve Bones' little puzzle, too. Adam supposed he was guilty of abandoning a task that he was finding difficult and unengaging, but sometimes there was no shame in passing work along to the person best suited for it, rather than expending a lot of energy on a job one struggled with.

The rest of the morning and the bulk of the afternoon passed quickly. There was a reasonably steady flow of customers, many in search of cheap copies of the latest Scandinavian murder-thriller, which, fortunately, the store had in abundance. Books purchased for beach reading tended to get jettisoned as soon as the end of the vacation, and some people cooled on recommendations from 'hot' lists fairly rapidly. There was even a thin faced blond man who came and scowled around the back library briefly, and then left without saying a word. Adam watched his departure with a little bemusement and then returned to negotiating with a customer over the price of a *Riverside Shakespeare*. Yes, he knew you could get paperbacks of the individual plays for next to nothing. No, that wasn't really relevant to the cost of a showpiece, hardcover compendium. Adam was quite relieved when they were interrupted, again, by the chime of the front door opening, and he recognized that the tall, thin arrival represented an escape from the discussion altogether.

The arrival of Eric Speirs also reminded Adam that this was supposed to be one of his rare evenings off. Eric was an art history student at the university who did a few shifts at the store around his studies and other commitments. His reliability was erratic, but Adam couldn't really be a choosy employer; the profit margins at W.M. Howard, Bookseller were small enough that they could offer only a fairly modest wage and reasonably modest hours on top of it. Eric knew enough about books to be helpful to customers, usually turned up when he was supposed to, and was responsible enough to lock up the store and secure the night deposit. He also seemed to be in a constant process of reinventing his look — currently he seemed to be trending towards goth, but it was always hard to predict.

Adam exchanged some pleasantries, handed off the Shakespeare negotiator to Eric, and then headed home. He arrived in time to find his telephone ringing. It was Jane Moore. "Father, finally," she said. "I tried you at the store first but I guess you had just left. Anyway, you need to come to the hospital right away. Bones is awake."

Chapter 14

Adam decided it was worth paying a cab to get to the hospital as quickly as he could. It felt important that Bones have his friends around him as soon as possible. It had occurred to him to call the other Guild members, but he would have had to look up their numbers. Jane would probably have them on hand.

"Hi Father," said Jane, as he came in the door. There was a doctor standing by the bedside, and Jane was sitting in the chair on the other side. "Sophia and Fred are on their way too." The doctor was explaining that Bones still needed rest and would need to limit his exertions severely over the next weeks, but he was interrupted again.

"Listen, someone write this down before I forget," said Bones, still quietly, but intensely. Jane fished out her tablet computer in time for him to recite six letters and numbers. Bones repeated them twice to make sure he, and Jane, had them straight. When he was finished, he laid back again with a look of rather grim satisfaction.

"Wait, did you get the license plate of the van, Bones?" Jane asked incredulously. It was a little strange to think of taking notice of a detail like that in the chaos of the assault. She had also noted the digits on a little notepad that Adam supposed she probably carried with her everywhere, and entered them into her Blackberry, backing up her information seemingly by reflex.

"I was lying there looking up at that van, and taking that beating, and knowing no one was coming to help, and so it felt like the one thing I could do was remember that plate. So yeah, I got it, so one day they could get what they had coming," Bones answered in a quiet, tight voice. He twisted the bedsheets in a clenched fist as he spoke.

"God will punish," Adam interjected, to his own surprise. The words had slipped out inadvertently. He had never pushed the idea of a God who provided appropriate consequences for people's actions, which was so often at odds with most people's experience with the world, and wasn't really even sure he believed it himself. Still, sometimes it was a comfort to think that there would be rewards and punishments that matched the things that people took in life, and he imagined the appeal of that idea was what had made him say what he did.

"I hope you're right, Father," replied Bones, with unaccustomed venom in his voice now. "If God don't do it, someone else better, you know?" He looked about as angry now as Adam could ever remember seeing him, and the doctor stirred uncomfortably.

"That's nothing to worry about now, Mr. Kale," Adam soothed. "You need to get yourself healthy again. I'm sure Inspector Kolb will want to know that plate number, though." Neither his own experience nor the doctor's incomplete explanation of Bones' condition told him very much about the ideal course for his recovery, but Adam was certain that this was not a good time to be getting angered and upset, as understandable as it was.

"I called the number he left," said Jane. "Some other cop who answered said he'd be by later." Having the license plate seemed like it should be decisive, to Adam, although it was possible the van had been abandoned by now. Even so, it surely had to be a strong lead for the investigation — the accounts of what forensic teams could accomplish with even the smallest pieces of evidence were greatly encouraging. With this, Adam felt real optimism that Bones' attackers would be found.

"Bella?" Bones asked. Adam realized he had left Napoleon's girlfriend out of his thinking entirely. Of course someone should have called her, but at the same time he had no idea how to reach her.

"Don't worry, I called her too," Jane assured him. "She's on her way as soon as someone comes to cover her shift. You're so popular, Bones." She smiled brightly and gave him a playful shove on the shoulder. Adam wasn't sure if she was deliberately trying to lighten the mood, but either way he admired the effect.

"Awww, who can blame 'em," replied Bones with a somewhat weaker version of his usual grin. "Where else are you gonna find something this good?" He preened as much as it was possible to do so, in a hospital bed, while attached to an IV and a heart monitor.

The doctor cleared his throat and asked, a little diffidently, if he could finish explaining the prognosis to his patient. Bones indicated that he should continue with an expansive, lordly gesture that produced a titter of amusement from Jane. Adam grinned broadly as well, if only because it seemed as though Bones' spirit was intact.

The doctor explained that the most severe crisis had passed; there was no longer blood on Napoleon's brain and the danger of intracranial swelling was now greatly reduced. However, there was no doubt that he had a serious concussion, and that the fractures to the skull would take some time to heal. Taken along with Bones' other injuries, which included broken ribs and a cracked collarbone, there would be a long period of mandatory bed rest, and then physical activity could be slowly resumed.

Jane rolled her eyes at these last directions. "You will do anything," she said with assumed severity, "to get out of doing work for a while. You know you were supposed to help Freddie move in a couple of weeks." She smiled and shook her head in mock disappointment.

"Oh yeah," Bones replied, "moving in with you, isn't he?" He grinned in enjoyment of his own joke, and anticipation of Jane's reaction.

"Ewwww, Napoleon, gross," she admonished him. "You should be nicer to people who spend half their lives at your hospital room, God."

"Sorry Father," Bones said immediately, "she knows not what she does. You know how it is for people in love." He broke off into a laugh that degenerated into a cough, prompting an intervention from the doctor, who insisted that Bones avoid excitement of any kind for at least the next several days.

"I apologize, doctor," Adam said soothingly, "we're just very pleased to see Mr. Kale doing better. I'm sure everyone will see to it that things stay calm here for the next while." He looked over to see Jane smiling sweetly and that Bones had assumed an expression of angelic innocence. Keeping him 'resting quietly' was going to be a challenge, but in Adam's experience having one's spirits raised was also key to a quick recovery. Jane and the others would be good for Napoleon, especially if they kept him from brooding about his attackers.

The doctor excused himself and Adam went to the cafeteria to fetch a coffee for himself and a tea for Jane. Along the way he tried to decide whether it was worth telling Bones any of the results of his research into the book, and decided that it was still such an agglomeration of educated guesses, assumptions and apparently unrelated trivia that it wouldn't make for a very satisfactory distraction. Probably it was best just to tell him that the investigation was underway. Bones might be pleased to know that Adam had resumed his connection to Professor Marchale, he supposed.

That chain of thought kept him busy until he was returning to Bones' room, and now chewing over some of the other puzzles that had appeared in his life lately — the unpleasant visit from Reverend Smiles, the strange confrontation with Hugh Thomas, and the gnawing sense that the two things were connected. Certainly it wasn't worth mentioning either of these things to Bones, not when he was meant to be keeping relaxed.

However, thinking of puzzles and Bones' remarkable recall of the license plate number led Adam to wonder if he might remember other useful things about the attack. Adam remembered reading somewhere that it was important for people to relate the details of anything they had witnessed as soon as possible. While Inspector Kolb would surely arrive soon, it seemed like a good idea to jog Bones' memory immediately, if he could.

Adam gave Jane her drink and Napoleon an apologetic glance — he was strictly forbidden anything from the cafeteria for at least the next few days. Once Bones and Jane finished another teasing exchange, Adam coughed quietly and broke into the conversation. "Bones, I know this will be difficult," said Adam, "but can you remember anything else about the people who attacked you? Did they say anything to you?" Having started, he realized he didn't really know what the right questions to ask would be, and hoped that Inspector Kolb wouldn't end up being annoyed that he had interfered with a witness.

"They didn't say a word," Bones answered flatly, his amused demeanor draining away nearly instantly. "That van pulled up, they jumped up, and they just went after me. I know they took my stuff but that was after I was down. They didn't ask for my wallet or anything." His jaw set angrily, and his hands clenched into fists again.

Adam nodded slightly and regretted asking the question at all. "I'm sorry, it just seems so senseless," he said softly. "I suppose I was hoping for something that might help us understand." Adam had never really believed in a divine plan that determined the path of events, and it had been a long time since he had thought that things happened for a reason either, but he did like to think that most things that people did, or that happened to them, could at least be explained and understood.

"Nothing to understand, Father," Bones replied firmly. "Some people are just no good. Some people are just bad fucking news." Adam was a little taken aback; he knew Bones and the rest of the Guild children had always made a point of minding their language around him. It had always amused him a bit, because swearing had always been among the least of his concerns, but it was a sign of respect as well and he had cherished that.

"There are good people too, Mr. Kale," he found himself saying. "Don't let yourself forget that." It was easy to let anger become the main reaction to any crisis, and Adam had seen it lead people in bad directions on more than one occasion.

"Nah, Father," Bones answered. "I know that every day. No idiot with a bat is gonna take that from me." Adam smiled and found a chair to sit and wait for the others to arrive.

Chapter 15

Over the next two days, Adam made as many visits to the hospital as he could. Bones was obviously tiring of mandatory bed rest fairly rapidly, beyond that he seemed to be recovering quickly. Every so often, the anger about his attack would resurface, but usually he seemed content, or at least willing, to let the police investigation run its course. Adam regretted that he had not had another opportunity to speak with the detective looking into the case, but the others told him that John Kolb had been in at least twice already to speak to Bones, take his statement and ask questions.

The case had never gotten beyond local news coverage but even that rapidly ceased; Adam had had enough conversations with Jane to know that neither *Victim continues to recover* nor *No new developments in investigation* were tempting story lines for the news media. It was reassuring to know that the case was still getting significant attention from the police.

Adam also tried to spend as much time as he could researching Charles Warrington, and quickly became thankful that he had not been a more significant or prolific author. Even with Warrington's modest reputation there was still a good deal of material relating to his work, usually trying to place him into the emerging speculative fiction genre of the post-war period, or comparing and contrasting him to more well-known writers. Unfortunately, there was nothing in the discussion of Warrington the writer that shed any light on his ownership of the strange book; he was not, or at least was never described as, a collector of antiquities, rare books, or occult curiosities, and even the more in-depth descriptions of his craft did not suggest that he used particular objects as the inspiration for his writing.

As a result, Adam was beginning to fear that this whole thrust of the project was ultimately a dead end. Warrington had not been a significant enough figure to have his life examined in detail, and so it seemed extremely improbable that the books in his library would be mentioned in any of the academic writing. It was possible that there might still be some connection to be found in Warrington's own works, although Adam increasingly felt that was a long shot too. With luck Marchale, or one of his colleagues, would be able to advance things from the manuscript studies end of the question.

Although the specific puzzle provided by Bones and his book increasingly appeared to be insoluble, Adam quickly came to enjoy exercising his mothballed research skills again. Perhaps he had abandoned his scholarship rather too completely upon taking up stewardship of his first parish, and certainly once he left the church he now felt he should have resumed some sort of academic pursuit rather than immersing himself quite so completely, and exclusively, in the world of W.M. Howard, Bookseller. It was still not appropriate, Adam reflected, to take up one of the research assistantships Professor Marchale had repeatedly offered, but there must be some contribution he could make as an independent scholar. The problems there were the lack of resources that came from attachment to an institution, and of course the lack of compensation. Even so, he resolved to try to give some thought to a direction for it all once the horizons cleared a bit.

Adam was pondering all of this during a quiet morning at the store, one unafflicted by yam boxes full of unwanted books or alarming alleyway discoveries, but also unfortunately free of customers. He had just made a second pot of coffee and settled down to a crossword puzzle when the door jangled open.

The man entering the store was immaculately and precisely dressed in a blue suit, but could really have been any of the thousands of urban professionals found in downtown Ottawa every day. His most notable features were a gleamingly bald head, which to Adam had the look of being shaved frequently, and a pair of round framed glasses made something like steel or silver. "Good morning, good morning," the man said pleasantly, smoothing down his tie as he spoke. "You are Mr. Howard, perhaps?" He gently lowered a soft leather briefcase to the floor.

The case seemed to be bulging with documents and Adam supposed it was probably reasonably heavy to lug around.

"Alas no," Adam replied with a friendly smile. "Mr. Howard is semi-retired and isn't in at the store today. Was there something I can help you with, or did you need to speak with him specifically?" From time to time they got inquiries from people who were interested in the store's location, in buying the business, and of course in selling them office or retail supplies. Adam had long found it a useful tactic to be able to defer all such inquiries up the chain of command to Walt Howard, who would genuinely intend to get back to these people, but would undoubtedly take several weeks before doing so.

"Ah, my mistake," the visitor answered. "Then would you be," he flipped open a small leather bound folder and glanced at a paper inside, "Mr. Godwinson?" He offered a tight little smile as he snapped the folder closed again.

"That's right," Adam said. "I suppose I handle a good part of the store's day to day business, so possibly I can assist you?" It was a little curious to find a salesperson that would have his name, but he supposed that speaking to the staff of other businesses in the area would obtain the information easily enough.

"Oh, I do hope so," his visitor said earnestly, extending a hand. "My name is Paul Bagot, and I have some interest in a book I believe your store may recently have acquired." Adam shook his hand, and Bagot then re-opened his little folder to extract a business card. "My card, before I forget." The folder snapped shut again promptly.

Adam examined it and laid it down on the counter. "A lawyer, Mr. Bagot?" he inquired. "I hope there isn't a problem regarding a sale?" Once, when he had first started working for Walt Howard, there had been an issue where they had bought a lovely old copy of Audubon's *Birds of America* and then been informed that the person who sold it to them was a relative of the owner who had not had any permission to sell the book. In the end, faced with a protracted legal wrangle and the costs associated with it, Howard had simply returned the book and absorbed the loss. Bagot's card didn't declare any affiliation to a law firm, as far as Adam could see, so presumably his practice, and, with luck, his potential for causing trouble, was relatively modest.

"Oh, I'm not here in a legal capacity today," Bagot said with a breathy little chuckle, "but as the grandson of Charles Warrington." He had a slightly expectant look on his face now, and Adam quickly had to decide how helpful he was going to be. The man's appearance at the store was definitely a curious development, and there was also at least one other reason to proceed with a bit of caution.

Adam glanced at him a little quizzically. "Mr. Warrington's grandson, you say?" he asked, with slight emphasis on the name.

"On my mother's side, naturally, of course," Bagot added hastily. "But in any case I am advised that your store recently purchased a volume from my late grandfather's estate, an untitled work of some age, perhaps?" He glanced around the shop quickly, as if hoping to immediately sight his objective prominently displayed on one of the shelves.

"You are quickly, if not completely accurately, informed," Adam answered with some surprise. It was always surprising how rapidly rumours could spread, but there were additional issues. "In fact a friend of mine bought the book, and although he brought it to me for an evaluation, neither I nor the store have purchased it." Of course there would have been a record of the book's purchase at the estate sale, but how that would have led to the bookstore was much harder to fathom. On one hand, Adam was glad that Bagot had not bothered Bones in the hospital, but on the other it was slightly alarming that the book's movements had apparently been traced at all.

"Ah, well, the important part, if I may, is that you have it," Bagot said eagerly. He had visibly brightened at the confirmation that the book was, or at least had been, here. Adam began to wonder if it was worth a great deal after all, but at the same time there were more pressing concerns.

"I'm a little curious as to how you know that," Adam replied firmly. "It only came into my keeping a few days ago and I haven't spoken to anyone about it." He decided to leave out Professor Marchale's involvement, for now. Something was not quite right about this visit and he decided against volunteering any information. Possibly the lawyer would inadvertently reveal the source of his intelligence.

"Well, I have made inquiries, you see," Bagot said, stroking at his chin. "The thing is, the important factor, if I may, is that the book was in all likelihood, I should say certainly, never meant to be included in the estate sale. The volume was of particular value to the family and it had been intended for it to remain with them, you see." He lowered his voice slightly as he spoke, suggesting that in offering this information, he was extending a significant confidence.

Adam thought this over for a moment. Bagot's story wasn't impossible, based on his experience with how estates got parcelled out after the death of a family member, when everyone was affected by grief and so many things needed to be done in what seemed like no time at all. Still, there were obvious problems. "Perhaps we should make certain we're talking about the same book before we go any further, Mr. Bagot," he suggested. "Do you have some documentation with you?"

"Oh, do call me Paul, of course," Bagot replied. "And I did bring some material to clear up any confusion along those lines, just bear with me for one moment, if you would be very kind." He laid down his folder on the counter, opened his briefcase, and searched through it briefly before finding a manila folder, which he opened and placed on the counter as well. "Here we are, if you would have a look at these, Mr. Godwinson, or?" he looked up inquiringly.

"Adam is fine," he allowed. The folder held a little sheaf of papers, secured by a bulldog clip. The page on top had what looked like two different photographs of the book Napoleon had brought in, but somewhat grainy and in black and white. From what little he knew about photography, Adam thought they were poor-quality digital images.

"Now, yes, here we are," Bagot went on, "Manuscript book bound in leather, brown, no title, shelf mark KD," he glanced up at Adam repeatedly as he read from the page. "Untitled and unsigned, age of work indeterminate. Text degenerate or obscure, length 326 folios in paper." He paused, licked his lips briefly, and then looked up again. "Does that sound like the, ah, volume in question, Adam?"

"It does indeed," he replied quietly. "And you say the book was of considerable value? I hope you're not suggesting anything improper has taken place." The last thing Adam wanted to face, and in fact one of the very last things the store could weather financially, was a lawsuit over a book in their possession.

"Oh, by no means, not at all," Bagot said soothingly, "No, no. Merely an unfortunate, ah, mistaken course of events, perhaps? An honest mistake. And the value, well, is primarily, overwhelmingly, sentimental, of course, and I did not mean to imply otherwise. No, the late Mr. Warrington had the book for many years, you see, and because of that and its, ah, unique character, the family views it as emblematic, or representative, perhaps, of his collection."

"A little strange," Adam observed, "that a book like that would end up being accidentally sold, then."

"Well, unfortunate, to be sure, or certainly regrettable, but you see," Bagot lowered his voice to just above a whisper, "without meaning to speak out of turn, in the immediate aftermath of Mr. Warrington's decease, owing to the, ah, bereavement, the family left the disposition of his estate in the hands of a second party, who I would not of course name, but who may not have been as respectful, or at least not as attentive, of all the family's wishes as might have been desirable."

"Dear me," Adam replied, "I hope the matter isn't being left to rest like that?"

"Oh, well," Bagot answered, "we are taking advice on the issue, of course, but I fear we are perhaps straying from the most important reason for my visit, and there are issues of confidentiality to consider, you understand."

"Naturally," Adam allowed. "What is it that you were hoping for?" It was important, he felt, to let the lawyer lay out all his cards and try to react as little as possible, for now.

"Well, to be forthright, Adam," Bagot said with a little smile, "I had hoped that you might see your way clear to returning the book to the family, allowing for some recompense in terms of the purchase price. Failing that, I am empowered to negotiate reasonable terms to buy the volume from you outright," he adopted a more serious tone, "although I should warn you that the family will not be taken advantage of in a time of grief and the opportunity for profit is, ah, slim."

"Dear me," Adam said again, "what a thing to suggest. Profit would be the furthest thing from my mind, Paul, and I'm certain we could come to some arrangement quickly, except for two difficulties." He reflected that he was going to enjoy the rest of this conversation, but also that Bagot's presence in the store did have some alarming implications.

"Do excuse me, please," Bagot said, betraying a little suspicion in his voice, "but what are these difficulties? My clients, that is, the family, we desire a quick resolution to the matter, if possible." He had drawn both his leather booklet and the manila folder towards him on the counter slightly, somewhat protectively.

"Well, the first problem," Adam explained, "is that the book is not mine to sell, or return to you. As I said it was purchased by a friend of mine and although it is in my keeping," he again allowed himself a little fiction here, "I can hardly give away or agree to a price on something that doesn't belong to me, you understand."

"Ah, well, yes," Bagot replied diffidently, "I can see the difficulty arising there, indeed. Perhaps you had best put me in touch with your friend, and negotiations, or conversation, can proceed?" Now the leather folder was flipped open, and he took out a pen, clearly poised to take down contact information.

"Well, my friend is currently in hospital," Adam said apologetically, "so I'm afraid you may need to exercise some patience, there." The pen wavered over the folder and then was slowly put away. The lawyer pursed his lips and then slowly flipped the cover closed again.

"How sad, and unfortunate," Bagot said, "I trust a full recovery is expected? Perhaps you might obtain permission to act on their behalf in the, ah, interim?"

"Well, all things are possible," Adam said solemnly, "but there is still the second of our problems."

"Yes, yes," Bagot replied, with perhaps a touch of annoyance. "And what is that?"

"Well, it's a curious thing, Mr. Bagot," said Adam, fingering the business card on the counter in front of him, "but I have spent the last several days researching the life of Charles Warrington, and I have learned a great many things, some interesting and some less, but one fact I discovered is of tremendous interest to me just now, and that is that although Charles Warrington did marry, and did have two children, neither had any children of their own. So you'll understand that there seem to be a number of things we need to clarify, yes?"

Bagot said nothing, and fiddled at the arm of his glasses nervously.

"I find," Adam continued, "that when people are conducting legitimate business, they do so honestly, and that when one begins to encounter mistruths, the motive behind them is suspicious as well. I think just about everything you have told me since you came into my shop has been lies, and I wonder exactly what you are really up to? What's your real interest in this book?"

"You ... you will hear from our lawyers," Bagot said, hastily grabbing his folder from the counter and retreating towards the door.

"I look forward to it," Adam called after him, "you evidently know where to find me." Bagot fumbled the door open and fled, leaving Adam to mull over whether it was worth calling the police, why the curious book Bones had bought on a whim was worth such a subterfuge, and yet time had apparently not been taken to construct a more plausible story. He fingered Bagot's business card and eyed the crossword again, trying to decide which puzzle to work on next.

Chapter 16

Later that evening, Adam had just finished washing the supper dishes and was debating the relative merits of watching *Jeopardy!* over weeding the garden. The carrots had come up enough that they needed to be thinned out, as had the radishes, and the apparently invincible lilies planted by a previous owner of the house had made yet another return this spring. Working in the garden was usually relaxing, and Adam found that extirpating a patch of weeds or caring for some vegetables gave a sense of accomplishment that was a pleasant contrast to life's more durable problems. Faced with an unusual array of difficulties, Adam decided to give garden therapy a try.

It had been clear and warm through most of the day, and although it was already starting to cool down, the evening promised to be a pleasant one. Adam knelt in the grass at the edge of his vegetable patch and began thinning his radishes. There was always a moment where he had to gather the necessary ruthlessness to uproot some of the fledgling plants, although he also always felt the hesitation was silly. He had once tried to use the process as a foundation for a sermon on the need to be willing to do unpleasant things that one knew was right, but he hadn't believed the congregation was very pleased with the metaphor, or perhaps the message.

Thinking back to his time at St. Michael's would always dampen Adam's mood and now there was a dour feel to the previously pleasing evening. The light seemed to be failing more quickly than expected, and there was a chill in the air. He stood up from the radishes to go back inside and fetch a sweater, not wanting to leave the job unfinished. As he crossed the tiny yard, he glanced up at the sky and found it thoroughly transformed from how it had been when he had stepped outside a few minutes ago.

The sky overhead was abruptly and heavily covered with what seemed to be very low clouds that had turned the early evening twilight into equally sudden darkness. The wind stirred through the trees and the garden in short gusts that seemed to be building in intensity. The mass of clouds roiled and squirmed across the sky restlessly. Aside from the wind the street was silent, and Adam stood under the patio light and watched the sky for a few minutes, expecting to see lightning soon and anticipating the spectacle of a thunderstorm at night.

The wind continued to increase in strength and Adam heard the sound of something blowing around on the street, or in a yard a few houses down, perhaps patio furniture or lawn toys from the sound of it. He also began to hear a few excited and alarmed voices, briefly carried by the wind and then suddenly cut off as it changed direction.

There was still not a speck of rain falling, just the darkening bank of clouds rolling in and the wind that began to lash down from the night sky. There was a sharp tearing noise and then a somewhat more muted crash; Adam supposed that a tree branch had come down and he began to feel a little unsafe out in the storm.

He flipped his patio chairs over, thinking that they might be less likely to catch the wind like that, and then went back inside. The glass shuddered in the window frames as another gust tried its strength against the house. The sound of the wind was steady, now, still no rain or thunder added to it, just a constant rushing noise that continued to build in intensity. Adam tried to go back to kitchen chores, wiping down the counter top and cleaning one of the burners on the stove, but found his attention drawn back to the wind, and his increasing impression that he could hear something in it.

It was another silly notion, he knew, and he was far past the point where he would have believed that he would be unnerved by a storm, but he was sure he could hear a whispering, a harsh-edged low voice, along with the sound of the wind in the trees and against the house and through the bushes. He stopped pretending to wipe down the backsplash and concentrated on the sound, and before long it seemed as though he could hear almost nothing other than the sibilant voice, although he could not make out any specific words, just a general sense that the whisper carried an edge of anger, or of scorn and loathing.

Adam stood in his kitchen debating with himself. He was certain that if he went back outside he would discover, right away, that the voice in the wind was an illusion created by some interaction between the air and the structure of the house, but couldn't quite convince himself to do it. That feeling of not being safe, even a few steps out his back door, was still there, and somehow the thought of even opening the back door seemed like a truly bad idea.

He felt an unfamiliar flood of relief when the phone rang, and grabbed up the receiver with uncharacteristic speed. It was Sophia. The familiar voice was a sudden bubble of warmth and calm that he seized on eagerly.

"Hi Father, are you all right?" she asked. He supposed his voice answering the phone had not been quite as steady as he had hoped.

"Just fine," he said in what he hoped was a reassuring tone. "The phone just surprised me, that's all. What's going on?"

"Oh, it's nothing," Sophia replied, "I just got home and I'm not really doing anything tonight, and I wondered if you might like some company for a while. I don't like to think of you alone in that house all the time."

"It's good of you to ask," Adam said, "and ordinarily I'd be more than pleased to have you come by, but I'm not sure it's a good idea to be out in this weather if you don't have to be."

"What weather?" Sophia asked, sounding genuinely perplexed. "I was listening to the radio in the car and they said it would be clear."

"It doesn't seem that way just now," Adam objected.

"Are you sure you're all right?" Sophia asked again, "Because I'm looking out the window right now and the sunset is beautiful."

Adam suddenly realized that he couldn't hear the whispering, or the wind at all, any longer. He looked out the window and the sky outside was indeed bright again. Somehow he found that almost as unsettling as the storm had been. "Yes,

Sophia, I'm just fine," he answered. "If you really don't have anything else you need to be doing then yes, I'd enjoy a visit very much."

They hung up, and Adam stepped outside and looked up at the sky, which was clear except for a small smear of high clouds lit slightly pink by the setting sun. Although his street was strewn with leaves and small branches obviously ripped from the trees, and he could see that it had been part of a large ash tree that he had heard coming down earlier, he could see no trace of the cloud bank that had covered the sky a few minutes previously.

The ordinary evening sounds of the neighbourhood were gradually resuming, although a couple people from up the street were having an animated discussion over whose responsibility the ash tree was. Adam stood and watched the sky for a few more minutes. Finally he went back inside to see if he had any of the herbal tea Sophia usually enjoyed.

Chapter 17

After Sophia left, Adam made himself something with caffeine in it and waded through the bulk of *The Eater of the Sun*, and although there was a fair amount of detail about the civilization-destroying entity and its presumed acolytes, he didn't find anything that connected to the book he and Marchale were studying. A book in a curious language or cypher fit the general theme of cults and secret rituals, but it wasn't mentioned specifically, and so the association, if there was one, was very loose indeed. He had tracked down some additional examples of Warrington's travel writing at the university library and had brought those along to work. It wasn't terribly likely that there would be anything useful in them but the possibility was there, and so the work had to be put in.

The following morning passed quietly. A few customers trickled in, and he had to send away several university students trying to sell their textbooks. He and Walt had discussed having a textbook section once, since the store was fairly close to campus, but there were too many problems for something that was unlikely to make money. It never felt good to tell someone who had paid over a hundred dollars for a book that he wasn't prepared to give them anything at all for it, but after watching a massive introductory text on European history sit on the shelf for two years — until he had finally taken it home — he had learned to harden his heart.

The store's door jingled open and Adam glanced up from a Charles Warrington discussion of hikes in the Pennines and was surprised to see Jane Moore. It was true that he didn't really know how a journalist's day was filled, but it was still an unexpected development to have her turn up in the middle of the afternoon, especially unannounced. He was about to offer a flippant commentary on her work schedule when he noticed that her face was drawn with what looked to be fatigue and worry.

"Good Lord, Jane," he said, getting up and meeting her just inside the door. "What's happened?" He felt that unpleasant tingle in his stomach again. "Did something happen with Bones?"

"No, Father," Jane replied. "I saw him at lunch and he was just fine. I've just been doing some research, and I kind of need to show it to someone to decide what to do next. Do you have a minute?" She was fretting with the strap and zip of her shoulder bag as she spoke and her posture was tense and uncomfortable.

"Of course, if I can help," Adam assured her. "Come over to the counter there, I think I can offer you tea if you'd like it." Jane had never asked him for input into her work before, so possibly this was something involving religion? If he were honest with himself, Adam didn't terribly enjoy discussing spirituality anymore, but if it was helpful to her article he would make an exception.

"Actually, I'd kind of like to do it a little more private, you know?" Jane asked. "I just don't want anyone overhearing this until I know what it means." Adam doubted that there was a very high chance of customers coming by, judging from the rest of the day's business, but Jane was clearly worried and it wouldn't be too difficult to put her at ease.

"Let me start the tea," he said, going into the back room and rummaging through a drawer until he found some single-serving tea bags that he suspected had been plundered from a hotel room. "Then we'll take a look at what you've brought me." Once the kettle was filled and warming, he returned to the storefront and gave Jane a reassuring smile. Adam flipped the store's sign over to 'Closed', shot the bolt on the door, and stuck up a Post-It declaring 'Gone for Coffee — back 10 mins', which would be a plausible excuse for most people who knew him. This done, he and Jane went into the store's office.

Jane took a seat at the desk and briefly frowned at the disarray surrounding her. "You remember the license plate number Bones remembered?" she began. She had her tablet out now and was calling up a series of documents as she started her explanation. Adam nodded encouragement and she went on.

"And you remember that cop said he ran it and there was no match?" She sounded frustrated, or angry, or perhaps both, and Adam couldn't yet discern why.

"Inspector Kolb, yes," Adam agreed. "Maybe the plate was a fake." Would it be difficult to make a false license plate, if you had the right tools? He remembered reading a story about a con man that stole license plates and altered them for his own vehicle, hammering out 8s into 0s.

"He said Bones must have remembered it wrong," said Jane disapprovingly. "After the way Napoleon said he made a point of remembering it, too." Now it was clearer who she was upset with. Jane was always defensive of her friends and would not have liked the suggestion that Bones had made a mistake about the license plate.

"The trauma…" Adam began, but trailed off. He really didn't know how likely it was that the injuries Bones had suffered would cause him to misremember something like that. The doctor hadn't mentioned memory disturbances, but perhaps it was sort of assumed in cases like this.

"No, you're not getting it," said Jane, a little frustrated edge in her voice now. "I know someone at the MTO and I asked them to look it up for me, and there was a match, and the plate is registered to a white van." She made a gesture on her tablet computer and brought one of her documents to the foreground of the display.

"You have people now, Miss Moore?" enquired Adam, somewhat amused. Actually, it was fairly impressive that she had already established contacts like that, but he supposed it was one of those things journalists had to learn to do.

"Yeah, yeah, you'd be surprised where I know people," Jane replied impatiently. "That's just the first part. He sent me a PDF of the registration and see, the van is owned by something called the Sunrise Foundation. I looked them up too and they're based in Ottawa." She made another little gesture with her fingers and magnified the relevant part of the document.

"The van must have been stolen," Adam mused. That explanation had immediate problems, though — a stolen van would certainly have been reported to the police, and then there should have been no way that Inspector Kolb should have missed getting the match for the license plate.

"Maybe," Jane said skeptically, "But if I found this out in an afternoon, what's that cop been up to? He's either stupid, a slacker, or he's screwing us around."

"Why would he be doing that?" Adam asked. "He seems like a dedicated enough man." In fact, Adam had expected the police investigating the attack on Bones to be doing only a very cursory job, and to offer very little hope of a resolution to the case. Instead, Kolb had seemed at least mildly optimistic, and had certainly seemed to be taking it very seriously.

"I'm sure they all *seem* dedicated," Jane answered. "But I'm already doing his job better than him, so something isn't right." Adam understood her tension a great deal better, now. Probably she didn't want her concerns about the police to accidentally become public.

"No, it's strange," Adam agreed. "Have you spoken with the Inspector about this?" Checking on license plates seemed as though it should be a fairly straightforward part of an investigation, but perhaps that was another false impression created by television and movies. Possibly it was another case where it was unwise to underestimate the problems presented by bureaucracy.

"That didn't seem like the best idea," said Jane tartly. "Not until I know what his angle is, anyway." Obviously she was well on her way to deciding what the explanation for Kolb's apparent error was. Adam knew there was a great deal of cynicism about the police these days and while some of it was justified, he supposed, he also wondered whether it was fair to generalize it quite this automatically.

"Your instincts have been good so far," Adam said. "I'll leave it up to you. But what about this Sunrise Foundation? I've never heard of it." There was no point getting in arguing with Jane, and in any case she had, apparently, turned up an important new set of facts in the investigation. What to do with them was another problem, of course.

"No, I looked into them a bit as well," Jane replied, with a bit of uncertainty creeping into her voice now. "There I didn't do so well. They have a website, but it looks like it's from the 1990s or something and there's almost nothing on it. It just says ... here it is, it says: *The Sunrise Foundation is a philanthropic organization dedicated to charitable endeavours both worldwide and especially in the Eastern Ontario region.*"

"That's both ambitious and vague," Adam observed. "There must be more than that." Some charities did start out with hopelessly broad sets of objectives, or hopelessly optimistic ones, but they didn't usually stay in existence for very long either. However, it was also possible that this particular foundation just didn't have very good publicists working with them, which was often the case for organizations that had almost no budget. In fact, that could also explain the lackluster web design. For a long time, the parish website at St. Michael's had been created and maintained by one of the children from the congregation, and they had only introduced a webmaster into the budget when he had gone to university in Alberta.

"You'd think, but there isn't much," Jane said. "If I were running a charity I'd have lots of copy about things we've done in the past and current projects all over my website; they don't have anything like that. I would also make sure there were a bunch of ways to get in touch with us and give us money, but all there is on their site is an email address." Her concerns certainly made a lot of sense for an organization that was at least making an effort to maintain a web presence.

"You'll find there are badly-run charities, just like everything else," Adam explained. "What else is on that website?" If they were keeping a page up, they must be doing something with it. Some outreach organizations maintained forums to share information, or had links to resources for the people they were hoping to assist.

"Not very much," Jane explained. "There's *About us*, which has that blurb I just read and the email address. There's *Challenges of Today*, which has a lot of junk about overpopulation, world poverty, and economic inequality that reads like it was lifted from Wikipedia or something. Then there's a page of links to some other charities with better much better websites, and most of them are broken links anyway."

"They really might just be not very good at maintaining a webpage," Adam said. "Have you tried sending them an email?"

"Uh, yeah," Jane replied, rolling her eyes, presumably because Adam had needed to ask. "I said I was doing a story on Ottawa charities and wanted to include them. Most charities can't get enough publicity, but no answer yet. It hasn't been long, though, especially if this bunch is as clueless as they seem to be."

"All right, that sounds good," Adam allowed. He was impressed as to how quickly Jane seemed to have devised a plan of attack for solving these questions. He had frequently struggled with not knowing where to begin with a research problem, and ended up doing nothing for long stretches of time.

"Charities need to be registered, too, so I'm trying to find out more about them from that end of things," Jane went on. She chewed at a fingernail for a moment before continuing. "I really wanted to know what we should do about this Inspector, though."

"I'm not sure we should do anything, yet," Adam replied, after thinking it over for a moment. "I know sometimes the police keep certain details of investigations to themselves, so they don't tip things off with people they're investigating. Inspector Kolb might not want anyone letting this Sunrise group know he's interested in them." The inspector had promised to keep them abreast of developments in the case, but he hadn't said that they would get every fact that was uncovered.

"I guess," said Jane, sounding far from convinced. "But if he's interested in them, then I think I'll keep digging on them as well." As long as Jane wasn't publishing any of her findings, there didn't seem to be much risk to the police investigation. Presumably she would know the legalities of interfering with police as well as anyone.

"I can't see any harm in that," Adam agreed, "But be careful what you say to them. We don't want to cause any problems with the investigation." Some people always benefitted from encouragement to get them over their doubts and into action. Others could always use a little caution to temper their enthusiasm. Learning to make the distinction had been one of the trickier things for a young priest to pick up, when parishioners came for guidance but, with people he knew well, Adam was confident, and in his experience, Jane was one of the latter.

"If you want to call it that. So far this guy doesn't seem to be getting anywhere," Jane said disgustedly. Adam was a little surprised that she was this evidently upset so quickly. It had still only been a few days since the attack, and it seemed a bit early to be too harshly critical of the police. However, you did often hear about the importance of solving crimes quickly, if they were ever to be solved at all. Perhaps Jane was reacting to that, or — more likely, in his estimation — she was still dealing with the trauma of having a friend badly hurt, and not having anyone to blame.

"We all want to find out who did this to Bones," Adam answered. "For now I think we should be patient." It was unfortunately true that in many crises, even when the situation was grave, there was still nothing to do but wait. Wait for someone to get better, or not. Wait to hear the results of tests. Wait to find out how the court ruled. Wait to see the grade you got on a test. Just as unfortunately, some people would tear themselves to pieces with worry during the waiting, and finding a way to provide calm was the most important service one could contribute.

"You be patient," Jane said emphatically. "I'm going to keep myself busy." Adam reflected that whether Jane was able to come up with any information or not, and whether the Sunrise Foundation turned out to be anything other than a rather eccentrically-run charity, might not ultimately be very important. Jane had found her own way to keep her mind off of Bones' injuries and the uncertain prospects for his recovery.

"All right," Adam agreed again. "Just let me know if there's anything I can do to help." He realized that the idea of providing help to Jane, and the other people touched by Bones' attack, was increasingly important to him. Possibly he had missed being able to be a source of comfort to people in need more than he had realized. Or, Adam considered, perhaps he was just finding his own strategy for coping with the situation.

Chapter 18

After Jane left, presumably to continue her research into the Sunrise Foundation, Adam found himself turning over the idea of there being some sort of group behind the attack on Bones in his mind. Surely the van being stolen, and used as an untraceable vehicle by the thieves in another crime, was a more plausible explanation. But then there was Detective Kolb's observation that the attackers had not behaved like muggers usually did. Bones' own description of the attack had sounded unusual, too, but who was Adam to judge?

Jane had been deeply skeptical about the whole idea that the van was stolen at all. But if it wasn't, then that opened up a whole new series of questions. Who, connected with a charity — even as apparently ramshackle an operation as the Sunrise Foundation — would be involved in a street assault? And what motive could they possibly have had? Was it a hate crime, as John Kolb had suggested? If so, it seemed strange that the attackers hadn't sent a more clear 'message,' although possibly the attack itself was supposed to be the only message necessary. Adam was prepared to discard the idea that this was some private trouble Bones had become entangled in — while Napoleon wasn't friends with everyone he knew, it was still true that Adam had never known him to have any real enemies or enmities.

What possibilities did that leave? Why else would someone attack a young man on the streets, especially people connected to a charity group? The one fantastic idea that kept recurring in his imagination was that the strange book from the collection of the late Charles Warrington, so recently purchased and yet already the subject of attention from at least one unscrupulous character, was the important factor. And yet, why? By its age alone the book had a chance of being relatively valuable, and as a curiosity it might be worth much more to the right sort of collector — someone who enjoyed oddities and mysterious artifacts. However, it wasn't the sort of thing that should attract the attention of many criminals. Rare books were not easy to sell (if one wanted anything approaching the full price, at least) and hard to care for properly. In any case, a collector would hardly need to resort to theft if they wanted the book. Even if they had missed buying it at Warrington's auction, Bones would probably be open to a fair offer.

None of it explained why the Sunrise Foundation might be interested in the manuscript. An old book no-one could read had no obvious value to a charity. Again, his imagination suggested an idea, spawned from Jane's suggestions that the results of her research might indicate something strange, beyond that of a poorly-run charity. What if there was more to the Sunrise Foundation than that? Still, Adam had no idea what that something more might be, and was also increasingly sure that he was embroidering a far more imaginative explanation than was necessary to fit the facts.

John Kolb's investigation might or might not be proceeding at a pace that satisfied him, or pleased Jane Moore, but then neither of them were privy to all of the difficulties associated with it or the discoveries the detective might have already made. It was never easy to find yourself faced with a problem that had no courses of action available to you, and the only thing to do was wait for solutions provided by someone else. Still, Adam told himself firmly that it was foolish to add to his stress by inventing problems that probably didn't exist, and to be patient while the police did their business. By the time he had worked through all this it was time to close up the store and bring an end to what now felt like a very long day.

Chapter 19

Adam arrived home to find a voicemail message from Professor Marchale demanding his presence at his office the next morning. "Vital stuff, demanding of time, attention, and careful thought," Marchale explained. "You have a tremendous supply of two of the three so you are also nominated. Your damned project anyway," he had growled, and thereupon hung up. Marchale hated leaving messages and could be relied upon to get annoyed by the end of the process.

There was essentially no chance of getting anyone to fill in at the store for the morning, Adam reflected, so he would either have to open somewhat late or take an extended lunch. Trying Marchale's patience by missing a meeting, albeit one he hadn't actually agreed to, was probably not a wise move, not when the professor's help was likely to be crucial to extracting some meaning from the book.

And now, it seemed at least marginally possible that there might be some connection between the book and this Sunrise Foundation unearthed by Jane. Had they been the real employers of Paul Bagot, who had so clearly had nothing to do with the Warrington family? There was something compelling, as well as deeply unsettling, about the idea of a group of people or formal organization that might be out there, making plans against Napoleon Kale, Adam Godwinson, and those associated with them. If they had a business large enough to own vehicles, what other resources might they have?

Jane's research hadn't included how many people worked for the Sunrise Foundation, officially. Suddenly that number, whatever it might be, was of great interest to Adam. How many people might be out there working for these people, and what might they be prepared to do? Probably the foundation would have to employ people who believed they were doing charitable work, to keep up appearances, so not all the employees would be a threat. But how would one tell, and how did you go about your life with even the idea of a 'threat' lurking out there?

Then again, Adam had never once heard of the Sunrise Foundation before today — never seen it mentioned in a local paper, or in a list of groups involved in a fundraising dinner or road race. It was possible the whole thing was a fiction, a paper creation to justify the ownership of things like white vans, offices where things could be planned and buildings where activities could be carried out in private.

Adam finished a glass of wine he didn't recall pouring and forced a halt to his imaginings. He could really terrify himself, or paralyze himself, coming up with increasingly daunting situations and obstacles in his path. Certainly he had just invented a great deal of menace surrounding a charity with a bad website, based on little beyond Jane's suspicions and the work of his own mind, or at least his imagination. Sometimes all one could do was deal with what was tangible and immediate — such as Marchale's insistence on a meeting tomorrow.

The store usually got more business around the middle of the day, as people took their lunches and tourists wandered the city. Few peoples' need for a used book was urgent enough to get them out early in the morning. Adam therefore resolved both to get to Marchale's office as early as possible, opening the store late once again, and not to think about anything related to the book, Charles Warrington, and the frustrations associated with them for the rest of the evening. He flipped through the channels, found a baseball game, and settled into the distractions of the Blue Jays' woeful bullpen.

The next morning he made his way to the university as quickly as possible, and not only found Todd Marchale already in his office, but also found him in an unusually presentable state. Marchale was wearing a dress shirt that appeared to have been ironed, and most unusually, a tie. "Ridiculous meeting later," he said, answering the unvoiced question Adam supposed must be in the expression on his face. "Got to convince the library not to cancel all the journal subscriptions. Strange idea, library having things people want to read, but such are the times we live in."

"Funding cuts, I suppose," Adam replied, settling into the chair in front of Marchale's desk. It was apparently the same chair that had been there during his doctoral supervisions, and for untold years before. There was a strange sense of comfort in that. "Difficult choices to be made all 'round."

"Oh, of course," Marchale agreed testily, "Though how you hear of things like that buried in Harlequin romances I don't know. Anyway, of course the library is angry about not getting any money, we're angry about having a library with no damned books in it, they shout at us and we shout at them, and the problems remain unsolved." As he spoke, he opened a desk drawer, banged it shut again, rummaged through his much-abused briefcase, and rooted through a heap of papers balanced on one corner of the desk.

"Frustrating," Adam said. "I'm not sure anyone knows what the solution is." Marchale had pushed his chair back slightly so he could examine the floor under his desk, and even rolled the chair over to his right so he could look into the garbage can. Adam was amused to see it still had a sticker for The Offspring on it, the appearance of which predated his time as Marchale's student and which the professor had consistently declined to explain.

"Everyone knows what the solution is," Marchale contradicted him, "give more bloody money to universities. But what the devil are you doing getting me going on this when you know perfectly well that's not why I called you here?" He went back to the original desk drawer, opened it, and now drew something out.

"I'm sorry, then," Adam replied bemusedly. "What was the urgent matter?"

"Fresh grist for your mill," Marchale said with relish, tossing a slender paperback book onto his desk top. "I won't tell you if I begged, borrowed or stole it but I will lend it to you. Further insight into our subject, perhaps." Adam picked up the book and found that it was another work by Charles H. Warrington, this time published in 1951, according to the date on the cover. It was titled *The Infection*, but was otherwise undecorated. He couldn't help but wonder if Marchale was taking satisfaction in having him slog through as many examples of Warrington's strange writing as possible.

"More fiction?" Adam asked. So far he had digested, to some extent, *The Eater of the Sun* and made inroads into three of Warrington's travel books, and he was not particularly eager to add to his reading list. With everything else that was going on it was hard to find the necessary focus, especially for writing like Warrington's.

"First of all, shouldn't you be able to tell me? You're meant to have been researching the man, after all," Marchale scolded. "Secondly, a travel book with that title must have been from a bloody awful trip, so I think you're on safe ground." He checked his watch and scowled at the verdict. Presumably the meeting was for later in the morning, which would explain the rather brisk pace of this conversation.

"Anything in particular I should pay attention to?" Adam enquired hopefully. If it was at all possible to avoid reading the entire book, he decided, he would do so. *The Eater of the Sun* had been interesting in a way, for its insight into the kind of writer Warrington was, but he couldn't say there was anything really useful about it.

"Well the whole thing, of course," Marchale responded cheerfully. "Look at you, still in hot pursuit of shortcuts after all this time. Hard time in the salt mines, it's the only solution, same as always." Adam did recall more or less that same advice more than once, during his thesis research. That was the way research often went. There was no way to tell, in most cases, whether there was something useful in a given document, or set of records, without reading through it. Adam had tried to learn to regard the time spent reading things that turned out not to be useful as valuable, rather than wasted time, because at least now a source could definitely be ruled out. Still, the process tended to be frustrating, especially with material that was difficult to get through.

"It's just that if it's only a pile of nonsense," Adam replied a little impatiently, "I have a lot of other things I can spend my time on." Normally he took a much more conciliatory tone towards Marchale and his suggestions, and he knew that reading *The Infection* was a logical thing to do, but that didn't mean he had to like it and for a brief moment he let the stress and fatigue of the past few days slip through.

"Dear me, no sense of scholarly intrepidity," Marchale said with assumed dismay. "Well in part this thing," he indicated *The Infection* with a jab of his unlit pipe, "is meant to 'continue the themes of his previous work,' according to its description, so it may be worth a look just for that. I also still think, with some regret for your troubles, that it is very much worth seeing whether there's any connection between his writing and the mysterious book — if I can't turn something up through the manuscript community that is genuinely our best chance at a clue to what the thing means." He glared sharply across the desk at Adam. "Unless you've a better idea, of course?"

Adam had to confess that he didn't. "I'll have a look through it," he said with some resignation. "I'm not sure I really understood that other novel, if you can call it that," he went on, "so I just hope I'm not missing something significant I suppose. That and there really is a lot on my mind just now."

To his surprise, Marchale did not offer up a caustic retort to this confession. "I know you have, Mr. Godwinson, I know you have," he said solemnly. "To be blunt I was hoping perhaps all this," he indicated Warrington's novella, and the scattering of notes associated with it, with a circular motion, "might distract you a bit from your troubles. Never does any good to spend all one's time chewing over things not under our control. Also, if I may say, I was also hoping to tempt you back to scholarly things again. Contrary to expectations you didn't turn out to be utterly inept at it and I really could use the help."

It took a moment for Adam to compose a response to this uncharacteristically empathic declaration. He knew Marchale had genuine affection for his students, even if it was often conveyed through sarcasm and critique, but it was rare, very rare, to have him directly express it. "It's good of you," Adam said eventually, "and I will keep on with the research."

"You are wasted in that bookshop, my boy, wasted," said Marchale with vigour. "You must do better." This was an old argument, but again it was rare for it to be advanced so directly. It was a compliment, Adam knew, to have Marchale still think he was suited for scholarly pursuits after so many years away from it.

"I do the best I can, professor," Adam replied mildly. "It doesn't have the hard practicality of theological studies, I suppose, but I think I sometimes do some good in my way."

"Oh, a touch," cried Marchale with evident pleasure. "Well, you can't say I haven't made an effort, can you? Now, if you're not going to make yourself useful, I have a meeting that promises to be nearly fatal, after which there's a horde of undergraduates due to storm the barricades, all perishing under the injustice of their grades, so make your escape while you can."

Adam made his goodbyes and went to the bookstore to open it up, only slightly later than usual. There were neither donated books to sort through, nor had anything appeared overnight that needed to be cleaned up, and as a result he had few demands on his time, aside from starting the coffee maker and readying the petty cash. He really had very little desire to start his day with *The Infection* which, if it was similar to *Eater of the Sun*, would be an annoyingly uphill climb. However, after trying to deflect his attention, first onto a crossword puzzle, and then onto trying to eliminate the squeak from the store's back door, Adam was forced to admit that *The Infection* would not become any less of a difficult read by being put off, and that it was probably better to tackle the problem with some urgency. He put the store's paltry collection of tools away in the basement and returned to the front counter where Marchale's latest assignment was waiting for him.

With some trepidation, Adam tried to tackle this new example of Charles Warrington's writing. His travel books were mostly light and relatively engaging pieces on different parts of Europe, the Middle East, and North Africa which Warrington had toured around, although perhaps a trifle heavy on architecture, and occasionally they included somewhat jarring observations about the "dark aura" of a rural church or the 'infamous history' of an apparently mundane village, interjections that went without further elaboration. Somewhat strange though they were, the travel books were at least readable, but Adam had not yet been able to force himself to finish *The Eater of the Sun*, and this fresh example Marchale had dredged up from the depths of the library's collection did not look any more appealing.

It was another slim volume, cheaply printed and bound, and therefore now in rather precarious condition. Like *The Eater of the Sun*, it had no characters or plot for the reader to follow. It was also written as though it were a treatise on perfectly straightforward material, but again the actual subject was bizarre. Warrington wrote about a disease of the mind, as far as Adam could determine, but it was poorly defined as to its cause, and whether he was referring to a literal disease, an inborn syndrome resulting from a physical cause, or a purely psychiatric disorder. Some of his descriptions seemed to indicate all three. There was also some kind of ill-explained social discourse to the book — Warrington would complain about unnamed politicians and writers without explaining exactly what his objections were, or what alternatives he might prefer. It was, overall, a deeply dissatisfying read.

The Infection was well known in recent years, began the first chapter, entitled *Summary*. *The paralysis of spirit, the belief that defeat was inevitable, and that there was no action possible which could avert us from a doomed course, must be recognized by all those who survived our late calamities.* Adam checked the publication date and found that this copy was, incredibly, a second printing, and that *The Infection* had been first printed in 1949. It was probable, then, that Warrington was referring to the Second World War. Perhaps his still-elusive war experiences had affected him after all, Adam mused.

What we must also recognize is that this was not a phenomenon unique to the times, and indeed was no accident at all, the *Summary* continued. *The Infection is a deliberate blight placed upon mankind by forces malevolent, for the purpose of*

our subjugation and destruction. Here was one of the problems
with the book. What were 'forces malevolent'? The connection
to the war could perhaps be taken to indicate the Nazis and
propaganda, but it wasn't explicit, and some of what Warrington
wrote seemed to contradict that reading. *It should be likewise
clear to any thoughtful observer than the Infection is with us
still, and will not be eradicated except through vigorous and
deliberate action.* Adam hadn't found anything to indicate that
Warrington believed that Nazism was a threat after the end of
the war, and he meant by *vigorous and deliberate action* was left
to the imagination.

As Adam read on, the *Summary* did not, in his mind,
improve. *This is our only reasonable course, for the spread of
Infection is our enemies' fondest wish. The creation of the set of
mind in which resistance is impossible, all action is useless, and
destruction inevitable, is the best and strongest weapon they
bring to bear. We must be ceaselessly on our guard against
tracts, symbols, and discourses which bring us to an Infected
state.* This really did sound like propaganda, but who was
Warrington's enemy? *For it is not only that the diseased mind
becomes pliable and incapable of mounting effective resistance,
but those Infected propagate their own disease to others. We
find all too many public servants, journalists, and writers who
produce work of a clearly Infected tenor. These must be avoided,
and if their creators cannot be cured then the work must be
suppressed.*

Adam laid the book down, pushed up his glasses, and rubbed
his eyes. There was a certain Cold War flavor to *The Infection,*
but the ideas didn't seem to have any political content. Perhaps
it would be easier to digest if Warrington had expressed a direct
concern with Communism, but as it was, his thinking was hard
to appreciate and in some ways disturbing. The call to suppress
journalists, for example, had an unsettling tone. Adam decided
that late evening was evidently no time to cross intellectual
swords with Charles Hope Warrington, and opted instead for a
crossword puzzle before bed.

He spent the afternoon studiously ignoring *The Infection* on
the shop counter, and trying to also dismiss his imaginings of

Professor Marchale's reaction to his lack of dedication. Fortunately, a number of customers presented themselves, including one who was looking for a copy of a long out-of-print fantasy novel, part of a series of which the Ottawa Public Library system had all but the first volume. Adam was sure he remembered having a copy come in — he had been deeply pessimistic about its saleability — was eventually able to find it in one of the boxes of overflow stock, and sent the rejoicing young man on his way. There was an undeniable pleasure in helping people find books they had been trying to find for a long time, and even more, he found, in reuniting someone with a lost favorite.

When Eric turned up to work the evening shift, Adam decided to go and look for Alex again. For one thing, Alex's comment, at the end of their last conversation, about 'the book' kept nagging away at the back of his mind. It hardly seemed possible that Alex could know anything about the manuscript and, although most of what he said never made sense to anyone but Alex, it had been a startling coincidence. It wasn't impossible that Bones had spoken to him before bringing the book to Adam. If Alex was in any way involved, it was possible that he might be bothered by people like Paul Bagot. Given that man's dishonesty, Adam was worried what else he might do in pursuit of the book. Alex was vulnerable, and not due to his mental difficulties. Perhaps more than any of us, Adam considered; a young homeless person could disappear completely and few people would even notice, and even fewer would make anything of it.

Adam tried several of the parks in the downtown area before opting for Parliament Hill. Security tended to move obvious transients along from there fairly quickly, but Alex enjoyed the little sanctuary for feral cats towards the rear of the complex, and it was worth trying before going farther afield.

As he made his way through the intersection at the War Memorial, heading for Wellington Street, he felt a creeping sense of uneasiness swim up from the pit of his stomach. By the time he was approaching the first entrance to Parliament Hill,

Adam was thoroughly on edge and looking, once again, at the people around him with growing suspicion and concern.

Had he seen the young man in the cargo pants and the blue shirt before, earlier in the day? Why was he wearing sunglasses and a ball cap, on a day that had been overcast since morning? Had that been him stepping out of the coffee shop on Dalhousie, and now here, near the Parliament buildings?

Adam tried to think if there were other times when he had seen the man through the day. Had he walked past the bookstore, perhaps glancing in as he went by? Had that been him in line at the ATM? Was it possible this thoroughly medium man — height, weight, build, face — had been sent to follow him by another person from Reverend Smiles' church, or, if Jane was right in her suspicions about the van used in the attack on Bones, was there a link between the man and the strange Sunrise Foundation, with its cryptic and pessimistic website?

Perhaps someone was hoping he would lead them to the book this way. The idea that there even was a 'someone' or a 'them' behind recent events that he needed to be concerned about was deeply unsettling, even leaving aside the presence of this disturbingly familiar-looking person. Then again, maybe the man was waiting for his chance with a knife or a gun, when Adam was alone in a place with no witnesses, or in a crowd where an attacker might never be recognized.

Or perhaps he was just another guy going about his business in the city, running errands and going to and from work, and perhaps it wasn't even the same man every time — how many young men could you find in a ballcap and blue shirt in the city, without even trying very hard?

Adam took a deep breath and looked around himself carefully. Yes, there was a man in a cap and sunglasses among the crowd waiting for the buses along Wellington. No, he couldn't be sure it was the same man he had seen earlier in the day. Even if it was, what was there to do? He could either go home and hide, or go about his day. There was too much happening to do nothing.

He turned deliberately away from the queue of people at the bus stop and made his feet start moving again. Sometimes the best way to be calm was to force yourself to take on the appearance of being calm. As he walked through one of the gates in the imposing stone and wrought-iron fence that enclosed the Hill, Adam took in the usual crowd of visitors and took a moment to enjoy the space. The buildings were lovely, but it was the Hill itself that Adam particularly valued. It was the seat of the government, and yet it was a place where people came and went freely, went for a jog or enjoyed a coffee break, and played Frisbee or, sometimes, rugby on the lawn in front. As centres of government went, it was about as open and public a space as it was possible to be, and Adam had always found that most appropriate.

On the other hand, he couldn't shake the feeling that all the events of recent days added up to something truly bad, even if he didn't yet understand how all the disturbing pieces fit together. Adam looked up at the Peace Tower, and at the statues of past prime ministers arranged around the Centre Block like a skirmish line, and tried to convince himself that he could rely on someone else to handle the situation. Not the federal government, of course, but surely the RCMP or Ottawa Police would ultimately resolve all these problems, and leave people like him to sell books and help friends through their convalescences.

However, there was nothing about the setting that really persuaded him that it was a good idea to rely on the situation to take care of itself. The Hill was open, welcoming, and pleasant, but it also wasn't a place that left you overawed or impressed by a feeling of authority, and Adam supposed that was appropriate too. Many times the problems you found yourself stuck with were also best solved by yourself as well, Adam considered.

By the time he had followed this train of thought along he had also walked around behind the Centre Block, past the bell commemorating the 1916 fire, past the Police Memorial, and found that his instincts had been right and Alex Sloan was indeed standing near the 'cat condos', perched on the forested slope down to the river. Tonight there was a large tuxedo cat out eating some of the food provided by local animal charities, and a slim ginger tabby stretched out in the light of the setting sun.

"Hello again, Alex," Adam said, from a few steps away. For once, Alex didn't seem to have noticed his approach, and at times he could startle easily.

"Hi Father," Alex replied, a little distantly. "How is it?"

"Things have been..." Adam paused and considered exactly how much to tell Alex. There seemed little point in making him worried or upset, and yet Adam did have some concerns for his safety. "Things have been difficult," he concluded.

"The dummies might be right, hey?" Alex asked with a flicker of a grin. "Father, you got to listen to me more, listen to her more, understand?" He took a light grip on the bars of the fence and leaned back a little.

"I always enjoy our talks," Adam assured him. "What do you think I haven't been listening to?" Alex often found it frustrating when people didn't understand what he was saying to them, and especially if he felt like he was just being ignored. Adam and the Guild children had always made a special effort to keep him feeling included and, where possible, to integrate his ideas into what they were doing.

"You don't look so good," Alex said flatly. "You got to be careful that you don't get the sickness. Some of the places you've been going get you sick real easy." He shook his head in disapproval, although whether this was of Adam and his behavior or something else was not entirely clear.

Adam sighed. It seemed as though Alex was still dwelling on the dangers of hospitals. "Now, don't worry," he replied, "I'm just fine. Well, I could probably use a little more rest but it's been a busy week so far." The fixation on sickness was a little concerning; Alex would sometimes get very focused on particular ideas or worries, but Adam had never found a better solution than just letting them run their course.

"Rest?" Alex demanded. "Last thing you need, last thing. Got to move, Father." He illustrated this last comment with a little disjointed set of dance steps, and then turned back to the cats. Adam could sense that they had attracted the curiosity of some other people out enjoying the evening on the Hill, but put it out of his mind. At the moment, Alex seemed to need attention.

"Oh?" Adam asked. "Where do I need to go?" He was increasingly inclined to write off the comment about the book from their last conversation as a coincidence now. Most of what Alex was saying tonight had no obvious connection to the situation with Bones and the manuscript. He chided himself slightly for imagining farfetched connections when the reality in front of him was problematic enough.

"It's not about where," Alex said firmly. "It's a question of what. Just don't forget that you can, that's what she says. Are you listening?" He turned to look directly at Adam, with a surprisingly stern expression on his face.

"Of course, Alex," Adam replied. A little tentatively, he reached out and rested his hand on Alex's shoulder. Alex not only didn't pull away, but also reached over to give Adam's hand an affectionate pat.

"Ok then. I don't want to talk any more anyway. Help me watch the kitties." He turned decisively back towards the cat condos and grinned at a little grey tabby sharpening its claws on one of the platforms.

Adam was about to reply that he had other things that needed to be taken care of, but stifled the idea. Surely there should always be time in life to spend part of a warm evening with a troubled friend who wanted to watch some cats in the sunshine. They stood and watched the black and white one washing its face after dinner, as the sun sank down over the river.

Chapter 20

When Adam woke the next morning he tried to make a mental agenda for the day. Obviously it was necessary to spend the bulk of it at W.M. Howard, Bookseller — whatever else was happening, having the store closed frequently was irresponsible and getting someone to cover for him was impractical. He wanted to find time to go to the hospital and visit Bones, though, and needed to spend more time at the library investigating the corpus of material on Charles Warrington, too. Visiting Bones could be pushed to the evening, he supposed, and some research shoehorned in around lunch. By the time he had figured this out, he had also eaten a bowl of cereal and an apple on autopilot, and was ready to head to work.

His notional agenda was almost immediately derailed when, partway through his morning routine of opening the store, Adam noticed the message light was blinking on the phone. He was fairly sure it hadn't been when he had left the previous day, but in his distracted state he wasn't certain. It was possible, given the early hour, that this was a call he had missed yesterday, and had now been fermenting overnight. To his chagrin, this turned out to be the case — there was a brief message from Jane Moore, sounding annoyed, perhaps at getting the store's voicemail, asking for him to call immediately.

Adam sighed, regretting the lapsed hours, and dialed. "Father, can you come over to my place, like, right away?" Jane asked without preamble. Adam couldn't quite decide if she sounded frightened, excited, or perhaps a mix of the two.

"I'm meant to be working," he replied. "Can you come to me instead?"

"I don't think that's a great idea," Jane said hesitantly. "I don't want to carry this stuff all over town."

"All right, I'll be right over," Adam agreed, with a slight twinge of guilt at closing the store again. Weekday business was never brisk but he certainly didn't want it to become common for potential customers to find the place closed. However, the urgency in Jane's voice was undeniable. "Are you still in the apartment on Bronson?"

It turned out she was now renting a condo in Lebreton Flats. Adam locked up the bookstore, wrote an apologetic note about a pressing 'personal emergency', and taped it to the door. Possibly he should speak to Eric about taking on more shifts until things calmed down, although that would be an additional expense. As he took a bus to Jane's, he marveled once again at his ability to be distracted by mundane details during a crisis, which he supposed the events that had started with the curious old book Bones had found now qualified as.

Jane buzzed him into the building and he took the stairs up to her unit. She must have been waiting close to the door, because she opened it almost immediately after his knock. "Thanks for coming so fast," she said, showing him into a remarkably clean living room, except for an explosion of paper centred on a low glass-topped coffee table and scattering out over the otherwise immaculate hardwood floor. "I had to show this to someone, and I really feel safer keeping this stuff at home."

"You mean you don't want to lose any of it?" asked Adam, indicating the mess. "You do seem to have a wealth of information, here."

"Partly," Jane said, sounding slightly distracted as she knelt down and started shuffling through some of the papers. "Also this stuff was hard to get and I don't want anyone to grab it back."

"Grab it back?" Adam queried. "You think someone might want to steal it?"

"Well, stop me having it, at least," Jane said. "This is everything I've been able to get so far on the Sunrise

Foundation, and when I show you some of it you'll see the other reason I wanted you to look at it." Adam wondered exactly what might have happened to make Jane this worried over her possession of whatever information she had uncovered. Given his own recent experiences, though, her suspicions were far from unfounded, and he knew she deserved a clearer picture of what she was getting involved in.

Adam briefly filled her in on his visit from Paul Bagot. This, in turn, meant explaining the book Bones had brought to the store, the manuscript that he suspected had been the trigger for the chain of events that he felt increasingly entangled by. "I don't want to alarm you," Adam finished, "but you might want to be on your guard from that kind of visitor."

"If they're after the book," Jane said, "that would explain their van being used by whoever attacked Bones." She hooked a stray lock of hair behind one ear in a gesture he had seen her use for many years, when she was deep in a debate with one of the other Guild children or trying to sort out the eccentric organisation of the parish archives.

"I don't know for certain that Bagot had anything to do with the Sunrise Foundation," Adam replied. Jane fixed him with a very steady, and very skeptical, look.

"That would be a pretty enormous coincidence, don't you think?" she asked. Adam did agree that it seemed unlikely that there wasn't some link between all of the curious, and increasingly alarming events surrounding them. "Anyway," Jane continued, "a weird old book kind of fits in with this other stuff I called you over here to see. Come and have a look, you'll see what I mean."

"All of this is on Sunrise?" asked Adam, squatting down on the other side of the table. Jane had obviously been working rapidly. Some of the papers looked to be ordinary computer printouts, but there were some that appeared to be photocopies of originally handwritten pages as well, and a few sheets that looked like typewritten originals. "But I thought they were a fairly closed book, so to speak."

"There are sources on everything," Jane said with some satisfaction. "You just have to know where to put the shovel.

Now, here's the first thing — it's a list of their assets from an internal audit. They rent some office space and some storage units south of town, they have a couple of vehicles, and they have a store on McArthur that they run like a Goodwill shop. Then a few years ago they also bought a chunk of land out the country that was supposed to be used for a summer camp."

"It all sounds vaguely charitable," Adam observed. "Not very ambitious, I suppose, but not unusual either."

"The thing is," Jane continued, "That they've never actually built any camp, or done anything at all with it," she took a moment to dig out another paper, "50 acres of land. As far as I can tell it's just sitting there growing weeds or whatever. I was thinking of driving out to have a look but then I got to the rest of it."

"What else is there, then?" asked Adam, trying to sound encouraging. So far he couldn't see why these papers had gotten Jane so excited, and why they had her worried. She picked up several of the handwritten pages.

"Ok, this is the good stuff. It's like, notes from some of their meetings, I think," she explained, worrying at a thumbnail. "This is the weird shit, sorry Father."

"Never mind, Jane," Adam said with amusement. "Why don't you just tell me what has you so upset."

"Ok, like I said these are from some of their meetings. They have official ones," she indicated another stack of papers that were neat documents from a word processor, "but these are like private, not part of the charity's records at all, really."

"You're sure they're genuine, though?" Adam asked.

"Uh huh," Jane confirmed, a little absently. She was riffling through the sheaf of papers and then seemed to find what she was looking for. "Ok, here we are: *Presentation of world trends from L. and S. confirms that the Resolution was correct and all present agreed to proceed as planned. M. presented results of her research and confirmed acquisition of Libri Fidei Verus.*"

"Book of the True Faith," Adam interjected. "This is all tremendously vague." Still, a book with a title in Latin fit uncomfortably easily into the pattern of recent events. He felt a fluttering sensation deep in his stomach and frowned out the window at the glass and concrete wedge of the War Museum.

"Probably deliberately, and you'll see what I mean when it gets clearer in a minute," Jane assured him. "*M. also confirmed from this source that freeing the King in Exile is the clearest course of action in pursuit of our goal. Once out of the darkness, according to the source, the King will rapidly grow in strength and consume the corrupted, the failed, and the worthless. Aliquid melius.*" Jane looked over at Adam expectantly.

"Anything will be better," he said softly. "Is there much like this?"

"That was the strangest one," Jane replied. "Most of the unofficial notes talk about recruitment of new members, or they complain about specific things that happened. Here's one about the oil spill in the Gulf, here's one about the shootings in Norway, and here is one about child soldiers in the Congo. Every time they say that *this new evidence confirms our Resolution.*"

"And is that Resolution in there, anywhere?" Adam asked. If not for the admittedly fragile links between Sunrise, the assault on Bones, and now the strange manuscript, these documents would have sounded like the all too common, fevered imaginings found in badly printed books and especially sprinkled throughout the internet, and would have been easy to dismiss. As it was, the trembling feeling in his belly wouldn't allow him that luxury.

"Oh yeah," Jane confirmed. "It's the strangest thing of all of them. Listen. *Resolved — by all these present assembled and dedicated to the dawning of a new age: We, being agreed that all the societies of humankind are irreparably corrupt and despicable, and under the control of the wicked, the useless, and the deceived, resolve to work in unity and all our strength to bring these to an end, and allow the sun to rise on a new world. Aliquid Melius.*"

"Anything will be better," Adam repeated. "You're sure of these documents, that they're real?"

"Father, believe me," she said firmly, "it sounds as weird to me as it does to you, but I'm absolutely positive about where this stuff comes from. I can't tell you who wrote them, exactly, but it's someone who's part of this Sunrise deal. Now, does it make any sense at all to you?" Adam rubbed a hand over his forehead and thought about it. It was all quite bizarre and fantastic, and yet some of it did sound eerily similar to the equally strange writings of Charles Warrington. He wasn't yet prepared to suggest any such connection, though, and in any case there was another issue nagging at him.

"Jane, I feel like I should ask," he asked with some hesitation. "The way you came to have this information — was it entirely legal?"

"Father, if my theory is right these people put Bones in a coma and tried to have you stabbed," Jane retorted. "I'm not all that worried about legal right now."

"I sympathize with feeling that way, I really do," Adam replied, "But there are concerns."

"If that's a polite way of saying that you might feel like you have to turn me in," Jane said acidly, "Just relax. If I just don't tell you where I got this stuff, does that get you over your guilty conscience?"

"Jane, I will always regard anything you choose to tell me as strictly between us," Adam replied firmly. "I suppose I've changed a lot since St. Michael's, but my ethics haven't entirely evaporated."

"I'm sorry, Father," Jane said, more quietly. "I shouldn't have said that, I know you're always on our side. I guess things have been more hectic than I thought."

"Never mind, Jane," Adam answered. "It's been a difficult few days, like you said. What I was going to say, though, was that you must be very careful. If any part of what we think about these people is accurate, they may be very dangerous, and right now you're the most exposed of any of us, as the one asking all the questions."

"I'm not so sure, Father," Jane replied. "From what you've said, and what they've actually done, they seem pretty single-minded about that book."

"They do," Adam agreed. "I think that means we don't understand things completely yet, because nothing I've learned about it suggests it should be so valuable to anyone. It's just an obscure curiosity, as far as I can see."

"I know this stuff sounds crazy," Jane said, "but I don't think these people are stupid. Things are very well organized, especially in keeping things hidden. If they're that interested in the book, there must be a reason here somewhere."

"Then I hope we figure out what that reason is," Adam declared, "while there's time to do something about it."

Chapter 21

He left her frowning over her piles of papers and walked along Booth Street, letting his feet carry him as his brain wrestled with these latest additions to the problems confronting him. This was a long-standing habit from his student days, one that had sometimes led him on 3 a.m. walks through less than encouraging neighbourhoods, but in general the results had always been good and Adam had eventually accepted that there seemed to be some connection between moving his feet and moving his mind. At least, he reminded himself, it had the side benefit of keeping him active and in some kind of shape, although he had been lax about his running in recent months and his walks had largely been restricted to ones between his house and the premises of W. M. Howard, Bookseller.

Now it seemed incontestable that he had a problem that would take some unknotting. The book Bones had brought to him, and Charles Hope Warrington, had been possibly intriguing puzzles, but recent events combined with the results of Jane's research seemed to take things into another realm. Adam wasn't sure he would have believed that there were truly people with such strange, dark beliefs in the world, but Jane seemed confident in the reliability of what she had uncovered and, to his untutored eye, the documents had seemed genuine enough.

It was also true, he supposed, that there were well-established groups of people who contended that the world was run by shape-changing lizards or that the human race had originated as extraterrestrial clones and, in that light, the beliefs of the members of the Sunrise Foundation weren't really uniquely bizarre. It was still hard for him to understand what might lead a person to start thinking that way, though. Did all those people, however many of them there were, really believe that anything would be better than the world they lived in? What could bring one person to such a place in their mind, never mind a whole group of them?

As Adam made his way along the river pathway, he recognized that part of the reason he had come this way was that he enjoyed the setting, but also that he was hoping to see Alex again. For whatever reason the area around Parliament was, apparently, currently appealing under whatever criteria led Alex through the world. It was, at least, a relatively safe place for him to be in, Adam thought, and that was something. Although their last few conversations hadn't made much sense to Adam, it had seemed to him that Alex was trying to say something he felt was important, and Adam wanted to try to understand the message.

If there was a message, he admitted to himself as he started up the hill beside the canal locks, and the Bytown Museum. One of Alex's doctors had explained, years ago, that although it was tempting to find significance in everything a patient with his condition might say or do, sometimes there would be nothing there to find. Sometimes there was no message, only symptoms. Even so, Adam told himself that he had neglected Alex, along with many other things, for long enough. It was time to try to do something with himself again, and reaching out to Alex again was a worthy first step.

However, first there were these more pressing issues to deal with, he decided. Recent events were coming together in a way he did not like. It wasn't only that he didn't yet understand how to solve the problem that was confronting him, it was that he didn't even understand what the problem was, yet. He needed more information. What Jane had uncovered was promising, but Adam admitted to himself that Charles Warrington and his strange publications were somehow enmeshed with this situation as well, so there was more work to be done there.

By the time Adam had worked his way through all this internally, he had also worked his way through the ByWard Market, the familiar streets of Lowertown, and arrived on his home street. It was only just after noon, and he should undoubtedly open the store for the afternoon and try to salvage some of the day's business. Perhaps he could be allowed a pleasant lunch at home first, he considered, and was starting to think about which among the contents of his refrigerator were most likely to still be palatable when his train of thought was broken, and he stopped.

Sitting on the walkway up to his door was a tiny plastic baggie, of the sort that people got ecstasy, and other drugs, in small amounts. Living close to downtown it was far from unusual to find this sort of thing scattered around, although street littler didn't usually make its way up from the sidewalk. Like many such baggies it was decorated with a little logo, probably to advertise the dealer's brand or perhaps associate it with a particular rave or whatever they were called these days, Adam reflected. What caught his attention now was that the logo in this case was a series of yellow cartoon suns, truncated to show just their upper halves, as if setting, or rising.

He stood looking down at the little piece of plastic, unsure what to do. His mind had immediately formed the link between the pictures on the baggie and a rising sun, and thence to the Sunrise Foundation that Jane had discovered, and had been lurking in the shadows of his thoughts ever since. The baggie was empty, and could have been blowing around the streets for a long time, he argued. On the other hand, it looked fresh and he couldn't escape the impression that it had been placed, just in the centre of one of the slabs of his front walk, where his eye would almost certainly fall on it as he departed from or arrived at the house.

Was it stretching things to make an association between those cheery little suns and this strange foundation Jane was currently researching? Had the baggie been left as an indicator that he, too, was under watch or study of some kind? Hugh Thomas had seemed as though he had been on drugs; was there a connection there as well? Should he pick it up? Was it important to get rid of it? Could he simply ignore it?

Adam finally convinced himself that he was being ridiculous. He supposed if he was being watched, and that someone had been waiting to see the effect of this little token of their attention, his standing and staring at the thing for however long it had been would be a sufficient reward. There are problems enough to worry about without inventing additions to them, he told himself firmly. He set off to find lunch, and then to the bookstore, and hoped that some hours of helping people plug holes in their collection of Harry Bosch novels would prevent him finding sinister meanings in anything else that afternoon.

That evening, Adam, Fred and Sophia surprised each other by each gradually arriving at Bones' hospital room. This time, they had made no plans to visit together but obviously, it was already becoming part of their routines. Bones continued to seem more like his regular self, and they spent a pleasant few hours amusing one another. They had just said good night to Bones and were leaving the hospital for the night when Sophia got a text message, which turned out to be from Jane. "She says she has found something very important," Sophia said, "and wants to meet together right away."

"She already showed me some of her research," Adam replied, "and she said there was more to come, but I don't think she expected the results quite this soon. Based on what she already shared with me, this is probably something that demands attention. Where is she?" The sources Jane had alluded to were evidently fruitful, or at least she was able to exploit them skillfully, but Adam couldn't help wondering what might be expected of her in return.

"She didn't say," Sophia explained, "but I can text her back. We can take my car and go together?" Fred and Adam agreed and headed across the parking lot to where Sophia had been able to find a spot, earlier in the afternoon. They had only gotten a few steps from the building when two men, one with dark blond hair and one with curly black hair, got up from a bench and seemed to fall into step behind them.

Without any comment, the three of them sped up their pace towards Sophia's car slightly, but right away they heard hurried feet behind them. "Hey, hold it a minute," one of the men said. Immediately Adam felt a tingle of nervous energy — his approach wasn't that of a person asking for the time, or a light, or even for spare change. There was no hesitation, from self-consciousness or embarrassment in how either man approached on the street, or how they first grabbed, rather than hoped to get, Adam's attention.

"Yeah, what is it dude?" Fred asked lightly. He would usually blithely assume that everyone he met was equally amiable, or at the very least inoffensive, until he was directly disabused of the notion by evidence. This meant he got along with almost everyone he met, but at times it meant he ended up in long conversations with panhandlers or solicitors that he was too polite to break away from. Sometimes it meant he didn't realize he was in an argument until it was well underway.

"I'm talking to him," the man insisted, jabbing a finger towards Adam, who suddenly noticed both of them were wearing puffy winter jackets, despite the warm evening, and both had a hand deep in one of their coat's pockets. The pair was taking care to keep some space around themselves, Adam noted now, and that little kernel of alarm started to become more insistent.

"Well, what is it?" Adam asked, with a conscious effort at keeping his voice steady. He tried to think of anyone he might have upset or annoyed over the past few days, someone who might now want to renew hostilities, or extract an apology. Unfortunately, or fortunately, it had been a peaceful week at the bookstore, and outside of that he had been devoting almost all of his time to Bones' hospitalization and research into Charles Warrington and his curious book. As a result, he couldn't help himself from starting to make some more ominous connections.

"You have something I want," the man said bluntly. "Now we're going to go and get it." Again, his manner was of someone who was not expecting any contradictions. Adam glanced around the parking lot, hoping to see a security guard whose attention he might be able to attract or, failing that, any other group of people. He was remembering a self-defence169 and 'street smarts' workshop that had been given at St. Michael's, many years ago now, by a pair of bluntly practical police officers. In many cases the presence of witnesses, they had explained, or the idea that the alarm had been raised, would make all but the most determined criminals retreat. Unfortunately in this case the parking lot was perversely empty.

"I don't have anything of yours," Adam replied firmly. "You're making a mistake." He recognized neither of the men and was briefly hoping that the whole thing might prove to be genuinely a case of mistaken identity, however unlikely that seemed.

"You have something I've been sent to get," the man said. "The only mistake will be not doing exactly what I say." As if to illustrate his point, he pulled his hand slightly out of his jacket pocket, to reveal that he was holding what looked to Adam to be a fairly significant knife, and not of the type you used in a kitchen.

"All right," he said as calmly as possible, "you do have my attention. Why don't you tell me specifically what it is you want." Keeping Hugh talking had proved to be the solution to that situation, Adam told himself, and possibly it would work again here. Surely someone could see what was happening from the hospital?

The man seemed to think about his response for a few seconds before answering. "Yeah, I'm pretty sure you know already, but I want that book, the old one you got a few days back. The one from the estate sale. That clear enough?" The other man — his partner, Adam supposed — was doing his own survey of the parking lot, keeping an eye out for anyone who might interfere. Every so often his attention would drift back to Adam, he would fix a flat gaze on him for a few moments, and then he would go back to monitoring his surroundings.

"Clear enough," Adam allowed. "I don't have it with me." For some reason, he felt very glad of that fact, although he was also concerned about Professor Marchale, who did have the book, either at his office or in his home. Obviously that connection had not yet been made, and Adam hoped very much it wouldn't be. Marchale had a formidable personality, but he was an old man and certainly not capable of handling a physical situation very well.

"If I thought you had it on you, I wouldn't be wasting time having this nice chat," the man said with some scorn. "I don't know where it is, but you and I are gonna take a nice trip over to wherever you're keeping it, and you're going to hand it over.

Then everyone goes about their business and has a nice evening, OK?" That internal warning that Adam had been feeling as they crossed the parking lot now suggested to him that if he allowed this man to take him anywhere, things would probably not end well at all.

Adam took a deep breath. "You can't really threaten me, though, can you?" he said. Mostly he was hoping to stall for a little more time and hope some potential witnesses happened into the parking lot, which was remaining obstinately deserted. "After all, I'm the one who knows where the book is, so you're not going to stab me."

"People say all kinds of things after they get stabbed, Father," the darker haired man said. His companion gave him a slightly annoyed look. Adam filed away the observation that these people knew his background. It wasn't any kind of secret that he had once been a priest, but it wasn't as though everyone who came into the bookstore knew it, for example.

"Anyway," the blond said, "I don't need to do anything to you, because it's nice and convenient that you have these other nice people here with you. Do we understand each other?" He offered this threat in a firm, but offhand manner, like a workman discussing a task he had done enough times that he could already be sure that it wouldn't be any challenge to do again. It might not even require his full attention.

"We do," Adam heard himself say quietly. These men were not high on drugs, or whatever had happened, or been done to, Hugh Thomas. These men were evidently used to confrontations, seemed to be used to violence, and Adam reflected that they must be getting paid quite well. He also doubted they knew much of anything about the book in question, except that they would have been told not to come back without it, and he was also suddenly seized with the conviction that giving it to them would be a terribly bad idea. Perhaps sensing his hesitation, both of the men quietly slid their knives out into view.

Adam was just about to break and run, despite the part of his mind screaming at him that it was a terrible idea, when there was a blur of motion from his right. Sophia had suddenly stepped past him, pivoted, and cracked her forearm into the face of the man closest to them. He stumbled backwards, dropped his knife, and collided heavily with a bike rack and light pole. His partner stepped forward, but Sophia was already in motion again. She grabbed his jacket with both hands, yanked him towards her, and rammed her forehead into the bridge of his nose. The second man went down, a fountain of blood pouring from his face, and stayed down. His dazed compatriot managed to get his feet under him, and after a wild-eyed look in Sophia's direction, took off at a sprint.

Sophia Beaudry rubbed her forehead vigourously with the heel of one hand and grimaced. "Ow," she complained. "But most people don't expect that one, especially from a girl." She turned to the others and grinned happily. "See Father, they teach you all kinds of things in the army that are useful in everyday life."

"I'm sorry I ever doubted you, Miss Beaudry," said Adam feelingly.

"Fuck me, Sophia, that was…" Fred searched for the right words, and quickly abandoned the effort in favor of a fist bump. "Fucking hell, woman."

"I'm inclined to agree with you, Mr. Wallace," said Adam. "I think I hear sirens, though." Presumably someone had seen the confrontation after all, which meant that deliverance might have been soon at hand in any case.

"Yeah well Father, I'm not real inclined to wait around for the cops right now, you know?" Fred replied, shifting uncomfortably from foot to foot. Adam could see he was seriously upset, but hadn't yet figured out why.

"What's the problem, Mr. Wallace?" he asked. It was true that he and Fred might have some difficult questions to ask about being involved in their second armed confrontation in only a few days, perhaps especially if Officer Tessier was present again. However strange the events were, though, Adam felt they were on fairly safe ground, at least legally speaking. It did seem improbable that they would avoid a long session of questions, though, which seemed to be where Fred's thinking had already jumped to.

"If we get hung up here," he explained, "what happens with Jane, waiting for us?" She had apparently said her news was urgent, but was it urgent enough to leave a crime scene?

"We can call her," Adam suggested, "and let her know we'll be late. Her news will keep and I don't want to make this situation worse." There must, evidently, have been some witnesses to the altercation and, even though Sophia had acted in self-defence, he wasn't sure what the consequences would be if they left prior to answering police questions. At least one of the men, the one Sophia had head-butted, seemed as though he might be seriously hurt. The legal consequences there could be substantial.

"I'm not thinking about being late," Fred objected. "I'm thinking about what if she's about to get a visit from some dudes like these guys." Adam felt that unpleasant tingling feeling once again. Especially if this attack had somehow been motivated by whatever Jane had uncovered, Fred's concern was a plausible one. Leaving Jane on her own might be a dangerous risk.

"When you put it that way, I think I agree with you, Fred," agreed Adam reluctantly, deciding that legal consequences could be handled but leaving Jane in danger might not be fixable. He supposed it was unlikely that either man disabled by Sophia would be pressing charges, and hopefully whoever had called the police would be unable to identify them. The attackers themselves would probably not want to share any information, and in fact the one Sophia had head-butted didn't look as though he would be very communicative about anything for quite a while. Adam thought about calling someone from the hospital, but that would probably also lead to a long session of answering questions, however, and leave Jane exposed.

As he thought about the situation, and the vague threat of the Sunrise Foundation, he also considered that whoever this opposition was, precisely, they had considerable resources. It might be possible for them to make this situation very serious, legally, for Sophia, and perhaps Fred and Adam as well, if they became officially attached to it. Squelching some ethical queasiness, he said, "I think we should be going."

There was still the other consideration as well, of course. Bones was still in hospital and presumably safe enough there, but Jane was on her own. "We should find Jane right away," Adam went on firmly, "And one of you should call her immediately and tell her to go someplace very public, with lots of witnesses. That should keep her safe until we get to her."

"Bar's the best bet for that at this time of night, Father," Sophia offered, as they hurried away from the scene of the altercation. "You don't mind, do you?"

"Lord no," said Adam Godwinson. "I think we all need a drink after that, and you probably need several. Now let's hurry, and hope that these people didn't move against Jane at the same time as they did against us."

"Do you know who these freakshows are, Father?" Fred demanded, as they hurried to Sophia's car. Nothing else stirred in the parking lot, a sudden silence that made their footsteps sound incredibly loud and the distance down the row of parking stalls immensely long.

"Not exactly," Adam admitted, "but I suspect Jane may help to clarify that picture. They may have been more friends of Reverend Smiles, I suppose. Whoever 'they' are, they're obviously not shy of hurting people to get whatever it is they want. We must get to Jane before they can."

Chapter 22

They arranged to meet at a cheery, but, more importantly, chronically busy pub on Elgin Street. Sophia emphasized that Jane should go there right away. They were all counting on her being surrounded by potential witnesses, providing her with some level of protection until they could arrive.

Sophia's call was also illegal, because she made it while driving as they left the hospital parking lot. As soon as they were moving, she had taken out her phone and dialed, without giving any opportunity for objections. Adam reflected that she had become a lot more decisive since their time at St. Michael's, which was generally a positive, as long as she kept some perspective.

"Sophia," he said mildly, once she had hung up, "you do know that Fred and I both have phones, right?" He assumed that she was more rattled than she was letting on, which was understandable, but if it led her to make bad decisions, that was a potential problem.

"Sorry, Father," she replied, "but what does it matter?"

"I don't think we want to give the police any excuse to pull us over just now," he said as gently as possible. "Let's try and stay calm, and think through what we're doing.

"Sorry, Father," she said again. "I guess I didn't think about that one too much."

"Not to worry," Adam replied. "You did very well earlier."

"Thanks," Sophia answered with a grin, "but now there's another problem, and we can all solve it together!"

"What's up?" asked Fred, squirming around in his seat to look out the back window. "Cops, or someone else following us, or?" He left the question hanging as he continued to crane his neck and scan the traffic around them.

"No," Sophia said, still smiling. "But I don't see anywhere to park, yet." The laugh they shared turned out to be something they had all needed. By the time they arrived at the pub, though, a lot of tension had returned. If Jane wasn't there, how would they go about trying to find her, and help her?

Fortunately, Jane was holding down a table towards the back of the bar from the advances of a group of university students, and waved them over eagerly. Adam felt a wash of relief as he and the others gathered around the table, together and, at least apparently safe for now.

"Are you all right?" Jane demanded. "You all look freaked out, and Sophia, you have a huge red thing on your forehead. What is going on? I wanted to talk to you guys but what's the deal with the 'go somewhere public, don't be alone' stuff?"

Sophia fingered the welt on her head and Fred attempted a somewhat confused explanation of the encounter in the hospital parking lot. "Basically, things are a little freaky, so you might want to take some advice," he said.

"It's been an interesting night all 'round," Adam said tiredly. "There'll be time to fill you in later, but I think your message was urgent, Jane." A cheerful waitress appeared and they ordered drinks. Adam, finding himself suddenly starving, also asked for a plate of fries.

"Yeah, kinda," Jane agreed. "You know I've been trying to find out more about this Sunrise Foundation thing, right?" She had waited until the waitress was gone to begin her explanation, and leaned forward over the table as she spoke. The music and conversation in the pub made speaking quietly an impossibility, but also made it unlikely that they would be overheard. It was hard enough to keep track of what the person you were trying to listen to was saying, Adam thought.

"I remember," he replied. Now that the danger had passed he felt completely exhausted, almost as if he could go to sleep right there in the pub. Possibly, sitting down had been a bad idea. If he drank the pint he had ordered he was sure he'd never stay awake. As he considered flagging down the waitress to change his order to a coffee, Jane was speedily outlining the fruits of her research into the Sunrise Foundation.

"Damn, that's messed up," Fred observed sagely.

"To say the least," Adam agreed, "but Sophia also said you had come up with something new as well?" Jane nodded and leaned down to rummage in her messenger bag.

"Well, I finally got someone to send me the paperwork for when they registered it as a charity," she explained. She had her tablet out on the little table and was flicking through a series of documents. Before she found what she was looking for, the drinks and food arrived, leading to a brief delay while everything was rearranged on the table.

"Remind me again why a bunch of dudes obsessed with the end of the world count as a charity?" Fred asked, taking a deep gulp of his beer. His usual irreverent manner seemed a bit brittle in the aftermath of the confrontation.

"Well I don't think that's what they tell you at first, Freddie," said Jane scornfully. "Finding out what they were like was actually pretty difficult, not that you'd understand." She still hadn't provided many details about exactly how she had obtained the first set of documents about Sunrise, but Adam supposed that was standard procedure for journalists and their sources. He was slightly surprised, again, at how many contacts Jane seemed to have, but then she had always been superb at getting to know everyone around her.

"Children," Adam broke in, trying to sound stern but mostly sounding fatigued. "Let's try to stay focused." He left his beer untouched, and the bulk of the french fries had already vanished. Evidently he wasn't the only one who had found a sudden appetite, although right now he mostly wanted a few moments in a quiet room.

"Of course, Father," agreed Jane sweetly. "It's probably past your bedtime." Adam opened his eyes to see all three of them grinning at him. It was a good sign, he supposed, that they were maintaining a sense of humor during all this.

"You're very kind," he said dryly. One of the things he had always admired about the group was that although they did tease and needle each other, no one was singled out as the target for long, and the person who was currently doing the teasing would get their turn shortly.

"Look, is it just a coincidence that Jane has been looking into these people and all of a sudden we're getting trouble on the street?" Fred demanded. "I mean are they spying on us or something?" Adam had been toying with that idea himself. It was certainly easy to start seeing malevolent patterns in everything if you allowed yourself too.

"I'm not sure they have the resources for that, Fred," Adam objected mildly, "And some of this started before Jane's research did." Despite his own concerns, paranoia was a real danger too, and it would become all too easy to become paralyzed by fear rather than taking prudent actions.

"Don't be so sure about the resources thing, Father," said Jane. "Among a whole bunch of other stuff I got their board of directors. Listen to who's on it: Stephen Smiles." That put a rather different tone on the Reverend's visit to the bookstore, Adam reflected. There did seem to be a connection between many events of recent days, and Fred's concerns began to seem more plausible again.

"There's a lot I didn't like about Reverend Smiles," Adam considered, "But I wouldn't have thought he was of an apocalyptic persuasion. Is there much money in this charity, after all?" He surprised himself, a little, with how automatically he assumed a financial motive for Smiles' involvement, but he supposed that money was what he associated with the evangelist most, after all.

"That's just the beginning," Jane went on. "The second member is Louis Flambard." She said this with disappointment in her voice. Adam had known her admiration of him was genuine, but he was now trying to see what the environmentalist and a religious fundamentalist would have in common.

"Flambard?" Sophia interjected. "Why would he have anything to do with a piece of slime like Stephen Smiles?" Adam couldn't help but smile at her vehemence. He really wasn't sure what Sophia's spiritual beliefs were, these days, but she had always been intense in her sincerity and a gladhander like Smiles would never appeal to her.

"He thinks the world is ending," Fred chuckled, "Do you actually listen to his speeches, or do you just dig the beard?" It was true that Flambard made a lot of dire predictions about the consequences of human activity, but he was just as passionate in advocating for action. There was still another piece to this that Adam couldn't quite see, yet.

"But he's not religious," Sophia objected, "and Smiles never talks about anything else!" It was true that it was difficult to imagine anything that Stephen Smiles was involved in not having some kind of religious angle to it, but there hadn't been a hint of spirituality in Flambard's speech the other night. Then again, religious beliefs were sometimes more of a complicating factor than an asset, in the public arena.

"You never know," Adam said. "Some people just aren't very public about it. But anyway, he doesn't have to be religious to see the value in Smiles' connections, and possibly his bankroll, in doing whatever it is these Sunrise people do. Whatever you think of his beliefs, Stephen Smiles could be a very useful ally." Devotion to a cause could often make for curious alliances, but it was still far from clear exactly what the cause was, in this case.

"Speaking of which," Jane resumed, "listen to the next person. If you want to talk resources and useful allies, you won't get much better than Matilda Damory." Adam recognized the name right away. Damory was something of a superstar of the business world, making her name in stock trading and then starting her own investment capital firm. Damory was also photogenic and witty, and so she was frequently on the news, commenting on economic issues, and sometimes appeared on other programming relating to money and investment as a panelist or judge. Damory never gave any signs of religion either, Adam reflected, but then any that she did have wouldn't really be relevant to discussions of the Eurozone crisis or corporate tax rates.

"I never understood her," Sophia said. "She changed so much." She looked a little sad as she made the observation. Adam wouldn't have expected her to know much of anything about Matilda Damory, but he was getting used to being surprised, recently.

"What do you mean," Adam asked. "Do you know her?" He was trying to think where they could possibly have crossed paths.

Damory was from Toronto originally and, as far as he knew, had never lived in Ottawa. She was certainly not involved in the military, and Sophia had nothing to do with television.

"No, no, I just meant she was so different when she was younger," Sophia explained. "I was at McGill when she was still finishing her Master's degree, and she was part of all these campaigns about social justice, against poverty and inequality and political corruption. Then all of a sudden she is wearing a suit and working for a bank." Adam chided himself for forgetting that Sophia's brief time at university might have brought her in touch with Damory. Sophia had enrolled in a social science degree, but decided that it wasn't for her after a year and a half. Even though he was no longer with the church by then, he had still tried to smooth things over between she and her family, with indifferent success, it seemed to him.

"Maybe she decided she could do more for her causes by promoting the right companies and stuff," Fred suggested. "Also maybe she thought it would be nice to have money to contribute to the cause instead of just painting some signs." Damory wasn't well known for charitable contributions, though, Adam thought. She usually said that handouts just created dependency.

"Maybe," Sophia said skeptically. "I've just never heard her say a word about any of the things she used to be so passionate about in school." Adam hadn't really associated Damory with any activist causes, either. When she appeared on TV it was usually to extol the virtues of free market capitalism and to suggest that entrepreneurs looking to make money were the best solution to any problem.

"People can change as they get older," Adam observed. "Some of us even make radical changes of career, you know." He wondered, though, why Damory had never, to his knowledge, spoken about the reasons for her change of heart. Explaining all the flaws of the causes she had once promoted, compared to her current philosophy, seemed very much in character. Perhaps it was out of respect for those she had worked with, he considered.

"And, maybe she never believed in any of that junk anyway," Fred declared, "maybe it was just how she fit in with people. You know, like how every boy in school pretended to be into carpentry whenever Sophia was around." He offered this last comment with a teasing little grin; Adam reflected that he seemed to be recovering from the confrontation at last.

"Freddie, behave!" Sophia scolded. "Anyway, I guess it doesn't matter why she did what she has done. She would mean a lot of money for these people as well." Still, she said this somewhat sadly, and Adam wondered if she was disappointed in Damory's apparent change of philosophies.

"Yeah but listen," Jane said. "That's not even the bad part. There's one more name on the list." She turned her tablet around and pushed it across the table for the others to look at. Adam looked down at the screen and it took a moment for his eyes to focus on the scanned document it was displaying. Once they did, he could see that Jane was pointing out where the members of the Sunrise board were listed, and after the names she had already discussed was one more.

The last member of the board of directors of the Sunrise Foundation was John Kolb.

Chapter 23

After they had damped down the shock of Jane's discoveries with more pints of beer, Adam wasn't quite sure how to proceed, both generally and in an immediate sense. Getting the entire Guild together in one place had seemed crucially important, but they couldn't really stay that way from now on. In a while, the pub would close and all of them would want to go home. Was it safe? Was there any rational alternative?

He realized that it was also going to be necessary to rethink how he had been approaching all of the problems that were suddenly part of his life. Even after Jane's criticisms, Adam had still been assuming that Detective Kolb would uncover whatever answers were out there. Failing that, if Kolb had been lazy or disinterested, presumably other members of the police force would eventually take up the slack. These latest revelations put Kolb firmly among the problems that needed to be solved, though, and left no easily evident course of action.

Fred and Sophia were obviously eager to leave by now, and Adam knew that rest was important, perhaps especially for Sophia, considering her role in the night's events. Ideally, she should probably see a doctor, but that might lead to questions that would be hard to answer. In any case, she didn't seem tremendously concerned and Adam decided, with trepidation, to trust her judgement.

He also had to settle, finally, for an agreement that they would not go home separately. Sophia would drive Fred home, and Jane would take Adam to his house. Unfortunately they would then each drive home alone, but there didn't seem to be an easy way around that, and unless they started moving in with each other, everyone would be on their own at home anyway. The situation was increasingly alarming, but there were limits to what Adam was prepared to suggest, and, he knew, to what the Guild members would be prepared to agree to in any case.

On the ride to his house, neither Jane nor Adam spoke very much. Adam felt the fatigue in his head like wet sand, but strangely he also didn't feel like he would be able to sleep any time soon. Jane's mind seemed to be far away, although whether she was fretting over the problems confronting them all, or strategizing her research, he could not tell. They said their goodnights and Adam felt that going to bed now, and lying awake, would be counterproductive. On the other hand, he didn't want to read; too many of his problems seemed to be rooted in a book just now.

Adam sat in one of the old plastic chairs next to his vegetable garden, watching moths commune with the light over his back door and trying to make sense of the last couple of days. The first thing was that the book Bones had bought on a whim at Charles Warrington's estate sale, whatever was in it, was clearly worth a great deal to someone. Why that was, he could not yet imagine: Warrington's fantastic writings seemed to be a dead end, and perhaps Professor Marchale had been right and the book was just a prop for a writer of strange tales after all. Except that it appeared that Bones had been beaten into a hospital bed because of it, Hugh Thomas had somehow been sent after Adam with a knife, and most recently there had been tonight's attack.

If the 'why' was still elusive, the 'who' seemed fairly clear: the van Bones' attackers had used was owned by the Sunrise Foundation, Hugh worked for them, if indirectly, and Adam was confident there would be some kind of link with the two men tonight, somehow. What he couldn't yet understand was what could connect someone like the Reverend Stephen Smiles to an environmentalist like Louis Flambard, and the two of them to corporate prodigy Matilda Damory. Inspector John Kolb was the most immediately disturbing name, though — it was surely not a coincidence that he was investigating the assault on Napoleon Kale, and his link to Sunrise made it very hard to think about asking for more help from the police, somehow. How far did Sunrise's connections go?

Adam sipped his wine and struggled for a few moments with a clenching feeling of dread. Maybe they had people all over the place, maybe he and all the Guild members were being watched, right now, as Sunrise waited for their chance to grab the book that, as yet, none of Adam's friends had even been able to read.

But it didn't quite fit, he realized. They had been after Bones, and after Adam, twice. Smiles had been to the bookstore, and Adam felt it was likely that someone had been watching his home, or had at least made a point of indicating that they knew where it was. However, the one person who had, so far, remained completely untouched by it all was the person who actually had the book in his possession — Todd Marchale. Sunrise was reasonably well-informed, but they hadn't made the connection between Adam and his old university thesis supervisor yet. Just as clearly, they didn't have him under constant surveillance or have his phones tapped, or they would have picked up on Marchale immediately.

Their resources were limited, and perhaps not even that extensive, if they had to use a van owned by the foundation to carry out a street assault. No doubt they were trusting that Kolb could squelch any connection between the van and Sunrise, and to make sure that the investigation into the attack on Bones remained dead in the water, but it was really a considerable risk. Somehow, that was comforting; the enemies — as Adam realized he had started to think of them — were clearly powerful, but not endlessly so. In fact, a lot of what they had done seemed like acts of desperation rather than those of a calculating organization with time on its side. There was still a large part to this puzzle that Adam couldn't see yet, he admitted.

There was, however, a more pressing concern. Sunrise hadn't yet determined that Marchale was involved, and was currently in possession of Warrington's book, but there was no guarantee that things would stay that way. Adam had no idea how he would react if he was told about everything going on in connection to what had previously been a piece of academic trivia, but it certainly didn't seem right to leave him in the dark about it. Probably it was best to take the book back, taking Marchale out of danger, and perhaps even leave him happily ignorant of the whole mess. Adam finished his wine and resolved to get the book out of Marchale's hands tomorrow, first thing.

Doing that, though, eliminated their best chance of figuring out what the contents of the thing were, he argued to himself. Without knowing what the book was there was no way to know what the whole disaster was even about. That led to another question: was it even important to do that? Why not just courier the damned thing to the Hand of God's offices and be done with it all? Adam could think of no clear reason, except that from what Sunrise had already been willing to do trying to recover the book, he was sure whatever they wanted with it wasn't anything good.

So who cared? Was it his responsibility to do anything about it? Bones had bought the book because he was concerned that his old priest was in a rut. Adam had only started looking into it because, yes, it was the kind of puzzle he enjoyed, he had missed research, and it was a much more interesting problem than how much to price *Birds of Ottawa* at. Did that make everything else that was happening his problem now? Bad things happened every day, and no-one could prevent all of them. Adam went inside, locked the back door, put his wineglass in the sink, and headed for bed.

That question could wait for the morning, once Todd Marchale was no longer unwittingly in danger because of a favour Adam had asked of him.

Adam called the professor before leaving his house in the morning, but got no answer either at his home or his university office. He left messages and tried persuade himself not to read anything ominous into failing to contact Marchale, who hated answering the telephone at the best of times and would frequently ignore it even if he was in the same room. He would go to work and wait for Marchale to call. If he didn't hear back by lunch time, it would be a short walk to the university to investigate.

As he left his house, he noticed that his front door wasn't closed properly — not swinging open, but not pulled fully shut either. At first Adam shook his head ruefully at his own absent-mindedness and the effects of advancing age but, as he thought about it more, he couldn't decide if he had left the door ajar, or if there was a more alarming interpretation — that someone had been in the house after he had gone to sleep. Adam tried to remember his arrival home. He had been drinking and had been upset by the night's events; it was possible he had been distracted enough to be careless with the door. On the other hand, he'd never done it before, and it didn't seem outside the realm of possibility that people willing to orchestrate an assault or a robbery might burglarize his home in search of the book that was evidently so important to them.

In the end, Adam couldn't decide which interpretation was more unreasonable, and chewing over the matter meant that he went through the usual routine of opening up W.M. Howard, Bookseller, without paying very much attention to it. He turned over the events of the past several days relentlessly, trying to reach a conclusion that indicated that the problem was merely legal, or criminal, but it was like the Rubik's Cube his sister had gotten as a present that Adam had scrambled up and the puzzle had never been solved again — the pieces now refused to fall into an acceptable order.

Adam realized that he might have been speaking these thoughts aloud as he unlocked the door to the alley and immediately took an involuntary step back. The ground directly outside the threshold was covered with green powder, scattered about in great sweeping lines that curved and zigzagged and looped back over each other, recalling ludicrously tangled fishing lines and electrical cords in children's puzzle books.

Somehow here, now, it was disturbing — the green was shocking, bright, yellowish — it made Adam think of acid and, at the same time, of flames, as if the powder might be some ignitable substance. Was the pattern significant, some hex or incantation drawn here by whatever bizarre association he had accidentally become entangled with? His imagination sped immediately to several books on Vodou in the back library, the power of special drawings that had made interesting reading when the volumes were first donated.

Now he stood and looked at the lines of powder and wondered if he should scrub them out with his foot, or if that was somehow the trigger, if there was something here to be triggered at all. His gaze eventually fell on a black and red tin lying on its side a little further up the alleyway, and saw the words 'Poster Paint' above smaller type that would probably explain the precise shade of green currently spilled and, he saw now, slowly turning into a thick sludgy paste from the dampness on the pavement.

Adam grinned and shook his head at his imagination, although he also decided that the alley did not require any further investigation this morning. He closed the door and returned to the front of the store, now speculating idly about whether the mess in the alleyway was the result of some art supply misadventure, or just of teenagers using whatever they had to hand to make one of the acts of angry defiance against not being grown up but not being children any more either that he had often needed to handle with care at St. Michael's.

And yet, as he sat at the register to await the day's first customer, there was something in that green that still seemed very flammable in his mind, as though it was something that would go into a firework. And there, the association finally came to him, pieces from his memory slotting into place and he remembered Sophia, in her early teens and newly delighting in chemistry, especially things that flashed, banged, or flared in bright colours, taking what might have been an alarming interest in pyrotechnics if not for the amused guidance of a teacher at her high school.

Sophia had kept it as a hobby for years, and probably it had helped guide her into her vocation in the military. Adam remembered a church picnic where she had been eager to provide a display of her skills for the evening, and had produced a quite impressive array of fireworks in reds and blues and, yes, bright greens. Sophia had been as proud of her work as any young person can be, Adam had been proud of her, and did his best to silence the muttered comments from parishioners that were of the opinion that the whole thing had been dangerous and proper fireworks would have been nicer. Fortunately he was at least successful in making sure that if such things must be said, that they were said well away from Sophia, and she had bubbled with joy in her accomplishment for a long while afterwards.

Adam sipped his coffee and enjoyed the memory, and chided himself for this new tendency to find dark portents in everything he encountered through the day. Surely, whatever the significance of the last few days was, it could not be as bad as his imagination made it. He smiled to himself and reached for the phone to call Sophia and ask if she remembered the picnic.

There was always something slightly eerie about the phone ringing just as you reached for it, Adam believed, and it was the last thing his somewhat frayed nerves needed this morning. The cheery, relaxed facade he had just finished constructing abruptly collapsed and he picked up the receiver hesitantly, expecting something unpleasant.

Todd Marchale in a foul mood was certainly that, but in a way it came as a relief. "What in the devil do you want," he said without greeting or preamble. "Phones ringing all over the damned place, and I've actual work to do. If you want a meeting it's impossible today, I've a legion of ghastly unavoidable things sucking the life out of me. If you've something to report it had better be damned interesting."

Adam was glad it was a telephone conversation so he could safely grin at this outburst. Knowing that Marchale was safe and well lifted one of the weights from his mind and the professor's colourful diatribes had an undeniable entertainment value. Still, there was a serious issue to be dealt with. "I'm sorry to disturb you when you're busy, Professor," he said, when he was quite sure Marchale had temporarily ceased fire. "It's just that there was something I needed to discuss with you, rather urgently."

"Oh, hell," Marchale replied. "Why not, I doubt you can make the day any more wretched than it already promises to be."

"The short version is that I think I should take that book I brought you back," Adam said. How exactly to explain this without getting into issues that he would prefer to keep Marchale safely ignorant of, and without bringing up theories that the professor would lacerate with scorn, was likely to be tricky. "It's just that it turns out that the person I know who bought it, well, there appear to be some questions about the legality of the sale." This was a slight injustice to Bones, Adam admitted to himself, but on the other hand it aligned with inquires that Paul Bagot might still be making and was reasonably plausible. "I wouldn't like to get you entangled with anything so I think it's better if it's out of your hands, don't you?"

"You thought what," Marchale growled. Adam suddenly realized how he had miscalculated as Marchale went on. "You want to let some foul legal creature interfere with a perfectly worthwhile piece of research?" This was perhaps an optimistic evaluation of their studies of the strange manuscript, but Adam was given no opportunity to interject. "Damn that, you craven thing. If you back down from these people they'll suck you thoroughly dry." Adam remembered, now, that Marchale had been involved in a libel case in the early stages of his career, and it had left him with a permanent disdain for the legal profession and lawsuits in particular. "And you are not my mother, needing to protect me from the great terrifying world, either. It's just as well you told me about this but I won't be pushed off of any project of mine and I won't have you falling on your sword in noble fashion either. I'm not done with the damned book so you can't have it back yet. Clear?"

"Very," Adam said. He was trying to marshal a new set of arguments that would convince Marchale to give up the book. It would have to fit with the legal scenario he had started out with, which didn't leave him much room to maneuver. This was always the problem with not telling the truth, Adam reflected, it was hard to keep all the fictions straight, and among the reasons why he found that honesty was preferable. He was trying to decide, quickly, how to explain the real situation before him to

Marchale, in a way that wouldn't be instantly dismissed, when the professor loosed another volley.

"Christ on the True Cross," Marchale snarled, "What is it now?" There was a brief pause. "That wasn't at you," he explained, "but I think that's the secretary at my door, no doubt with more horrible news, so I shall have to let you go. Call me later if you've done any damned work." This was followed by an unpleasant clatter as, Adam presumed, Marchale wrestled the receiver into its cradle and broke the connection.

"Well," he said to himself quietly, drumming his fingers on the countertop, "that was less than successful." Forgetting Marchale's antipathy for the legal profession had been a fatal error, and although he was relieved that the professor had apparently not suffered for his possession of the book or his involvement with Adam, there was no way to guarantee that would continue to be the case. Adam supposed he would have to find another strategy for getting Marchale to return the book to him. As a last resort, he could risk offending his old advisor and simply demand the manuscript's return, although Marchale did not, in Adam's experience, react tremendously well to demands.

Still, the professor was at least potentially in danger due to a situation he didn't fully understand, which Adam couldn't bring himself to accept. There seemed to be no alternative to explaining the entire tangled mess to him, and hoping that Marchale could somehow be convinced that the crisis was genuine. That was likely to be impossible while he was in one of his tempers, and was therefore unlikely to be accomplished today.

This train of thought, Adam was surprised to discover, had taken him through most of this morning, the bulk of the contents of the latest box of "donations" to the bookstore, and the best part of a pot of coffee. He also remembered that he had meant to call Sophia this morning so, once lunch had been obtained, he sat down to call her at last.

Chapter 24

It turned out that Sophia had nothing planned for her evening and that she was eager to come to Adam's and spend the time on a quiet talk. They sat in his living room, drank coffee, and tried to steer the conversation away from recent troubles to happy reminisces. Adam finally asked her about the picnic, trying as he did to ignore the morning discovery in the alleyway that had brought it to mind.

He was relieved that she apparently didn't carry any memory of any negative opinions of her fireworks display, and after she was finished gently mocking his imaginings about spilled poster paint in the alleyway, they had moved on to other memories of the Guild and their various projects and causes. As it continued, though, he conversation about bake sales and Christmas pageants felt increasingly strained and its light tone increasingly like a pretense. Adam could see an unasked question vibrating below the surface of Sophia's cheery demeanour. Finally, abruptly, it forced itself through. "Why did you leave us?" Sophia asked, with a softness that cut painfully.

Adam stared at the bottom of his coffee cup as though a useful response might be there among the sludgy accretion of grounds. He had been through this decision so many times that it felt like a topic that should be long dead, but for whatever reason it refused to rest quietly. "I tried to explain at the time," he said eventually. "People said I had lost my faith, but that wasn't the case. I still feel that there's something larger than us, something that does care and offers hope and a way out of the darkness. I just," he paused and wiped at his glasses, and settled them carefully back into place before continuing. "What I couldn't continue to believe in was this thing we created, people created, that we use to judge each other and condemn each other and make some of us powerful and others weak. I've spent most of my life thinking about faith and religion and I think I decided that while my faith would never go away, I couldn't find a religion I liked very much, any more. I tried to explain it at the time, I thought," he finished, trailing off as he tried to remember exactly what he had told his soon to be former congregation those years ago.

Adam glanced back at Sophia, then, realizing that he hadn't been looking at her the entire time he was speaking. Her gaze was heavy on him. "I remember that," she said, mastering a slight quiver in her voice as she spoke, "but that's not what I meant. Why did you leave us? You had told us for years that we were important to you and then you disappeared out of everyone's life into that bookstore. No more visits, you don't call anyone. Before this, you didn't know who Bones was dating. You didn't know where Jane lived. Before this, you hadn't spoken to me since last year." There was no need to explain what 'this' was. Adam risked another glance over towards Sophia in time to see that her eyelashes were matted with tears.

He looked back into the coffee cup, at a pile of magazines he had never finished reading, and then at a chip on the corner of the doorway to the kitchen that he kept meaning to fix. This was not, after all, the conversation he had had so many times before. "I suppose I've never really thought about that properly," he admitted. "Honestly, I don't know what I'm doing with myself, right now. I haven't for a long time. I guess I didn't know what good I could really do any of you when I don't have many answers for myself. And I don't feel that I'm the best source for guidance anymore, when you look at how my life has been since I left the church. I'm hardly a success story."

Sophia seemed to think about that for a moment. "So," she said, "I'm only someone to give advice to, and if you can't do that there's no point in anything else?"

"That isn't what I meant," Adam replied quickly. "That's not how I think of things."

"I thought we were your friends," Sophia answered back, a little accusingly.

"You were, you are," Adam tried to assure her, feeling that this conversation was rapidly slipping out of control, into a direction he had been unable to anticipate.

"Then what is this bullshit about not being able to provide guidance," Sophia demanded. "If you feel this way about how things are in your life your friends are supposed to be the people you talk to about that. It's what you let your friends do for you."

"That's just never been how things have worked," Adam replied. "Not before. And I suppose I didn't want to place any burdens on you, on any of you. You've all got so many things to focus on for yourselves without my worries added to them. In the end I suppose I didn't feel like I had much worth sharing with you all."

"Oh, Father," Sophia said. "You're either going to be my friend or you aren't. Which is it?"

"I would like to be," Adam answered quietly. "I always wanted to be. I suppose I thought I was."

"You can't do this then," Sophia replied firmly. "You can't tell people they're important to you and then disappear because it's easy for you to do it."

"All right," Adam said after a moment. "I should have something to say, I suppose." He turned the coffee mug in his hands and looked back up at Sophia. "I'm sorry."

"Father," she said with smile abruptly breaking through, "It's all right. It's kind of reassuring that you can be as big of a twit as anyone else. Anyway, if we didn't think you were worth it I wouldn't have bothered with this. Just promise you won't disappear in another month until the next emergency that lets you give advice again."

"All right," Adam said again. "I promise."

"And one more thing," Sophia went on.

"All right."

"Promise me that you'll buy me a better cup of coffee and let's really talk for an hour or so." Adam nodded, stepped over to Sophia and embraced her gently.

"Let's go and do that," he said.

The next morning Adam found that someone from the pita bar adjacent to the bookstore had unwisely put some garbage out back without bothering to put it into a trash can or dumpster. Something had eviscerated the garbage bags and strewn the contents along the length of the alleyway. Adam tried not to take this an ominous sign for the rest of the day, closed the door and started rearranging some of the shelves in the back library. He knew that this was ultimately pointless work; there was no perfect book deployment that would suddenly cause someone to discover an overpowering need for a copy of *The Traveller's London*. However, shuffling things around was a reliable way to stop his mind wandering off in unwanted directions.

"Good morning, Father Godwinson," said a voice from the front of the store, rich with what sounded like cheer. "I thought we might have a talk." Adam stepped through the door to the back library to find a woman idly leafing through an illustrated book on gardening near the front of the store. Her face, and especially her hair, a shade of red that had to come from a very expensive bottle, were immediately familiar.

"If you like, Ms. Damory," he said as neutrally as possible. "Lately I seem to be telling almost everyone I meet not to call me 'Father' anymore, though." It might not be a battle worth fighting, he supposed, but there really was a principle behind the thing.

"Oh well, some things are more important than titles, Mr. Godwinson," she replied. "Do you mind?" She smiled in what Adam expected was a very effectively friendly manner, for board meetings and public relations occasions. Somehow, though, he immediately felt reluctant to take any of her manner at face value.

"Again, we can talk for a bit if you like," Adam said. "Assuming we're not interrupted by your celebrity, of course. Are autograph seekers a problem?" The comment was out of his mouth before he had thought over whether it was a good idea, or not. He wasn't sure where the impulse to agitate had come from, but it was a little late now. Damory gave no sign of being bothered.

"Rarely," Matilda answered firmly. "In fact, most of the time people just don't believe someone is who they really are until the time has passed, in my experience. And anyway, I love a good book as much as anyone." She picked up a hefty novel from the 'New Arrivals' table at the front of the store, glanced at it carelessly, and set it down again.

"So I've heard," Adam said softly. He made his way to the counter, sat on the stool, and took a sip of his coffee, finding it cold. "Do you know, I think you used to be a hero of a friend of mine?"

"How lovely," Damory replied distantly. "But you say I used to be — what do they think of me now?" She offered another sharp little smile as she continued to examine the shelves towards the front of the shop.

"I think we're all not quite certain what to make of you at the moment, Ms. Damory," Adam said. He had an uncomfortable feeling that the conversation was being guided towards a particular point, and saw no reason to help it along.

"Oh," she said with a touch of a pout, "and I thought I was quite straightforward."

"No," Adam declared, "It's quite a change from student activist to darling of the corporate world in the space of a few years."

"Oh that," Damory said tiredly. "Is that really what has you curious? Maybe I'll indulge you." She put down the gardening book as well, and began strolling between the bookshelves with exaggerated languor. Adam reflected that her whole posture was likely calculated to be unsettling, and that it worked rather well. "Yes, I really was quite devoted to causes while I was in school," she continued after a few moments. "Reforms in government. Sustainability in the economy. Social justice." She said the last two words with surprising bitterness. "But do you know what I really learned, Father? I did everything I was supposed to do at university. My grades were, I'm sorry, outstanding, I was active in campus life, I had more professors wanting to write me recommendations than I needed. But two years after graduation I was still sharing an apartment with three other people because it's all we could afford, I was working at a vile little restaurant in between volunteering, and I realized this was all I was going to get. I did everything I was supposed to do and all I got was debt and a minimum wage dead end."

Adam watched her toying with random volumes from the shelves as she spoke. "So you what, sold out your ideals for a nice place to live and designer clothes? You'll forgive me, but that's hardly," he glanced at the book in her hands, "novel." He wasn't sure why he was deliberately trying to provoke her, but for some reason he was.

"It isn't, is it," Matilda said with a mirthless smile. "Still, once I dropped the Guy Fawkes masks and the marches on embassies and the 'No Justice, No Peace' and all the rest of it, once I started to play the little games I was supposed to, well, you know how it went as well as I do."

"Yes, more money than you know what to do with," Adam agreed. "Are things like this," he indicated a pile of books on the counter, "because you're bored?"

"Not at all, not at all," Matilda demurred. "In fact, I have lots to keep me interested, Father."

"And you left your friends behind," Adam said. "Your friends from school who didn't have the revelation you did. I suppose it never occurred to you to use your position in society, or at least your bank account, to help them, poor lambs."

"Lambs, yes," Mathilda answered with surprising relish, "and our enlightened society will slaughter them in the end. Everyone thinks I love my world of board rooms and bank accounts, but it's just as hateful from the inside as it was from the outside. Actually, once you're closer to the centre of things, it becomes even clearer that what's wrong with our society isn't fixable."

"So, you quit twice," Adam observed shortly. "Once on your principles, and then on society, is that it?" He wasn't enjoying fencing with her any longer. In fact he very badly wanted to escape the conversation, and the gloom of Damory's words, as soon as possible.

"I don't think of it as quitting," said Matilda, without apparent offense, "and I only did it once. I gave up losing, Father. If we don't play the way this poison world we've created wants us to, we're crushed without a thought. And when we do, well, all we've had to do is become hateful people doing horrible things. Not much of a price." She paused for a moment, as though catching her breath. "I decided that, quite literally, anything would be better."

"I'm sure I don't know what you mean by that," Adam said mildly. Now, he was hoping, he would find out exactly how far she was into the rhetoric from the Sunrise documents.

"Oh, of course you do," Matilda replied in an exasperated tone. "I'm quite aware that your little journalist has been poking into things. In fact it's now that you have some idea of what's going on that I think we may be able to reach an understanding."

"You want my help in smashing the state, is that it?" asked Adam. "I'm not really a revolutionary."

"Neither am I, Father, you know that," Matilda said with intensity. "It's time to start again. When the King returns, he will tear it all down, down to shreds. I have no idea what will come afterwards, but it can't possibly be worse than the way things are right now." My God, Adam thought. She either really believes in these things, or she knows how to perform.

"It's an interesting enough theory," Adam replied, trying not to show any reaction to her mention of the King from Warrington's fiction. From Warrington's book, anyway. "I'm not sure why you needed to tell me about it, though."

"You know what I need, Father," Matilda said. "I need the book your inconvenient little churchmouse bought, after we had spent so long tracking it down and then waiting for it to become available. It's not too late to stop losing, Adam."

He looked up sharply at her use of his first name. "Friends already, are we?" he asked. "Even assuming this isn't all complete nonsense, what's my incentive for doing as you ask?"

"Well, I would say money, but I doubt that would tempt you," Matilda answered. "Perhaps I'll just say you don't want to be in my way?"

"Or I might end up in the hospital, like Napoleon?" Adam demanded. He could feel his temper slipping and fought to keep hold of it. "Not a very subtle argument, Ms. Damory. And I think perhaps you've already explored that particular avenue."

Did her blandly pleasant facade flicker? If it did, Adam thought, it was only for a moment. "Perhaps you might consider that there are other weapons to use on you," she suggested with a little smile. "Priests, or even former priests, are uniquely vulnerable these days to the right sort of allegations. It would be a shame to see you in prison, Father." Matilda waited to let that sink in before continuing, "But I don't really want to extort things from you at all, Father. Give me my book and we can be great friends."

"You'll have to excuse me," Adam said, "but I'm a bit confused. Even if I grant that everything we're talking about is possible, I should save myself by giving you the book so that, what, I can be burned to a cinder? It's not the best recruiting pitch I've ever heard, to be blunt."

"Oh, Father," Mathilda replied impatiently, "Kings have always rewarded those who put them on their throne, or back on it. But you're right in one way — you want to be very sure you're standing with the right group when the time comes."

"That's something to think about, I suppose," Adam said. "It's not here with me now, if that's what you were hoping."

"Of course not," Matilda replied. "If I thought it was here we might not be talking, to be honest. Your store is charming, but not really impregnable. In time we can find the book, wherever it is, and take it whether you want us to or not. I thought you deserved an opportunity to do something for yourself, and perhaps for your friends, though."

"Just as your friend Reverend Smiles did, I now realize," Adam observed. "How nice to be popular."

"You won't be for long, Father," replied Matilda, moving towards the door. "Not if you don't make the right moves, anyway. You are rapidly running out of options. Give us the book, send it to us if you don't want to deliver it yourself. Just don't take too long to think about it, or I shall have to take steps."

"Good day to you," Adam said. "I'm sure we'll talk again soon."

Chapter 25

Throughout that evening, Adam's attempts to finish studying the articles about Warrington's writing were interrupted by the phone. Unfortunately these were not calls from Sophia, Jane, or Fred — in fact there was no one on the line at all, just a quiet digital hiss on the line, punctuated by a regular, soft, beep.

At first he was just annoyed, assuming some kind of autodialing program had gone wrong or that someone with a fax machine was being persistent with a wrong number. As the calls continued to come, Adam began to wonder if there was something else going on. He tried staying on the line to see if anything else would ever happen, but there was nothing but the electronic noises.

Even the interval between the calls seemed strange, and very regular, so finally he timed it. They were exactly 5 minutes apart, each time, which seemed too regular to be accidental. And still, just the white noise, and the rhythmic tone on the line.

Gradually, even though Adam recognized that he was letting his imagination get away from him, he began to feel as though there was something more to the phone calls than just a nuisance — his mind strayed back to the Sunrise Foundation, the signs of the resources that they had, and the suggestive indications that they had been working against him.

Were the repeated phone calls an attempt at harassment, to distract him and keep him from working, and unlocking answers that might be useful? Were all the Guild members also receiving the repeated calls? Could it be an attempt at intimidation, to show that they knew where he lived, and to make him feel unsafe in his own house?

Was this one of the 'steps' Matilda Damory had alluded to? Her parting shot had been a strange one. Sending thugs to confront him in a parking lot certainly seemed as though steps were already being taken. Had Damory not been involved in that decision? If she wasn't threatening him with attack, what else might he need to expect? The phone calls were annoying, but surely no more than that.

When the phone rang again, Adam jumped nervously, even though the timing of it should have been expected by now. He realized that for nearly an hour, he hadn't been doing anything other than sitting and waiting for the next call to come in, and then trying to construct meanings behind it all.

Finally, he took a deep breath, got up from his chair, walked across the room, and unplugged the phone from the wall. It was possible that he would miss an update on Bones' condition, or another problem from one of the Guild members, but at this point it was a risk he was prepared to take. As an additional precaution, he turned off his cell phone. Nothing would happen tonight that couldn't wait until morning, he told himself.

Adam decided that returning to the papers on Warrington was probably a bad idea now. For one thing, he was too unsettled to really focus on them, and he might miss something important in them. They were also likely to keep the problem of the book, and the Sunrise Foundation, in his mind, and what he really needed now was to focus on something else.

It was a bit late now for gardening, and his nerves were still a bit jangled to work on a crossword. Instead, Adam poured himself a glass of wine and tried to focus on a historical novel, and a mystery set a safe 1100 years in the past.

The decision to drop by the Hand of God Ministry's Ottawa offices was something Adam had been turning over in his mind for the last couple of days. His first impulse was that there was little point, but Smiles was a politician, however he might want to avoid the label. Perhaps if he was presented with a threat to his carefully built name and reputation, he might be shaken loose from cooperating with the other members of the Sunrise Foundation. Perhaps that would be a breach that could be leveraged into collapsing their entire plan.

Moreover, whether the phones last night had been a technical malfunction or something more sinister, the feeling of being under siege in his own home had persuaded Adam to try going on the offensive. With this in mind, Adam broke from his usual routine and took his much-neglected and rather road-worn Honda Civic to work. He only used the car for travel outside the city or shopping trips involving large purchases, such as bags of topsoil for the garden or a flatpack from Ikea. However, the Hand of God had moved to the premises abandoned by one of Ottawa's failed high-tech companies, and was therefore awkward to reach by bus, and an expensive trip by taxi.

Adam's plan to shake something useful out of a confrontation with Smiles was an optimistic scenario, but not an impossible one, and doing something proactive had a positive feel to it. As a result, Adam enjoyed the drive to the city's western fringe, rehearsing his strategy on the way. Upon arrival, he was greeted politely, if not enthusiastically, by a chastely attractive receptionist, who asked how the Hand of God could be of service to him today. Adam explained that he was hoping to speak with Reverend Smiles, gave his name, was offered coffee, and asked to wait. It was no surprise that the wait was a short one — Smiles was probably hoping Adam had brought the book with him, was accepting his offer to join the Hand of God, or both.

Adam was ushered into an office that had been decorated in soft wood and light-coloured stonework; the furnishings and the equipment were clearly high quality but also seemed to have been chosen to avoid being ostentatious. It was a subdued, plausibly deniable kind of luxury that Steven Smiles enjoyed here.

"A pleasant surprise, Father Godwinson," Steven Smiles greeted him, getting up from behind the desk to walk over and offer his hand. "Perhaps you've reconsidered our last conversation?"

"Not yet," Adam said. "I was hoping we could talk about something else, for now."

"Well, I have many demands on my time, indeed I do," Smiles replied, "but I'm still pleased to make time for you, Father."

"Please, Reverend Smiles," Adam said, "We've discussed the use of that title before."

"My apologies, then," Smiles answered, holding up a placating hand. "Now, then, if none of your positions have changed, what is it that you wanted to discuss, Doctor?"

"I was actually hoping to talk to you about Hugh Thomas," Adam explained, settling into one of the leather upholstered chairs in front of the desk. It was either very new or hardly used. "I believe he had been working for you?"

"Indeed he was," Smiles said slowly. "A young man with some vision, I believe, and with a desire to serve his fellow man. A former member of your flock, as well, I think — perhaps your influence led him to me?" Smiles sat down behind his desk and arranged a stack of papers so that all the corners were perfectly aligned.

"Anything's possible," Adam admitted, although the idea that his teachings might have encouraged Hugh to end up working for a man like Steven Smiles was not a pleasant one. "You'll have no doubt heard about what happened to him, then?"

"Of course, of course," Smiles said. "Even the well-intentioned are sometimes beset with troubles, as you will know. I fear Mr. Thomas must have chosen to hide his demons from those he was close to, unless you were aware of them, of course."

"I wasn't," Adam replied. "But I am hoping to take an interest in his recovery. I was hoping you might be able to provide some insight that would be helpful, since you were apparently so much a part of Hugh's life."

"As I said, the young man must have kept his difficulties carefully concealed," Smiles explained, "I believe that's often the case with people suffering from such trials. However I must also confess that I was not as close with Mr. Thomas as you imagine. I would not like to sound proud, indeed I would not, but my ministry is of a fair size, and not all those who serve alongside me are personally known to me. There was a time when we were much closer, almost a family, but increasing our ability to serve the Almighty has brought with it a cost, indeed it has."

Adam finished his coffee and tried to think of another approach. The questions about Hugh Thomas had been effortlessly deflected, as Smiles had probably learned to parry inquiries into the finances and political connections of the Hand of God Church. Perhaps there was one other card worth playing, if only to see the reaction. "Perhaps I expected too much, then," he said diffidently.

"Oh, your interest is commendable," Smiles said warmly, "and you may be assured that the ministry will do all we can to aid in his return to health, of course we will. So perhaps we will find a common cause, after all. Now, if there was nothing else?"

"One other thing, while I'm here," Adam replied. "I was wondering if you might know anything about an organization called the Sunrise Foundation."

Smiles looked at him sharply. "A local charity, small in scope but devoted to a good cause," he answered finally. It had the sound of a practiced line. "Why do you ask?"

"Oh, I'd run across the name," Adam said blandly, "I've been thinking that I should be more active in the community and didn't know much about what they do. Possibly I could pitch in, that sort of thing." The friendly, open expression was finally gone from Smiles' face.

"You'll forgive me," he said, "but I think you're not being quite honest with me, Doctor Godwinson. It's not by chance that you raise this with me." Smiles was visibly calculating now, trying to determine what sort of a threat Adam might present, and how serious a one he was likely to be.

"Isn't it?" Adam asked. His concern now was keeping Jane from being exposed to anything from her investigations, but he supposed the best way to have done that would be to avoid revealing her results to Smiles. Still, it had seemed a worthwhile chance of shaking loose useful information.

"I work with the Foundation, as I believe you are well aware," Smiles answered. His face was set sternly now, as though admonishing a wayward member of his flock or rebuking a reporter who had strayed from an agreed line of questioning.

"Well, what if I am?" Adam said. "You've been wanting me to work with you. Why don't you tell me all about what the Sunrise Foundation does, and perhaps I'll have something to think about."

"I can have some literature sent to you, at your store or at home," Smiles replied. Another practiced sounding deflection, which suggested that he might no longer be thinking of Adam as a potential recruit. Perhaps it was just a well-conditioned reflex for dealing with inquiries into the operations of his charities and church, however.

"Oh, but I was hoping you might be more specific," Adam said. "Maybe you can explain the philosophy behind the whole thing, for example? Or, on a practical level, you might be able to tell me about activities — the sort of things that get delivered in those vans of yours, say." Perhaps it was time to show a little bit of what he had uncovered, and see if that would unsettle the Reverend's handling of the conversation.

"Now, Father," Smiles said. "I'm unsure what you've heard, or may think you've heard, but you should be cautious. It's a great shame that in these latter days if one says things without being able to prove the truth of them, the, ah, resulting entanglements can be significant. And I'm sure you'll understand that I couldn't allow the reputation of my ministries to be smeared with spurious allegations."

"I may be able to prove more than you think," Adam replied, thinking again of the documents Jane Moore had uncovered. "Without of course imagining that you would be personally aware of any wrongdoing, there may be more vulnerability than you expect."

"Nothing happens in my ministries without my knowledge and approval," Smiles said. "I am dedicated to my cause, and if you've come here hoping to upset them then I can only advise you to tread carefully." Of course Smiles had long experience with legal troubles, and had fought numerous cases of alleged fraud successfully, often following up with his own successful suits for libel and slander against his accusers.

"I'm learning to be careful," Adam replied. "The world seems more dangerous all the time, but so far I persevere." He had hoped, or at least considered, that Smiles might have been misled into cooperating with Sunrise, but it was increasingly clear that this was not the case. Adam reflected that he should have known that someone as image conscious and meticulous as Smiles would never have gone into anything blindly.

"To your credit, I'm sure, even if we cannot agree philosophically," Smiles nodded. "It is a sinful world, Doctor Godwinson, and it is a sad truth that we must all do what we despise in our hearts to accomplish the will of the Almighty."

"So you're like Ms. Damory, then, are you?" Adam asked. "Pretending to be something you hate so you can be in a position to enact these plans of yours. She's filled with despair about the secular world, and you've given up on religion, haven't you, Reverend?"

"Given up on religion?" Smiles replied with a smile. "You mistake me, indeed you do. I acknowledge that Matilda, and many of the others, have nothing but loathing for the world we live in, but who can blame them? Look around, and you see nothing but sin, and victory for the unclean. Despite it all, though, I cleave to the purity of faith in the Almighty, and I pray that will never change."

"Isn't it the role of faith to provide people like that with some comfort and hope, Reverend?" Adam asked. He had always tried to encourage people against succumbing to pessimism. It was easy to believe the worst of things, but that could easily become self-fulfilling, in his experience.

"But when the church, the churches, are as much a part of the problem, Father Godwinson, what then?" Smiles answered back. "No, religion, in the way most people understand it, is just as fallen, just as tainted, as anything else, I fear. I made that case to you when we last spoke, you may recall."

"But you understand it differently," Adam said. He didn't bother to hide his skepticism, now. He had tried pretending to be sympathetic, or at least potentially sympathetic, and gotten little information that was useful. Perhaps the Reverend would be more forthcoming in the face of opposition, even unintentionally.

"I do, and I had hoped that you might share that understanding, indeed I did," Smiles insisted. "My offer to you was genuine, and I would make it again if I thought there was any prospect of acceptance. Perhaps if you had read, as I did, the words of William of Anjou, you might yet have joined us."

"I'm not familiar with the name," Adam admitted. It was a little familiar, though, and he scoured his memory, trying to turn up the association. It sounded medieval, so perhaps it was something Professor Marchale had mentioned, or something from one of his classes. But no, somehow Adam felt the connection was to something more recent.

"You wouldn't be," Smiles said. "His works were sadly suppressed by the corrupt church, of course. He wrote as long ago as the twelfth century, his *Book of the True Faith*, and even then he saw that the world did not work according to the precepts of Christianity, and in fact often the reverse — he saw the will of the just thwarted and the godless rewarded, and knew that the world could not be a creation of good, but was the design of sin and evil."

"Not that unusual an argument," Adam observed, remembering parts of some of his theology studies. "It's basically the Manichean view of things, ascribed to the Cathars and the Bogomils and I can't remember how many others." That was it. William of Anjou had written the book described in the documents Jane had found, cited by whoever had written that mission statement of the Sunrise Foundation. Perhaps Smiles had even written it. Certainly there was little doubt now that he was aware of it.

It was possible, Adam imagined, that William of Anjou really had been some disaffected medieval writer, as much in despair about his world as Damory and her followers were about theirs. Such people were not uncommon in any age, as any historian soon discovered. It was also possible that William, and his book, were later creations, written by members of the strange movement Charles Warrington had described in his own works. He supposed it didn't matter; the idea had clearly resonated with Steven Smiles, and given him an impressive certainty of purpose.

"All condemned for heresy," Smiles said, "and yet they saw the truth. This world is not under the control of a good and just Lord, it cannot be. No benevolent Creator could allow things to be done so contrary to His design. No, we are prisoners in a world controlled by dark forces, Father." It was one simple answer to the dilemma of how a benevolent creator could allow bad things to happen — conclude that the creator was not benevolent.

Adam admitted that his own solution to the paradox tended to change depending on the situation, and that the usual answers religion provided often rang hopelessly hollow to people in the midst of a crisis.

"And so your solution is surrender, then?" Adam asked. "Surely, if you're right, there is a need to provide guidance, to lead people towards better things?" He suspected he knew what the reply to this argument would be, but perhaps it was still possible to shake Smiles' conviction, a little. Sometimes an argument just needed to be made, too.

"The duty of the faithful is plain, Father, it is clear indeed," Smiles went on. "The world being as it is, our mandate must be to hasten the end of this dark creation, so that something better can be put in its place. There can be no correction of a world built on a foundation of sin and evil, I fear. Even Augustine said we must turn away from the City of Man, Father. I merely take that advice to its logical conclusion."

"And Ms. Damory, and Louis Flambard, and Detective Kolb, they all share this vision, do they?" Adam asked. Flambard was, at least publicly, a staunch atheist. Had that been part of the media persona as well? He couldn't imagine Matilda Damory embracing a faith in anything other than herself, somehow.

"They discern a part of the picture," Smiles said. "Perhaps I use them in the service of the Almighty, as they no doubt believe they use me towards their goals as they see them. I have prayed on the matter, indeed I have, and I am persuaded that in a righteous cause even imperfect allies are acceptable."

"And what do you expect of me," Adam asked, "to become another ally?" It was not really a compliment, he considered, that

Smiles had felt he might be sufficiently alienated from society to find the ideas behind the Sunrise Foundation appealing, nor that he might have been thought to be sunken so far into pessimism and sadness. Was that really the image he had shown to the world for the past few years?

"I am past hoping you might join our cause," Smiles admitted. "I still believe you might see things as I do, given time, but time is in unfortunately short supply. No, all I suggest is that you simply have the courage to stand aside, avoid further trouble for yourself and allow things to unfold as they should, as they must." He gave a light, but emphatic, thump to the immaculate surface of his desk to punctuate this last point.

"Oh, I've become surprisingly devoted to seeing that things unfold as they should, Reverend," Adam said. "You can depend on it." It had been, he reflected, not a very useful conversation after all, except he had learned two things. First, Samuel Smiles was fully aware of all aspects of the Sunrise Foundation's planning. That eliminated him as a potential weak point, but it was worth knowing. The second point was more interesting.

Smiles had said time was in short supply. Why that would be was still an open question, but it did help explain why Sunrise had been willing to do some of the things they had. They had exerted themselves fairly publicly on more than one occasion, probably including whatever had afflicted Hugh Thomas. To do that was a risk, which someone might start to investigate as Jane Moore had, and uncover the strange underpinnings of the organization. If they had some kind of deadline, some limit on the time available to them to complete their plans, that would help explain why they would risk exposure.

Adam doubted that it would be feasible to simply play a delaying game and run out whatever clock the Sunrise Foundation was on, but it was a useful factor to be aware of. Perhaps when so many other things seemed to be in the opponents' favour, it was useful to know that time was not on their side.

"Thank you for your time, for the coffee of course, and an illuminating conversation," Adam said, as he rose and left the office. "I suspect we'll be seeing one another again soon."

"As you wish, Doctor Godwinson," Smiles replied, "and if you insist. I shall pray that you find the wisdom to know the things you cannot change, before that comes to pass." As Adam left the office, he decided there was one other thing he had perhaps learned. People kept telling him to stay out of things and not to interfere. That suggested that interference was possible, and was another encouraging thing to take away from his time at the Hand of God.

Chapter 26

Adam left the encounter with Smiles with a feeling that was not precisely not knowing what to do next — rather, he felt that there were three or four things that all needed to be done immediately. Unable to choose, feeling his insides clench at the failure to do so, he decided to do something that was always worthwhile, and go to visit his friend in the hospital.

En route to the hospital, Adam began to find things that worried him in the traffic surrounding him, or at least in his perceptions of it. Had the grey compact been following him through most of his journey, or was the one he saw now, three cars back as he waited at a stoplight, just one of dozens of smallish grey cars you saw on any car trip? Did that police cruiser just happen to pull out moments after they had driven past the Metro parking lot? Had the pedestrian with the expensive looking DSLR camera merely seen something photo-worthy as Adam's happened to drive by?

He slid his hands along the steering wheel and tried not to stare into the rearview mirror. Jane's discoveries about the Sunrise Foundation were alarming, but they couldn't really be everywhere, surely. Was he becoming a bit like Alex, seeing things in the world around him that weren't there, or at least meant something different to him than they did to everyone else? Of course, Adam thought, he might easily object that he had reasons for thinking the way he was, now, but maybe Alex would say the same thing.

The sharp blast of a horn startled him out of his thoughts; the light had turned green. Adam whacked the turn signal in his alarm, fumbled to get it turned off again, accidentally turned on the windshield wipers. Finally he drove through the intersection, accompanied by more horn-blowing. He took a couple of deep, slow breaths and tried to let his jangled nerves settle. If his mind was this much on other things, he reflected, he probably shouldn't be driving at all. Hadn't he read somewhere that a distracted driver was as bad as a drunk driver?

He signaled his next turn, made it smoothly, and tried to enjoy the sunny day and the music on the radio. There was no reason to allow his problems to consume every moment of his day, and in fact that was giving people like Matilda Damory and Stephen Smiles entirely too much power over his life. He was only as distracted as he allowed himself to be. Although, was that the grey compact, again?

Arriving at the hospital came as somewhat of a relief.

∴

The increasingly ominous tenor of Adam's conversations, with Damory and then with Smiles, as well as the steps they had — apparently — already been willing to take made him certain that he and everyone else involved in whatever this situation was needed to protect themselves. He was also particularly concerned with Alex, an easy target on the street or wherever he might happen to have wandered. He explained as much to the group when they met at Bones' room after dinner the following day.

"I, uh, don't mean anything by this," Fred began cautiously, "but this is Alex we're talking about. You don't really think he's involved in anything that's going on, do you?"

Adam considered for a moment. The truth was that based on his recent conversations with Alex, he did feel that there was some sort of connection there. Exactly how that might be possible was far from clear — perhaps Alex had overheard something, perhaps he knew something from rumours — but ultimately it didn't matter. If there was even a remote chance that Alex Sloan knew something about the book and the Sunrise Foundation, then Adam felt it was vital to finally puzzle out what that was, and also to see that their troubled friend was protected.

That last concern seemed like the best way of persuading Fred and the others that searching for Alex was a good idea. Adam had only a vague impression that Alex knew something relevant to the situation they found themselves in, and even he had trouble understanding why that was.

"I think," Adam said finally, "that the people we're dealing with seem to be pretty well informed about us, and they're also obviously not above going to extremes to get what they want. It wouldn't have been hard for them to learn about Alex, that he was — is — our friend, and to decide to use that against us. He's very vulnerable, wherever he is."

"Ok, I see what you mean," Jane agreed, "but what are we going to do, exactly? You know what it's been like trying to get Alex off the streets." Adam reflected that he didn't really know how any recent efforts might have gone, but that yes, he was familiar with the general problem.

"He can be reasonable," Sophia interjected, "but you have to give him choices and not just tell him what to do." She had been the one who had managed to get Alex into shelters on previous occasions, and once had even persuaded him to check into a psychiatric facility. "The real problem is that he probably won't stay there. He won't know the people, he doesn't like staying in one place, and he'll wander away as soon as he can." That part of the issue hadn't changed either, then.

"Would it be any better," Adam suggested, "if one of us took him home instead of trying to put him into a shelter?" The idea of accommodating Alex, his strange behavior and erratic hygiene in his home was not a very attractive one, Adam admitted, but if it would keep his friend safe longer he was prepared to try.

"I doubt it," Sophia replied. "He would still want to be able to wander around all day, he wouldn't want to stay indoors, and then he would probably forget to come back in the end. It might be easier to get him to try it, maybe," she shrugged. Well, Adam thought, having Alex safe for even a day or two was better than not having him safe at all, and perhaps he would be more cooperative than usual.

"We can try, anyway," Adam said. "I'd go alone but I'd feel better if we stayed together right now, especially at night, after yesterday."

"Father," Jane objected, "we can look after ourselves, you know."

"Sure," Fred answered, "but maybe it's not such a great idea for him to be running around by himself in parks at night right now either. I'll come ride shotgun or whatever, Father."

"I want to come," Sophia said. "I might be able to help you with Alex."

"Please don't stay alone, Jane," Adam said. "I know you think I'm being silly, and honestly I hope I am, but I would feel a lot better if you came along."

"Oh, don't make a huge thing out of it," Jane relented. "I was only going to watch TV anyway."

They got into Jane's car and drove around the downtown core, hoping to sight Alex in some of the green space scattered through the area. Unfortunately one of the appeals of the city's parks were that most of them were insulated from street traffic, so there was only so much they could do from a vehicle. Jane finally parked in the Market so they could strategize their search a little more systematically.

"I know he likes it by the Canal," Adam began, "but we could spend all night along there. Maybe we should eliminate some places closer to home before we opt for that?"

"Sounds good," Fred agreed, "if we don't find him anywhere else first we can cruise the Canal for the rest of the time."

"Well, I think you talked with him most recently, Father," Sophia said. "Where was that? Sometimes he'll stay in the same place for a while."

"Once at Parliament Hill," Adam replied, "and before that down at the canal locks."

"If we walk over from here," Jane suggested, "we can do the locks first and then go to the Hill."

"Where next after that?" Fred asked.

"God, I don't know, Freddie," she replied tartly. "We can talk about it on the way, but let's get going."

Rather than let Fred and Jane settle more completely into their banter, Sophia and Adam hastily assented with this suggestion and the four of them walked over in the direction of the Wellington Street bridge. It was another pleasant evening, warm and clear, and the streets were relatively busy with people out enjoying the early summer weather.

Fred and Jane continued to snipe light-heartedly at each other all the way to the stairway that led down from the bridge to a wide pathway that led down past the canal locks, the Bytown Museum, and finally to where the Rideau Canal emptied out into the Ottawa River. It was a popular site for cycling and jogging, although it tended to clear out as darkness fell since the area was not especially well-lit.

As they walked down the slope towards the river, they were met by a sizeable crowd, buzzing with conversation. They would have just gotten off the last sightseeing cruise along the river, and were heading back to hotels or planning the rest of their evenings. Adam didn't immediately see Alex among them, and large crowds were not usually were he felt comfortable, but having come this far it still made sense to check thoroughly. It was still possible that Alex would be further along the river path, where things would be quieter.

Alex was not near the museum, nor the locks, but they continued down near the dock the tours used and watched the boat pull away. The evening was still warm and the river breeze was soothing. At times like this Adam understood Alex's attraction to the city's green spaces.

"I didn't see Alex on our way down," he observed. "Should we go up the river or back up and check the Hill?"

"If he came down to the river," Sophia suggested, "he would probably look for somewhere quieter than this. If we follow the path it loops around anyway." The riverside path did eventually come back up to meet Wellington, but it was a bit of a walk and Adam increasingly felt as though the goal of finding Alex and getting him somewhere might not be accomplished tonight.

"Well, let's do that," Adam assented. "Then we'll see what our next move should be."

"This is kind of going to take forever," Fred observed. "It would be a lot quicker if we did this in teams."

"Freddie," Jane replied quickly, "the whole point is that we're safer in one group. If we get split up it just creates more problems."

"I just don't want to be wandering around parks at 1 a.m.," Fred objected. "I mean some of us like to sleep sometimes."

Adam decided it was time for him to intervene again. "We're not going to do this all night," he said. "If we don't get enough rest we won't be able to handle anything and we'll make mistakes. I don't think it's a good idea to split up yet, though. We'll try a few more places and if we don't find Alex tonight we'll make a better plan and get an earlier start at it tomorrow. Sound ok?"

There was no answer, and Adam felt a little flare of annoyance — Fred and Jane were probably still sniping at each other somehow. Usually it was harmless and often it was amusing, but sometimes their bickering derailed anything else that was meant to be going on. On this occasion, though, he noticed that the pair was actually standing perfectly quietly, and there was another reason for their inattention.

Quite suddenly, there was a chill in the air and Adam noticed the park was deserted. The light seemed to have failed abruptly as well, and he looked back at the horizon to see that the setting sun was now obscured by a bank of clouds that had risen up in the west. The wind off the water was picking up and for a moment, Adam thought he heard a malicious little whisper in it.

"Heh, was it something we said?" Fred wondered. All the boat tour passengers were gone, and there were no cyclists or runners to be seen. Even the fishermen who often clambered down onto the rocks to cast into the river were absent.

"Who can blame them," Jane replied, "It sucks out here all of a sudden. Come on, let's look around for Alex and get out of here, OK?"

Adam could understand her impatience; what had been a cheery and pleasant evening was quickly turning uncomfortable. Even so, neither Jane nor any of the rest of them actually started to move, either back up the hill to leave, or down along the path to continue searching for Alex.

Adam had the feeling of waiting for something, albeit nothing he would welcome when it arrived. Despite the mounting sense of something about to go wrong, he felt unable to do anything but wait for it to happen. Fred, Sophia and Jane were looking around themselves uncertainly too, and Adam was abruptly reminded of herd animals from nature documentaries, unable to outfight or outrun some predator, and forced to hope that staying together would provide some obstacle to attack.

He looked back up the hill, the way they had come, and wondered why the ordinary little park suddenly felt as it did, and if he had missed some important detail on their way down beside the locks. Was there someone here watching them, or preparing to do more than that? He scanned the museum buildings and the lock gates for anyone trying to use the growing shadows to hide themselves, but could see nothing. Adam caught another snatch of angry whispered words in the wind, and then all at once, he had his answer.

It seemed to rise up out of the canal, between two lock gates, a patch of flowing darkness many feet across. The murky shape moved down the slope towards them, a motion somewhere between a liquid and rolling fog. It was only possible to see where it was because of what it blotted out, and how much darker it was than even the normal shadows of the nighttime park. It is rarely truly dark in a city, and this was a piece of genuine darkness, slithering and oozing down the hill towards them, seeming to pick up speed as it came, a sense of eagerness about how parts of it, like tentacles and cilia, flickered out towards them.

Adam couldn't think what to do, and he would later castigate himself for standing and watching whatever the thing was get closer, with a soft rattling sound like leaves in the wind that was increasing in strength. It was true that none of the others took action either, their attention was just as fixed as his on the encroaching mass of shadow. But he had brought them here, it had been his insistence that finding Alex was important, and so he felt it was his responsibility to bring them out safe again.

It had no eyes, no features at all in its inky mass, but it approached which such unerring directness that it seemed impossible to think that it did not know exactly where they were, and that it was interested in them, in particular. The sense of alarm was a pulsing beat in his chest now, but he still couldn't decide what to do, besides stand and watch the darkness approach. There was no scent, just the gentle, relentless skittering noise of its approach, and then a thin tendril of blackness flickered out towards Jane like a tongue and found the contour of one leg.

Her scream jolted Adam into action; doing anything at all was vital, to do nothing was death. Jane was clutching her leg and blood was running from underneath her hand, her flesh evidently laid open by the touch of this black form that was nearly upon them. "Quickly, quickly, move!" he cried, pulling Jane towards him and away from the shadowy shape.

It was between them and the path leading up beside the canal locks, past the Bytown Museum, and to Rideau Street. Even Jane's cry of pain might not have carried quite that far, and there was no time to wait for help, and there was no way to know what kind of help might even be provided.

The path leading along the river was deserted and dark, and it was a long winding way to where it would meet the Portage Bridge. There was nowhere that would provide shelter, and many places that would provide shadow, and Adam had little desire to go into any further dark places. Instead, he led Jane, and the others, towards the last lock gate, and hurriedly across its narrow walkway.

The need to change direction seemed to slow the thing; despite its shapeless form and nearly silent movement it seemed to have a certain inertia, to need to gather itself to a stop and redirect itself towards them. They were across the lock before it reached the wooden step up onto the walkway. Adam suddenly remembered old tales of evil things being unable to pass running water, and a flickering hope that perhaps it would be thwarted by the canal. But it had come up out of the locks, he recalled, and the crossing proved to be no barrier, as it seemed to wrap parts of itself around the ironworks atop the gate to pull itself along.

"What is that thing?" Fred shouted, leading the way down from the canal. "What is that thing?" The decision to move, or Jane's injury, seemed to have brought them all out of their daze.

"Dangerous," Sophia said with decisiveness. "Move!"

"Up the hill, quick as we can," Adam directed. There was a path that wound its way up from here to meet the road just outside the National Art Gallery. In the daytime it was a pretty walk along a forested hillside, and it was a popular way for cyclists to bypass the busy intersection around the War Memorial. At present it was empty of bike or foot traffic, which was perhaps just as well, but it was also prodigiously steep, and not the best path for a retreat. Runners used it for hill training and Adam hoped his own conditioning wouldn't fail him now.

He waited to be sure Sophia, Fred, and Jane were on their way up the slope before starting to follow them up, giving him a moment to watch the thing flow over the gate and pool itself to follow them again. There was no room for doubt now that it was directing itself towards them, and it seemed to Adam that it was trying to hurry, now, throwing out long pseudopods of darkness onto the ground and yanking itself forward. He wondered, irrelevantly, if it would leave tracks, something to show to authorities later.

"Father, come on!" shouted Sophia urgently. He turned to look and she had almost reached the hairpin switchback in the path, her army training serving her well. Adam supposed she had probably spent a lot of time running up hills, and she had also learned to work with a team. Sophia had paused to be sure the others were following and found Adam, mesmerized again, at the foot of the hill. He roused himself and started to run up the hill, catching up to Fred, assisting Jane, and helped them both hurry upwards.

As he reached the switchback he could hear crashing and snapping in the forest undergrowth — was it possible that the thing was cunning enough to try to cut through the woods and get ahead of them? There was no time to consider options and he supposed they could easily reverse themselves back down the hill if it did cut them off, although he was suddenly desperate to escape the isolation of the deserted park.

"Hurry now," he urged, finding Sophia waiting on the path again, just ahead of him. His breath was already failing him and his legs burning with the effort of climbing the hill, but above all else he felt they must reach the top.

"Where are we going, Father?" she demanded, directing him up the path and taking over helping Jane with her wounded leg.

Jane was making impressive progress up the slope, and Adam hoped that meant her wound was not serious, although sometimes adrenaline and need could make people ignore surprisingly grave injuries.

"We need to get to where people are," he shouted, although he had no clear idea why. The certainty was strong in him, though, and they followed on without question. They reached the point where the path met the sidewalk above, and the road that went up past the National Gallery in one direction, and down across the bridge to Gatineau in the other.

"Cross the road!" he yelled. Whether the thing had cut through the woods or just increased its speed, it was hard behind them now and the slope seemed to have no effect on it. The flowing motion looked deeply unnatural coming up the steep grade of the path, ignoring everything that had made their own ascent so difficult. "Straight across!" Adam shouted.

They dashed across the two lanes of the street to reach the grass shoulder on the opposite side, and Adam turned to look back again as soon as he hit the curb. The thing billowed out across the road, its movements bolder than they had been at first, and it was spreading itself wider and it seemed as though it must envelop them, but then a car swept down the road towards the Alexandra Bridge and it was caught in the headlights.

The thing shriveled and dissolved like plastic wrap touched by a flame, and disappeared entirely in moments. The car sped on; Adam imagined the driver may have seen nothing clearly. They took a moment to rest and then continue on the little distance towards the well-lit intersection at Sussex Drive. The spindly, towering form of the metal spider sculpture in front of the art gallery had never been such a pleasant sight.

Chapter 27

They made their way to Adam's house, which was only a few blocks away. Fred advanced the idea of calling the police, but abandoned the idea when the question of what he would tell them was brought up. Adam suggested calling an ambulance for Jane, but she insisted her injury wasn't that serious. In fact, she didn't seem to be having too much trouble walking on it, but Sophia still wanted to take a look at it once they got to Adam's.

The wound was not deep, and was straight and clean, as if done with a blade. In fact, Adam imagined, they would have trouble persuading anyone that the cut was not made with a box cutter or similar instrument. The only unusual part was the flesh around it, which was pale, almost bleached looking, like skin that has been in the water a long time.

Sophia inspected it closely and allowed that it probably didn't need stitches. She retrieved Adam's first aid supplies from the bathroom and set to work dressing the wound. When he had been a parish priest, he had made a point of keeping lots of first aid things around his house, because sometimes what was needed most was a Band-Aid and some antiseptic, not spiritual advice. Perhaps it was fortunate, now, that this had become a habit and he was still well stocked.

As Sophia cleaned Jane's leg and began to apply butterfly bandages along the wound, Adam followed up on a nagging feeling. He went to the table in the kitchen and retrieved the envelope of papers on Charles Warrington that Marchale had given him. He took out *The Eater of the Sun* and flipped to a page towards the end. It was more or less exactly as he remembered.

"Listen to this," he said. "It's from Warrington's book, the one we thought was a bad piece of fiction. *The devotees of this foul creature, who they call the King in the Darkness in its* banishment and binding, seek above all else the ability to bring their champion to Earth and pit it against all civilization, to our inevitable ruin."

"Father, no offense," Fred broke in, "but I think that really is just a bad piece of fiction. Like I think I read a book like that once." Fred was probably understating things; he was a voracious consumer of science fiction books and movies and could in all likelihood provide several examples similar to the content of Warrington's book.

"I'm sure you did," Adam agreed, "And I'm beginning to think that isn't accidental. But for now, listen to the rest of this: *The most puissant among them often have other, lesser abilities passed down through the centuries. They may be able to twist the minds of others to their ends, in particular to incite confusion and violence. Some are able to summon forth a lesser version of the King in Darkness they call a Piece of Shadows, a thing of creeping blackness that can seek its quarry and kill it with its touch. The Piece of Shadows is of infinitely malleable form but cannot abide the touch of bright lights, which will dissolve it back into nothingness with great rapidity."*

"Ok, that part sounds familiar," Fred conceded. "When did you say that thing was written?"

"1946," Adam replied. "It seems a little similar for coincidence to be a good explanation."

"So, what, you think the things from that book are real, Father?" asked Sophia. She was wrapping a gauze bandage around Jane's leg and securing the edges with surgical tape.

"It doesn't make a lot of sense to me," Adam said, "But it's hard not to start to think so. That thing tonight was exactly like Warrington describes, and some of the other things he wrote about are starting to make sense too."

"So did someone send that thing after us, Father?" Jane demanded, "Or were we just lucky enough to run across it?"

"I have no idea," Adam answered. "We went to the park looking for Alex, but no one knew that besides us. We didn't even know if Alex was there, I just thought he might be because that's one of the places I found him recently. I can't see how they could have known we were going there, but it doesn't make sense that it was an accident."

"Maybe it's like they don't have to know," Fred suggested. "Maybe they can just point that thing at a person and it tracks them down itself." He paused before going on, "Gotta be honest, that's like a lot of books too."

"I'm sure," Adam replied. "But I think you might be right. Anyway, let's not take any chances. From now on I think we should have some new rules. This is at least the fourth time there has been an attack of some kind on one of us, and if any of the rest of us had been alone like Bones was it might have been just as bad. From now on, no one goes anywhere by themselves. We'll use sick days from work if it's necessary, but I don't want anyone out by themselves until we figure this out."

"Even without that thing tonight, I think it's a good idea," Sophia agreed. "On our own we're much easier targets. What about Napoleon, though? He's still alone in the hospital."

"So far whoever is behind this has been cautious," Adam said. "I don't think they'll attack someone in a hospital unless they become very desperate. They wouldn't be able to accomplish anything without a great many people noticing."

"Ok, buddy system then," Fred declared. "What about Alex?"

"No, they didn't know where we were going and they didn't know why we were going there," Jane said. "They couldn't have been after Alex with that thing. It must be like you said, it found us."

"For now, we'll hope you're right," Adam agreed. "Tomorrow we'll try again to find Alex and perhaps we can convince him to come somewhere safe. Sophia, you always used to be good with him, will you come?"

"Of course I will," Sophia answered immediately. "And for now?"

"We'll call a cab to pick you three up. You can all go home and we'll pick this up tomorrow," Adam suggested.

"Sophie can take Jane home," replied Fred firmly, "But I'm crashing on your couch tonight. No one on their own, for tonight at least, OK?" He plopped himself down on Adam's rarely-flipped-out flip-out sofa with a determined air.

"Ok, Mr. Wallace," said Adam with a gentle smile. "That's very good of you."

⁙

Adam went to see Professor Marchale first thing the next morning. The schedule on his office door had included office hours early in the day and Adam felt that recovering the book was now quite urgent. After last night, any delay seemed to carry a very real risk, one made all the worse because Marchale would have no idea that he was in any danger.

Adam had prepared a whole series of frfesh arguments to use on Marchale, to convince him to return the book that was the focus of Sunrise's interest. Marchale's stubbornness with a problem that had engaged him was substantial, and after his earlier misstep with suggesting legal issues, Adam had decided to try and explain to the professor something of what now appeared to be going on. It was true that he couldn't really explain how the book fit into things, even though it was clearly the focus of the interest of Damory, Smiles, and however many others. Just as clearly, there was a danger in being possession of the book, and so Adam was resolved to do whatever proved necessary, even if it exposed him to Marchale's lacerating scorn or offended his old supervisor.

As it turned out, he didn't need to do very much at all. As soon as he hesitantly raised the subject of the book's return, again, Marchale almost instantly agreed. "Yes, yes, you do that," he said, a little dully. "Still can't make head or tail of the damned thing, complete waste of time, in the end." Adam felt a curious need to comfort the professor, who looked drawn and tired.

"Well, we've made some progress," he said lightly. "I'm sure the answer is there to be found. I just wanted to spend a little while studying it myself again, see if there's anything I might notice that connects to Warrington's writing, that sort of thing." Marchale didn't appear to be fully listening to these rather vague suggestions.

"You do as you think best," he agreed heavily. "As you know I've piles of work, mounds of it, and no more time to squander on the thing. Let me know if you turn up anything, of course, but I'm afraid I must wash my hands of it." Adam chewed over this apparent eagerness to dump their enquiries for a few moments. "Probably a damned forgery, anyway," he concluded dismissively.

"All right, Professor," he said finally. "Thank you for all you've done so far, I can tell it's been a strain on you." Marchale rooted around in one of his desk drawers and retrieved the book, which he had apparently stored in a box that Adam supposed was made of archival cardboard. At some point, at least, he had thought it was potentially valuable.

"Never mind," Marchale said with a weak smile, as he passed the book over. "What are teachers for if not to bring problems to? I just apologize for not being much help with this one. Hopeless from the beginning, I fear," he finished, closing the drawer with a hand that seemed to tremble slightly.

"You've been of great assistance," Adam assured him quietly. "And I know you've been very busy lately. I'll bring the things you loaned me back soon, is that all right?"

"You take your time, take your time," Marchale replied, with a baleful look at the pile of term papers on his desk. "Between you and me I doubt there is much pressing concern in most quarters about Charles Warrington."

Adam made his goodbyes and left, mulling over the apparently indecipherable book, and how it must fit somehow into the bizarre situation Warrington had, apparently, equally bizarrely, described or predicted in a book that a few days ago, had seemed so irrelevant.

When Adam arrived home that evening, his first feeling was of great relief. Now he didn't need to worry that his old professor might be exposed to danger. Adam wasn't sure how the conversation would have gone if he had tried to explain the situation to Marchale — it was possible that might have galvanized the contrary old man into insisting on staying involved. Adam didn't want that responsibility, and so he had decided not to take the chance.

It was concerning how deflated Marchale had been, though. Adam couldn't remember seeing him that discouraged in all the time he had known him and worked with him, but he imagined that the professor probably didn't have all the energy that he once had, and he was very busy with the work he was actually responsible for. It was also true that Marchale could be just as critical of himself as he was of anyone else, and was probably disappointed in himself for not making any headway with deciphering the book.

Fortunately, Adam had also never known anything that could keep Marchale's enthusiasm blunted for long, and he imagined that as soon as a fresh problem, or especially aggravating or challenging student, presented itself, Marchale would be back in fighting form quickly enough. Still, Adam resolved to call or visit as soon as he could.

His second feeling, as he closed the front door and locked it behind him, was one of trepidation. Getting the book back from Marchale had been the right thing to do, because of the danger possibly associated with it, but now of course he had brought that danger home with him. It was likely enough that Sunrise would think to look for the book at his home, too.

Adam looked around his house and rubbed the back of his head. It was a nice enough house, and he had a lot of affection for it after having lived there so long, but it was by no means an impregnable fortress. The doors had decent locks but he knew that they were like most home door locks; they wouldn't deter a really determined burglar. The intention was to make it difficult enough to get in that a thief who was looking for an easy mark would move on, but the theory didn't work if the thief was after something specific that they knew was in your home.

He sat down in his recliner, set the book on the table next to it, and tried to think. There had to be somewhere he could put it that would be at least difficult to find. Carrying the book around with him all the time seemed to be inviting the kind of attack that had happened at in the hospital parking lot, and Adam imagined that might not have ended very well if Sophia hadn't been there. On the other hand, the house was the first place they would think of to look. A desk drawer or under the mattress would not suffice.

He looked over at the book, sitting closed on the table in the lamp light. When Bones had first brought it to the store, it had been an exotic and captivating diversion, and then an interesting challenge. Over the past several days it had transformed in Adam's mind, first to an unexpectedly frustrating puzzle, and now he had a sense of menace and danger connected with it. The worn, leather-bound volume now made him a little uneasy, just sitting there.

Originally Adam had intended to spend the evening studying the book one more time, to see if there was anything he might have overlooked on his first examination, or if some of the symbols might somehow resonate with things he had read by or about Charles Warrington. It didn't seem likely, but it had also seemed like a waste of an opportunity not to make the effort.

Now, though, the idea of looking through the book was deeply unattractive, almost repellent. It had done nothing but frustrate him, and Professor Marchale, as well as bringing harm and danger to Napoleon Kale, Jane Moore, Adam, and to the people connected to them. As he sat there now, Adam didn't want anything to do with the old book at all, and if he wasn't convinced of the harm Damory and her people could do with it, he would gladly have disposed of the thing.

He didn't believe there was anything to be learned from it, or at least, not by him. However, he insisted to himself, even if he was incapable of figuring out what was written in the book, there was an undoubted value in keeping it from the Sunrise Foundation, and preventing them from using it. First, however, he had to find a way to keep it secure.

Adam turned on the television to break the silence, which seemed to be amplifying his worries, and went into the kitchen to pour himself some wine, hoping that would also settle his nerves. "First place they'll look," he said to himself, swirling the drink around in the glass. "And maybe that's it," he mused.

Searching his house for the book would, probably, have literally been the first thing they would have thought of to do. Surely they would have done that before trying something as reckless as the confrontation in the parking lot, and it had to be easier to hire someone for a break-in than for a knife-point extortion. Further, if it had been done well, by someone who was careful, he might not have noticed they were in the house at all.

Obviously kicking down the door and tearing the house apart would have been simpler, but Adam would also have reported it. Another investigation would have started, and John Kolb might not have been able to control where it went. If Adam's sense that Matilda Damory's plan had a fairly tight schedule to it was right, they wouldn't want to risk that disruption unnecessarily.

Adam smiled as he sat back down. If he was right, there was a good chance his house had already been searched, and that was why Sunrise had moved on to more drastic measures. A place they had already searched might be one of the last places they would look now, he considered.

Still, he couldn't be sure he was right, and even if he was, it wasn't impossible that as they became more desperate, Sunrise would search again. The book still had to be hidden, and he still didn't know where. Adam picked up the phone and dialed Fred Wallace. For a moment he wondered if they should talk in person, but surely worrying about phone taps was taking things a bit too far.

When Fred answered, Adam took a moment to frame his question. Fred had a vast store of movie and novel-related 'experience' that Adam had hoped might be relevant to the problem, and it turned out that he did have a suggestion, albeit one that he emphasized came with no guarantees. After saying his goodnight, Adam triple-bagged the book in progressively larger Ziploc freezer bags, stashed the book in his toilet tank, and tried not to imagine how Marchale would react to the situation of a centuries old manuscript being immersed, albeit carefully, in water.

Chapter 28

The next morning, Adam went to the hospital again, to ask a question that was going to be difficult at best but had to be resolved. It hardly seemed likely that Bones had known anything about the importance of the book when he purchased it, but if he had, it was a crucial piece to the puzzle Adam was trying to solve. His experience with Napoleon Kale was that directness brought the best results, so after a few minutes of chat he plunged in and asked.

"I do need to ask you something about that book though, Bones," Adam said, a little tentatively. "Did you really not know anything about it when you bought it?" If it was really just luck that had brought the book into his possession, and triggered everything that happened since, Adam wasn't sure if it was good luck or bad, considering.

"Nah, Father," Bones replied, "it was just a weird old book and I thought it might do you some good, that's all."

"Do me some good?" Adam prompted, although he felt he had an idea what was coming. Bones looked up at him with some intensity.

"Yeah, exactly," he said. "How long have you been doing nothing but working at that bookstore now, huh?"

"It's been..." Adam paused, knowing the exact length of time but suddenly not wanting to say it, "a while now, I suppose."

"Father, I don't mean this in a bad way," Bones said, "but it's time you did something a little more, you know? You're a smart guy, you got all those degrees, and all you do is work in a store that doesn't make any money."

"I was grateful to have it at the time," Adam replied, which was true enough. When he had resigned from his parish, and the church in its entirety, there hadn't been a great number of opportunities. Jobs were scarce to begin with and someone whose only qualifications were either spiritual or academic wasn't ideally positioned to take advantage of the market. Professor Marchale had made offers, of course, but Adam could never persuade himself that these weren't charity. Worse, Adam never forgot just how hard he had to struggle to produce his thesis and the few papers that had come out of it. Being surrounded by accomplished scholars who, by all appearances, created much more insightful work with far less effort left him with the sense that he was some manner of academic fraud.

Bones shook his head. "Nah, Father," he said, "you never liked it if we tried to bullshit with you. Sure you needed whatever at first, but you could be doing something else by now." He looked sharply at Adam, now. "What are you doing, man? You ain't lazy, so what is it?"

Adam rubbed his forehead with the heel of his palm. How to explain? In part he knew Walt Howard depended on him to keep the store running, now, but honestly someone else could easily take that over, if Adam had something else to move on to. Partly he did just like the store, working with books, which he had always loved and spent so much of his life with. However, in part he knew that it was easy, and that no one bothered him, mostly, and no one made him think about what he should be doing instead. Instead the people in the store either wanted to sell him their old, terrible paperbacks, or buy their books cheaply. None of it was challenging, and that had become comfortable, he justified it all because Walt Howard was grateful he was there.

He had settled, and it was easy not to think about how much time had really passed. But there was no way that he could think of to say that to say that, not when he had always tried to encourage Bones and the other members of the Guild, to keep them inspired and believing in what they could achieve. So instead of admitting that he had stopped trying to achieve much of anything, Adam sighed and said, finally, "I appreciate the thought very much, Bones, I really do. I'll give it some thought, I promise."

"You better," said Bones, pointing a finger for emphasis. "Wasn't just me, you know. All of us have been saying the same thing for a while. I just happened to find that old thing and thought it might light a fire under that ass."

Adam nodded his understanding. "It's just that it's a strange coincidence, then," he said, hoping to steer things back to his original point. He sighed again, expected that Napoleon would not be very happy about what he was about to say. "I think a lot of what has happened lately has to do with that book, you see." He explained about what he had learned from his research, about what Jane had found out regarding the Sunrise Foundation, and how, bizarrely, they seemed to fit together.

"For some reason they're in a hurry," Adam explained. "It's why they've been so reckless in trying to get the book, and it's why they didn't think they could just wait and try buying it from you once you were out of the hospital. They're up against some very specific deadline, and when they missed getting it at the estate sale I think they panicked."

"The secret doomsday cult of devil worshippers panicked?" Bones demanded incredulously.

"They're just people after all," Adam replied. "I think they've been working towards this for a very long time and they're desperate enough that they're depending on it happening. The idea of missing their chance must terrify them."

Bones thought it over. "So, you think when I got jumped, they were after that book?" he asked.

"I do," Adam said. "Even Kolb admitted it wasn't like a normal mugging. They were looking for you, specifically, and hoped you'd have the book on you."

"And the rest of it," Bones said, his eyes flashing, "Parts of it I already know, but when they came after you in the parking lot out there, that was about the book too?"

"I think so," Adam agreed.

"And then when Janey got hurt," Bones went on, voice taut with anger. "That was why. No one wanted to tell me the details, but that was it, wasn't it?"

"I think so," Adam said again. "What happened that night, well, it was very strange, and it's part of why I think these people are serious about everything."

"They're some kind of serious," Bones declared. "So what are we going to do, then?"

"I haven't been able to figure that out, yet," Adam confessed. "We're still no closer to being able to read the manuscript to even understand what they might want it for, you see. It's important, but we don't understand why. Presumably it can be used for something, but we don't know what." He realized this wasn't very encouraging so he fished around for something optimistic to offer. Finally he put his finger on it. "One thing in our favour is that time seems to be a problem for our adversaries. Smiles said as much directly, and a lot of their actions might indicate that they have a deadline, perhaps one that isn't too far off."

"So you're saying we could just wait them out," Bones suggested. "Keep the book, make sure they don't get it, and run out the clock on whatever it is they're up to."

"That seems the easiest way," Adam agreed. "The problem is that right now we don't know when their deadline is."

"So, we don't know how long we have to wait," Bones said, "and we won't even know when we've waited long enough."

"That's exactly the problem," Adam nodded, "At least, that as far as I've gotten."

"Well, what are we going to do, ask 'em?", Bones asked. "Maybe they booked a nice dinner or something?"

"That I don't know," Adam allowed. "It's part of why I also think it's important to keep on with the research. There must be a solution in the material somewhere."

"What do they need it for anyway, if they can already do that shit down by the canal?" Bones asked.

"I'm still trying to figure that out," Adam admitted. "So far I still can't figure out how to read the book at all, so I don't know if it can help us. I'm hoping it can. It seems as though they might need it to do whatever it is they want to do, so as long as we have it, they're in check. But I need to know more, you see."

"And as long as we have that book, they keep trying shit, though, don't they?" Bones asked. "This doesn't seem like the best kind of plan."

"Perhaps," Adam said. "Probably. It's been all right so far. We're all looking after each other, now, and it really must be only a matter of time before I make some kind of headway with understanding the book. If they can read it, to use it, there must be some kind of solution." How to get that solution, the private key to a cypher, if that's what it was, or the trick to reading the writing, was still a very steep hill to climb, but Adam decided that sounding confident was important.

"I don't feel good that I brought all this down on all of us," Bones said. "When you figure out what needs doing, you make sure you let me know."

"Of course," Adam agreed, although inwardly he was sure that it would be a lot better if Napoleon could be kept out of it. "And don't be hard on yourself, either. If you didn't buy the damned thing, they would have, and perhaps no one would have known what was happening at all, until it was too late."

"Heh," Bones chuckled darkly. "Someone looking out for us?" he asked. Adam was a little surprised, and not sure if Bones really meant the suggestion, or if he was making a joke. Adam was a long way from believing in a divine plan for things himself, these days.

"You never know," he allowed. "But it doesn't matter if it was luck or something else, the important thing is that we have a chance, it seems."

"Well," Bones said with a little smile now, "at least that gives you something to do, I guess."

Adam said goodbye to Bones and left him to rest, but he knew there was something else that needed to be done before he left the hospital. He had used concern for Hugh Thomas as a ploy to fish for information from Steven Smiles, but Adam was also genuinely concerned about how his former parishioner was recovering, or if he was.

The hospital, however, had been unwilling to give out information over the phone, and Adam had managed to persuade himself that there hadn't been time to visit in person, with all of the various other concerns he was currently juggling. He also knew that this was not the real reason for failing to make the trip two floors down from Bones' room to where Hugh lay in recovery.

Seeing someone he had considered a friend turned into a threat had been deeply disturbing, and he also knew that he had been very lucky in how the encounter had turned out. Hugh was large and strong enough to do a great amount of damage, if he had really wanted to, and surely it was only good fortune that had enabled Adam to talk him out of the attack.

Hugh lay very still, and seemed to be asleep. Even against the immaculate sheets of the hospital bed, his skin still looked tremendously pale. He was attached to an IV and a heart monitor, and despite his athlete's build, he still looked very small, as if he had somehow collapsed in on himself. A nurse was there, taking a blood pressure reading.

"He's been resting," she said, glancing up. "He's quiet most of the time, now."

"Do you know what's wrong with him?" Adam asked.

"Not exactly," the nurse replied. "He has many symptoms you'd expect from drug use, or withdrawal, but there don't appear to have been any in his system when he was admitted. We're waiting on a psychological consult, now."

"I'm a friend," Adam said, "an old friend from his church. Would it be all right if I spent a little time with him?" The nurse said that it would, and Adam sat down in the single chair next to the bed. Instantly, Hugh's eyes opened and fixated on him. Adam managed to stay seated only through a considerable effort of will. Hugh's eyes filled with tears and he moved his lips silently for a few moments.

"There were so many whispers," Hugh said finally. "Whispers, and the blood." The few words seemed to exhaust him and he sunk back into the mattress, his eyes rolling up to stare at the ceiling.

"It's all right now, Hugh," Adam said, and hoped that it was true. Warrington's writings and their encounter by the canal locks suggested that Damory, or her followers, might have been able to exert some influence on him, inflict some damage on his mind. If that was true, was there any hope of understanding what had really happened to him, or of repairing any of the harm?

"I was supposed to hurt someone, I think." Hugh said. "Did I?"

"No, Hugh," Adam replied. "You didn't harm anyone." He hoped that Hugh would never remember the details of what had happened, a few evenings ago. Enough damage seemed to have been done. Some of the tension seemed to leave the young man's features.

"Am I safe now?" Hugh asked, in a small voice.

"Yes, of course," Adam reassured him. "Quite safe, now." He hoped that was true, too. Between Bones, Jane, and Hugh Thomas, he had seen quite enough harm come to the people around him. He also felt Matilda Damory and her allies had a great deal to answer for, even if he didn't yet know any way of calling them to account. For now, though, he took Hugh's hand and sat bedside telling stories about summers long ago, until visiting hours ended and the nurse told him he had to leave.

Chapter 29

Adam was just about to leave the house for work the next morning when the phone rang. It was Fred Wallace calling from the hospital, and he was so upset that Adam had to ask several times to figure out what the problem was. At first he assumed that Bones' condition had taken a turn for the worse, but that wasn't it at all.

"No, it's not that they don't know what's wrong with him," Fred explained, taking the time to choose his words carefully. When he was upset he tended to talk faster than he was thinking and it could be hard to follow what he was saying. "It's that they don't know where he is. Like, he's not in his room and everyone here says he must have left."

"That's ridiculous," Adam replied. "Of course he didn't leave. Are they looking for him?"

"They say they already did that," Fred answered. "I'm not sure they're going to do anything else, you know?" He sounded not just flustered, but deeply upset, and Adam supposed that they had all been assuming Bones was well on the way to being back to his usual self and was out of any danger. Then, suddenly, this instead.

"All right," Adam said. "You stay there, and I'll be there as soon as I can. Perhaps there's been some sort of misunderstanding." He hadn't wanted to say that unfortunate though it was, people in authority tended to brush off the concerns of young people, and that it was possible the arrival of someone obviously older would change their attitude. Then again, that tactic had been most effective when Adam had still been a priest, and might not work as well any longer.

He hung up with Fred and called Eric Spiers, who was fortunately, and unusually, available to work a morning shift. Adam promised to be there for the afternoon, and then headed off to the hospital. Along the way he tried to make sense of this latest turn of events. It didn't make any sense than Bones would have left the hospital — he had been feeling better, but not that much better, and if he had decided to go home he would certainly have told at least one of his friends about it.

The only scenario that Adam could imagine Bones leaving the hospital under would be if there was some kind of threat, some reason why he didn't feel safe and felt like he had to leave suddenly. Bones knew most of the details about the troubles surrounding the Sunrise Foundation; was it possible that he had seen or heard something that had made him think he was under some sort of threat in the hospital?

Adam arrived quickly, thankful for a decent day of downtown traffic. He hurried up to Bones' room and found Fred, Jane, and Sophia in a discussion with a nurse that seemed to be teetering on the verge of becoming an argument. He coughed emphatically and asked the nurse exactly what the problem was. With luck, if he took over the conversation for a while, the others could cool down a little bit.

"The problem is that your friends aren't listening to me," he said, "when I explain to them that it is not our fault that this patient is gone." The nurse was clearly exasperated with the whole conversation but Adam had little patience just now.

"What do you mean," Adam asked the nurse, "that Mr. Kale is gone?" He was trying very hard to keep from sounding angry because, in his experience, people would become less helpful the more they felt they were under attack, but it was difficult. Patients in hospitals were not supposed to disappear, and hospitals were meant to keep good track of where the people in their care were in the building.

"I don't know what else to tell you, sir," he replied. "At evening rounds last night the nurse on duty reported that Mr. Kale was not in his bed. I'm told we did a full search of the building and he's not been found. Our assumption is currently that the patient left against medical advice." Sophia made a disgusted noise, walked a few steps away and began to dial her phone.

"Quite an assumption," Adam said, "but when he was first discovered to be missing, why didn't anyone call?" If they had done that, they would have discovered immediately that Bones was not at home, not with any of his friends, and that whatever had happened, he hadn't simply checked himself out of the hospital. Bones had been a bit impatient with his recovery, and was certainly eager to be discharged, but he wasn't foolish enough to simply walk out.

"I'm sorry, sir," the nurse answered, "but are you a relative? If not then we wouldn't telephone under any circumstances, even if we had your contact information." He looked quite satisfied to be able to offer that reply and Adam supposed he was probably feeling quite besieged by people asking questions he had no answers for. Still, the solution was to see that the answers were found, instead of pretending there was no serious problem.

Sophia hung up her phone and walked back over. "I just spoke with Bella," she reported, her voice tight. "She hasn't seen or spoke with Napoleon since her last visit. He's not there." Bones wouldn't have been able to get home on his own, and if he hadn't left with Bella, there were not many other alternatives that could explain where he was.

"I think it should be clear your patient didn't discharge himself," Adam said to the nurse. "I assume you'll start a more vigorous investigation?" As long as they assumed that Napoleon had checked himself out they wouldn't, for example, make a more thorough search of the hospital, or begin to consider other alternatives, although Adam wasn't sure what other possibilities made sense. Still, it was important to shake the complacency of the current assumption that Bones had simply gone home.

"I really can't say," the man admitted. "I'm not the one who makes those decisions." That, Adam reflected, was probably a very fair point. Probably haranguing this man had been futile and a waste of time, as well as a bit unfair.

"All right," Adam said, trying to adopt a conciliatory tone again. "I'm sure you can understand that we're quite concerned about our friend, who we're sure would not have simply left the hospital. Perhaps instead of making your life difficult you could put us in touch with someone who might have access to more information than you do."

The nurse allowed that it might be possible for one of the directors to come and speak about the situation briefly, and told them to wait in the room while he went and inquired. A few minutes later he returned and said that the director would be down shortly. Adam sat with Fred and Sophia and tried to be reassuring. Bones had not been in critical condition anymore and would probably be fine for a while even if he had left the hospital. Once they figured out what was going on, Napoleon would be back in care in plenty of time. Jane spent the time on her phone, and from the pieces of conversation he overheard, Adam thought she was talking to people she knew in the local media. He supposed that was a good idea, although if the hospital felt like Bones' friends had brought down a media attack on them, they might not be too cooperative in the future. Adam decided he didn't mind very much; the hospital could easily solve the problem by figuring out where Napoleon Kale had gone.

When he finally arrived, the hospital representative was polite and sympathetic, but also persistently vague about exactly what was going to happen in the next few hours to determine what had happened to Napoleon Kale. Adam tried several times to pin him down to more specifics, without success. They were directed to a lounge area away from the patient areas of the hospital and asked to wait for updates. The neatly-dressed representative swept away leaving very little enlightenment in his wake.

"He's already worried about lawsuits," Jane opined darkly. "He's not going to say anything he's not forced to, now." Adam decided she was likely to be right. The hospital administration was probably waking up to the fact that their patient had not simply left, and was now faced with the possibility that the situation was, to some extent, their fault. They would want to be sure they had all their facts carefully arranged before provided much more information, now.

"Should we speak to Kolb?" Adam asked. Contacting the detective investigating the original attack on Bones seemed like a natural step to take, although of course given what they now knew about John Kolb, there were complications.

"What's the point of that?" Jane replied. "We already know he's not doing his job on the first case, and he's with those Sunrise weirdos on top of it. He's not going to help."

"Yeah, but maybe we can talk to a different cop," Fred suggested. "I mean there's more than one detective in the city."

"Kolb will still be able to mess with their investigation," Jane countered. "He'd probably say it's related to his case and take it over, or something, and then do nothing again."

"In any case," Adam said, "the hospital will likely make its own report. It's frustrating, but I'm not sure what any of us can do right now." Hospital staff had almost certainly been told not to discuss the case by now, so even the impractical idea of investigating themselves seemed very unlikely to be useful.

"Father, you know this is related to all the other stuff," Jane objected. "We know who did this, we can't just not do anything!" As always, it was deeply frustrating to be faced with a problem that one could, at least temporarily, do nothing to help solve.

"But what can we do?" Sophia asked quietly. "We don't even really know what happened, just that Napoleon is gone. If we confront any of them they will just deny it, and if we make accusations it will sound crazy." Adam was grateful that she was also advocating caution.

"Let me think," Jane replied, "there has to be something we can do to rattle their cage." She sat down and started working furiously with her Blackberry. Fred seemed about to say something to her but Adam motioned him to keep quiet; Jane had found a focus for her crisis energy and it was best to leave her to it for now.

He did feel more than a little frustrated for not having a better course of action to suggest than 'wait', though. It made perfect logical sense but the urge to be doing something was strong and he knew they would need to find some way of harnessing it before long. Fred and Sophia went for coffee, leaving Adam to sit and watch Jane scowling at her mobile device.

Eventually, his own phone rang. He answered, and was surprised to hear the voice of Matilda Damory. "Hello, Father," she asked cheerfully, "have you lost something?"

"What?" he demanded. "What are you saying?" Adam felt a dead space growing in the middle of him. Somehow, despite everything they had learned about what Damory and her people were apparently capable of, he hadn't considered that there might be further danger towards a young man who has already in the hospital.

"I'm sure we understand each other, Father," she replied smoothly. "I think I can help you recover your lost item, and I think you know what I will want in return. Do you think we can come to an arrangement?" Damory sounded, Adam imagined, as though she was talking to an interviewee at one of her companies. To be honest, she sounded as though she might be ordering coffee.

"I think you're extraordinarily foolish," Adam said vehemently. "Don't you think you'd have some problems explaining this call to the police?" He knew he was failing to keep his voice under control and that his reaction was exactly what Damory wanted to hear, but he wasn't able to clamp down his emotions this time. He was tired, he had spent the last few days confused and frequently frightened, and now suddenly the crisis had escalated dramatically.

"The police?" Matilda asked innocently. "Has a crime been committed? Oh dear. Do call them if you wish of course, but I suspect you know what the results will be, and this is a one-time offer." She was clearly amused, probably at having unsettled him so easily. He presumed she was also enjoying having checkmated him so effortlessly.

"Is it," Adam said coldly. "And if I decline it?" Even as he made the comment he knew it was a bluff and he assumed Damory did too. Still, for some reason it was important not to crumble completely. Not right away.

"Well, then I doubt you'll ever find what you're looking for," Matilda said. "It's a frustrating feeling, Father, I don't recommend it. Why don't we just do ourselves a favour instead, hmm?" She spoke as if to a child who had been misbehaving, but not in a really significant way, who just needed a firm but gentle reminder who was in charge.

"This is despicable," Adam replied helplessly.

"If you say so, Father," Damory answered. "Listen, you're clearly having a difficult day and I suppose our arrangements aren't too time-sensitive. I'll call again in a little while, and you tell me what you think then." She hung up without further comment.

Adam realized that Jane had stopped working at her Blackberry and was staring at him instead. "Who was that?" she asked. For a moment Adam wasn't sure what to tell her. He didn't want to confess how utterly he had, apparently, failed them, but there was nothing else to do.

"Our friends again," Adam answered bitterly. "They want to exchange Bones for the book." As soon as it had become clear how important the book really was, he should also have anticipated what Damory might be willing to do to get it. He should have realized it from the attack on Bones, and the one in the hospital parking lot.

"What, that crazy book he bought from the old guy?" Fred asked. He and Sophia had just returned with a tray of coffees. "But isn't that supposed to be for ... you know, the ritual thing?"

"That's certainly how it looks now," Adam said heavily. "I should have known that Napoleon would be so vulnerable here." He knew the guilt was self-indulgent but couldn't quite pull himself out of it.

"Vulnerable how?" Sophia asked, "He was in a hospital with people working in it all the time. He should have been safe. Anyway, what are we going to do?" Her usual practicality began to pull Adam out of his blame-born paralysis.

"Well, Damory all but confirmed that there's no point in calling the police," Adam explained. "We know they're ruthless, and they seem to believe this strange mythology of theirs. I think we may have to give them what they want."

"But if they can really do what we read about with it," Fred observed, "how can we do that? I mean, we already know they can do the one thing with the shadows and all. What if they can really do the rest of it?" Adam reflected that in many ways Fred was right. Was it just selfish to give Damory this book, to protect their friend? Did they have some obligation to, perhaps, put the 'greater good' ahead of Napoleon Kale?

"I don't know, Mr. Wallace," Adam said tiredly. "But if they don't get the book I have no doubt they will take it out on Bones. They've given us some time to consider but I'm not sure that's any real benefit." He looked around, realized that the three of them were watching him expectantly, and forced something that resembled a smile. "Never mind," he said. "We'll come up with something." Now to find a way to choose between a friend and, if Charles Warrington was to be believed, the rest of the planet.

Chapter 30

It was Sophia who suggested that he go and search for Alex, again. Their earlier efforts to find him had failed, but Damory and her people had clearly established, fairly well, the connections between Bones, Adam, and the other Guild members, and it wasn't that unlikely that they might have added Alex to their picture of things as well. Possibly they would consider using Alex as additional leverage to go along with Bones. Keeping Alex completely safe was probably impossible but he could at least try and make certain that nothing had happened to him yet. Adam realized that his own nerves and pessimistic mood probably wasn't helping the others, either. The distraction would probably do him good and there seemed to be little for him to do here. Sophia, Jane and Fred promised to call immediately if the hospital came forth with any information, although that seemed unlikely now, and Adam set out on his search.

He tried to plan a strategy for finding Alex, along with one for convincing his troubled friend to go someplace safe. Adam toyed with the idea of trying to talk Alex into a shelter, or perhaps just one of their apartments, for the night or two that he would likely stay there, just as a hedge against whatever plans Damory might have. The problem was that it would be a struggle, and his last conversations with Alex had been relaxed, if more than a little cryptic.

Upon some reflection he decided that there probably was one very good reason for spending some time with Alex. There was still a feeling that Adam couldn't quite shake that somehow, Alex knew something significant about what was going on. Reading some grand importance into Alex's fleeting mention of a book and the rest of his ramblings was a stretch, Adam told himself, and yet the instinct wouldn't go away. At least, he decided, he was doing something.

He tried most of the parks in the downtown area without success, and was beginning to feel that he was wasting valuable time when he finally turned up Alex in a location suggested by Sophia, who had convinced him to accept a winter coat there the previous November. On the top of the Rideau Centre mall was a sparse and unattractive courtyard, with trees planted in concrete sockets and uncomfortable cement form benches. However, you could stand at the edge and look down onto the street below, and it was there that Sophia had found Alex without anything warm to wear, and it was here that Adam found him again today.

Alex was right up against the railing at the edge of the courtyard, his hands wrapped around the bars. It was really more of a fence than a railing, made of lengths of steel that were angled inwards at the top and ended in points. That, along with their peeling, neglected paint and resultant blooms of rust, suggested something institutional, almost penal. Adam supposed the railing was really a precaution against suicides; the suggestion of something designed to prevent escape was unavoidable.

As he got closer to Alex, he could hear over the wind that the young man was shouting something out into the space above Rideau Street. "Does it look infected to you? Is that really a good deal on underpants? These are the questions we have to be asking. It's in your mailbox, in your ballot box, on your Xbox. Ask about it, try before you buy. Don't wait, we are building a better tomorrow if we don't pay attention at the right time. Missed your bus, but it's all out there, all out there, and you've just got to be careful what you grab on to. You're going to regret that latte." The words flowed in an unbroken stream, as if they were something Alex had practiced for a long time, or if was reading them, although he had no notes or papers in his hand. It was almost like he was doing a routine of some kind, Adam thought, or preaching from a particularly odd pulpit. He wondered whether Alex meant to address the crowd of shoppers and people waiting for buses to Gatineau, and doubted they could hear him over the traffic and city noise. Had any of them noticed the odd figure above them, or did it all blend in to the background of a commuting consumer's day? Adam stood beside him and looked down himself for a little while, the scene dominated by massive, brightly Calvin Klein encased crotches filling the windows of the Hudson's Bay Company store. What did Alex see in all this? Adam wondered.

"When you have doubts," Alex said, "It's usually because someone is trying to mislead you. Hello, Father." He hadn't turned around, and Adam was a little taken aback. Possibly he had glanced behind him before Adam got close enough to notice.

Adam took a moment and couldn't decide if that was the end, or at least a pause, in Alex's address to the street below, or if the comment was meant for him. "Hello, Alex," he began. Sometimes it was best just not to get distracted from your original purpose. "I wonder if we could talk a little."

"Sure, Father, sure," Alex replied immediately. Then he looked at Adam a little curiously. "Did you lose your voice? Do you see it now?" Adam wondered if he was trying to make a joke, a pun on the question about whether they 'could' talk. Alex's sense of humour had always tended towards the strange, even before his issues had overtaken him.

"I'm not sure what I see, to be honest," Adam said, looking down at the street and its busy passersby, waiting for buses or buying books or meeting for a drink after work several stories below, feeling just that far away from such everyday things in his own life just now. He glanced over to see that Alex was looking at him with palpably intense scrutiny.

"Yeah," he said eventually, bobbing his head back and forth like a cat judging a jump it was considering making, "I guess you're pretty much infected now, aren't you?" There was a note of resignation in his voice, as though this was something Alex had long foreseen.

"Oh, Alex," Adam said tiredly, "I've been at the hospital, of course, but I'm not sick. You can't keep being so afraid of people who are trying to help you, you know." He knew he was sounding impatient, and that wouldn't be helpful in dealing with

Alex, but he also couldn't help it. This was going to be another waste of time, and although he still had no idea what could be done, he knew time was something that was in short supply.

"Not sick," Alex said emphatically, "Just not doing anything, that simple, right? Can't do anything, can't find your way home, can't touch this. Can't, can't, can't. Infected." He drummed his hands on the bars of the railing, punctuating each 'can't' with a whack against the metal.

"What are you talking about, Alex?" It wasn't a helpful question, not for Alex, usually, but it was out before he thought about it, again. Adam's mind suddenly felt like some geared mechanism, slowly activating, parts meshing together as it worked its way up to performing an operation.

"You got to pay attention," Alex said, the way one encouraged a child who wasn't keeping his eye on the ball or didn't trust that they would float in the water. "You read it, you hear it, maybe you watch it, or, or, they give it to you. That's how you end up infected, that's how you end up doing a whole lot of nothing."

Adam thought this over. The language was too similar to be a coincidence, but what did it mean? "That's the infection you've been," he paused for a moment. Was it fair to characterize things this way? "Warning me about," he decided to say, finally. "That's what you think I have." Hadn't he been thinking, ever since the conversation with Damory, that there was nothing to be done?

"Now you're where I am," Alex agreed. "The good word is that a full recovery is possible, with treatment." He was looking back down at the street now, tilting his head back and forth as though trying to get a different perspective on the view.

"And what," Adam asked carefully, "is the treatment?" He still couldn't quite decide if he was merely humouring this particular meandering of Alex's imagination, or if there was, somehow, a useful direction here. He was sure it was important to persist, somehow, and recalled a neuroscientist talking about a feeling of knowing, on the radio, and wondered if that was what he had now, or if he was just seeking any distraction from his various dilemmas.

"Don't do nothing," Alex said, as if explaining what the solution to two plus two was. "Now do you see it?" He was shifting his body around slightly now, as if enjoying music, from somewhere.

Adam leaned back against the railing and watched Alex again for a moment. He was still looking down at the street, and hardly seemed to be paying attention to Adam's presence at all. At the same time, he was holding perfectly still, something Adam had rarely known him to do at the best of times. "I think," he said slowly, "I think I may be starting to." Adam opted for a direct approach now. "Have you heard of a man named Charles Warrington, Alex?"

Alex scrunched up his face as if he was concentrating. "That's not a very good question," he replied, seeming to have reached a decision. "Does it matter? Last minute of play, ladies and gentlemen, last minute of play in the third period." Sports, and especially hockey, had been one of the things that had almost always been possible to focus Alex's attention on, even though he didn't understand the rules and wasn't invested in which team won. Something about the action captivated him.

"It's just that some of the things you and I have talked about, recently," Adam explained patiently, "are very similar to some things he wrote about. I was hoping you could tell me why that was." Alex had always been clever, and probably would have done very well in school if he had ever been able to keep his attention on his classes. Adam had spoken with several of his frustrated teachers, who told him about Alex's increasingly frequent absences, and his habit of suddenly walking out of those classes that he did show up for. He had never known what to tell them. Even so, when he was in the right mood Alex would blaze through books with astonishing speed, and it wasn't impossible that he might have read something Warrington wrote. It was even possible that the man's strange style would have resonated with Alex.

He was shaking his head emphatically, however. "Why is another bad question, Father. When the church gets hit by lightning all it means is that there was a storm," Alex explained. He seemed resigned to the direction the conversation was going in but not particularly interested in it; if experience was any guide his attention would soon wander off to something else.

"All right," said Adam, trying to keep frustration out of his voice. There was something important, here, he was sure of it now, but he wasn't sure how to get it out of Alex. Most of the time, he would say what he felt like saying, talk about what he felt like talking about, and directing his attention in particular directions was a difficult puzzle that never seemed to have a consistent solution. "What sort of questions do you think are good ones, Alex?" He remembered one of Alex's doctors telling him that some of the time, you had to let Alex suggest directions rather than having everything imposed on him.

"I knew a girl named Mary Carter, you remember?" Alex said, starting to tap one foot rapidly on the cement. "You've got to decide how you react, reaction time, it's reaction time. You know we can't do this all day." Although he was speaking in more animated tones now, and very earnestly, Adam conceded to himself that he really didn't know what to make of it. Fred had once suggested that it was as though Alex was thinking of three things at the same time, and wanted to talk about all of them, and at the moment it seemed like an apt description.

"I don't think I know what you mean, Alex," Adam admitted. "I'm not sure there's much we can do, right now." He felt very tired, not physically, but mentally. The past few days had been deeply upsetting, and that, combined with trying to come up with solutions to these sudden problems, was taking its toll. Possibly coming to have a talk with Alex, such as it was, had been a mistake. Some quiet time at home, away from everything, might have been more valuable.

"That, that," Alex broke in excitedly, "That's the infection again. It's like that weed in your garden. You have to understand this. That is what they want you to understand." Adam turned this over in his mind a few times. It was still tantalizingly close to some of the things Warrington had written. Was sheer coincidence more or less likely than Alex having read some old, out of print books by an obscure author?

"What about the book, Alex," he asked. "You mentioned it before." It had been Alex's comment about the book, that time they spoke after Bones was first in the hospital, that had first planted the idea in his mind that somehow, Alex knew or had heard something about that end of the problem. Maybe it would be possible to deliberately steer him back in that direction.

"Waste of time," Alex sighed. "Like sand through the hourglass, so are the days of our lives. How many times have you been told?" He sounded bored again, and was starting to trail the fingers of one hand back and forth over the bars of the railing, tipping his head as though listening very closely to the sounds they made.

"But it can't be a waste of time," Adam insisted. "Not with what ... they seem to be doing to get their hands on it." Even talking with Alex, it seemed unwise, somehow, to mention the Sunrise Foundation out loud. He wondered if he was overreacting, and then remembered the names on Jane's list, and Bones' disappearance from a hospital full of doctors, nurses, staff and patients. Perhaps not — Alex was alone on the streets and most people didn't pay any more attention to the city's dwellers in the margins than they absolutely had to. Adam also wondered if it was at all reasonable for Alex to have the slightest idea what he was talking about, but having started down this road, he decided he might as well follow it to the end.

"And if all your friends jumped off a bridge, would you jump too?" Alex asked, singing the words in an odd little tune. "I want to believe, but why, if you don't clearly know it to be such? The truth is out there, but you'll have to stop taking the word of your friends as gospel, that and your enemies." He didn't seem confused or taken aback by Adam's questions at all, which was possibly a good sign. On the other hand, that didn't make any of Alex's responses any easier to interpret.

"Alex, you need to try a little harder to be clear with me now," Adam said as calmly as possible. "I believe this is important. Are you telling me the ... others are mistaken about the book being important?" That was surely impossible, wasn't it? The whole sequence of events had been triggered by the book, by Bones' more or less accidental acquisition of it, and Damory's apparent need for it to serve her purposes. They wouldn't be so ruthless in the pursuit of something that wasn't important, surely.

"It's as true as you want it to be, Father," Alex said, gradually sinking down to a sitting position. "It's as true as you need it to be." He looked up at Adam intensely while unwrapping a Three Musketeers bar he produced from his jacket pocket.

"As true as I need it to be," Adam mused out loud. He sat down beside Alex and let his train of thought run for a few moments. It really did fit, in a way, with what Warrington had been writing about. If he left aside the question as to why that was, the next question became what it all signified. What did it mean? Adam had a growing feeling of those gears working together, operating towards an understanding, about which he didn't know if he should be pleased or worried.

"That's what she said," replied Alex with a grin, evidently amused. Sometimes his sense of humour was really very strange, Adam reflected. He sat and thought a little while longer, trying to put together Alex's rambling commentary with the results of his research, and with what they had learned about the manuscript Bones had purchased. It did all fit together, he thought, albeit in a surprising and alarming way.

"Thank you, Alex," Adam said after a while. "I think that's very helpful." He thought about trying to take Alex for a meal, or to a shelter, but somehow he knew it wouldn't work. Alex seemed not just content, but utterly delighted, now, to be exactly where he was. "We'll talk again soon, Alex," he said, "You must take particular care of yourself for the next while, do you understand?" Eventually when Alex didn't answer, or give any sign that he had heard the suggestion at all, Adam said goodbye and started to walk away.

"You miss a hundred percent of the shots you don't take," Alex called after him cheerily. "Keep your stick on the ice! Keep your head up, kid!" Adam left him there, eating his chocolate bar, and headed back home, to re-examine his notes on the writings of Charles Hope Warrington, and wait for a phone call.

Chapter 31

Adam went directly home and retrieved the book from its hiding place in the toilet tank, took it out of the Ziploc bags, and sat down to examine it one more time. He reflected that he was probably fortunate that Sunrise hadn't broken into his house searching for it; the toilet tank was the best place he could think of but was by no means safe. The hiding spot would probably have occurred to many potential searchers as well.

Again, Adam considered that they might all have been overestimating exactly how many resources Damory and her people had to throw at things like this; people willing to break into houses were probably either hard to find or expensive, and actually hiring them would probably be potentially difficult without exposing yourself to legal risk. Possibly he had just fallen into a trap of assuming that Sunrise was essentially everywhere, when really their abilities were much more limited. Just as possibly, he admitted, they just didn't think Adam was foolish enough to actually keep the book in his house, and assumed it was out of reach in a secure location.

What did it say, Adam reflected briefly, when the most secure location you had available was the tank of your toilet? Whether through good fortune or otherwise, at least the book was still in his hands. The exchange with Damory to get Bones released was possible, and Adam was convinced now that it wasn't a dangerous move to make, not really.

Adam once again picked up *The Infection* and found the section titled 'Conclusions'. There were connections between Warrington's ideas here and some of the things Alex had said. Somehow between that, and the apparent relevance of Warrington's other writing to the events of the past days, Adam felt as though he needed to pay more attention. He had read through *The Infection* during the last couple of afternoons at the bookstore but admitted he had only been half focused on it, although there was a particular passage that he wanted to look over again.

Eventually he found it, towards the very end of the curious little volume. *Overall we must recognize that while the Infection has a purpose, to persuade us to accept atrocities and even welcome our own demise, its ability to do so is far from unique. It is, after all, our convictions that make resistance possible, and our expectations that shape the form all our confrontations take. Our ideas define what is possible, and we must take great care not to have our possibilities defined for us, by those who wish us harm.* Adam hadn't paid what seemed to be a fairly standard piece of thinking from literary criticism very much attention, but now he wondered. He sought out another passage that he now wondered if he had failed to appreciate.

He found it in a subsection entitled 'Countermeasures', which had an alarming proposition to isolate 'infectious' discourses and preventing their spread. Adam wasn't sure that Warrington was calling for censorship, precisely, but his writing here certainly suggested that certain ideas could be dangerous. *We must never discount the importance of the symbolic. The infected will have their symbols, and so will we. Many objects we assign immense importance to have, in fact, no intrinsic worth whatsoever, except in that we insist that they do. When we insist upon such things they become as true as we allow them to be. We must be certain we have a superior alternative to any infected symbol that may appear.* Not censorship, then, but having opposing arguments, Adam supposed.

Adam thought about the Conclusion, and everything that had been said to him recently, especially by Matilda Damory, and wondered if there was a pattern to it all. If he was right, there was a way to understand everything that Sunrise had been doing, and perhaps a way to understand how to go about opposing them. It was even possible there was a solution here for the puzzle of the apparently indecipherable book Napoleon Kale had brought to him.

He leafed slowly through the pages of the manuscript, looking at line after line of incomprehensible writing that might, if you could somehow unlock the trick of reading it right, have all sorts of amazing things to say. It might tell you how to end the world, and it might also tell you how to stop that from happening, and Adam supposed every book was that way, until you learned to read it. All just symbols that could mean all sorts of things, intractable little puzzles until you were taught the solution. Whatever the meaning inscribed into this text was, whatever the solution to this puzzle was, Adam and Todd Marchale were out of time to figure it out.

A few days ago, even a few hours ago, Adam might have despaired about losing this possibility to gain some form of help from what was written in the book, or at least of the consequences of letting Damory have it, but now he felt certain it didn't matter, or at least not in the way he had thought it did. He felt a brief flutter of doubt, that perhaps he was just persuading himself to accept an inevitable situation, finding ways to rationalize defeat as we so often do. Adam took a deep breath and banished it. Either there was something to be done, or there was not. He believed there was. The first thing to do was to get Napoleon Kale out of further danger and back under proper medical care.

He was actually starting to feel slightly impatient when the phone finally rang. He let it ring a couple of times before answering.

"Hello, Father," Matilda Damory greeted him cheerfully, "have you had some time to consider my proposal? I'm afraid the time has almost expired."

"Dear me," Adam said, "you must be in a hurry. One would have thought you had all the time in the world." There was a long pause on the other end of the line. He wondered briefly if it had been unwise to sound so relaxed, but it was something he hadn't really considered and anyway he had discovered that he wasn't much of an actor.

"I'm glad to hear you're in better spirits, Father," Damory said, after a moment. "I do hope you haven't decided on anything unwise." Adam considered, too late now of course, that her implication that going to the police would have been futile might have been a bluff. Possibly their influence there didn't extend much beyond John Kolb. In any case, he reminded himself, if the perspective suggested by his last conversation with Alex was correct, it didn't matter.

"Not at all," Adam replied, in what he hoped was a somewhat more neutral tone of voice. "I've just considered your offer, and decided to go ahead with the exchange you proposed."

"Very good," Matilda said. "Pay attention and I'll give you the time and location." She gave him an address on Prince of Wales Drive that didn't immediately convey very much to him; he would have to look it up. "Be there this evening, 7 o'clock. I'm not willing to involve anyone else, so if you're not alone I'm afraid our business can't proceed. Is all of that clear?"

"Clear enough," Adam answered. "But vague. How will the exchange work, exactly? I like to know what I'm getting in for."

"No doubt," Matilda said, "but you'll have to remain curious for now. You'll have no trouble figuring things out when the time comes, I'm sure. Don't be late, Father."

"You really do need to stop calling me that, Ms. Damory," Adam replied.

"Ah, well, I think we'll probably have more important things on our minds before long," Damory said. "Don't be late."

"You said that," Adam answered. "You do seem very worried about time. Don't worry, I have no intention of taking any risks."

"Very wise," Damory replied. "I'm glad you're able to be practical." She hung up without further comment, and Adam went to pin down where he had to go for this meeting. He briefly considered whether there was some kind of strategy they could employ to trap Matilda Damory and avoid giving her the book, but in terms of practicality and legality it was all very doubtful. Once again, he reminded himself that if he was right, most of this was ultimately irrelevant and securing Bones' release was the only significant part of it.

Still, it was only prudent to let the others know where he was headed. He picked up the phone again to call Sophia, so that if things went badly wrong at least there would be some hint as to what had happened.

Chapter 32

Adam followed the directions from Google Maps and found they led to a motel south-west of the city called the Traveller's Haven. It was nondescript, didn't appear to be busy, and was sufficiently out of the way to make it a reasonable place to exchange the book for Bones. Damory hadn't given any further instructions, so he parked his car by the roadside and waited — there was still around a half hour until the specified time.

He took a moment to look around at the cars parked in the motel lot, none of which had anyone sitting in them. Fred's warning that the exchange was some kind of trap didn't seem likely, but Adam found it nagging at him. He couldn't imagine what Damory could hope to gain by a double-cross — she wanted the book and was about to get it. On the other hand, she was clearly willing to do virtually anything to people who were in her way; it wasn't inconceivable.

Adam watched the traffic go by and tried to think if any of the cars looked familiar — had they been following him, or were the same cars driving past, keeping the motel under observation? Did Sunrise really have enough people to do that kind of thing? Adam sighed and admitted that even if there was some kind of surveillance going on, he wasn't the right sort of person to spot it.

Fred and Sophia had been right; it would have been much better to have one of them along. On the other hand, his instructions had been explicit that he come by himself, perhaps for just that reason. He had finished his now-tepid coffee and the sun had just about gone down by the time another car pulled into the Traveller's Haven. It was an extremely new looking luxury car of the sort Adam would have expected Matilda Damory to drive, but he decided to wait and see what happened, for a moment. If there was some kind of subterfuge underway, the safest place for him was in his vehicle.

After a few minutes, the car's headlights flashed several times. As clear a signal as he was likely to get, Adam supposed. He got out, picked up the book, and walked across the interlocking brick of the parking lot. As he approached, the car's window wound down and a cheerful voice wished him good evening. To his surprise, however, it was not the voice of Matilda Damory — the car's driver was Louis Flambard.

"I was expecting Ms. Damory," Adam said, putting some effort into keeping his voice neutral. "We had an arrangement."

"The arrangement is the same," said Flambard blithely. "However Matilda asked me to make the exchange instead of her. I'm sure it doesn't matter to you?"

"As long as Mr. Kale is released, I suppose it doesn't," Adam replied, "but I'm confused as to why she would have chosen to involve you in this."

"Oh, I was already involved," Flambard assured him, "and I think Matilda may have had other things to arrange, but in fact she thought it was important for us to meet."

"I can't think why," Adam said.

"She thinks you're a problem," Flambard explained, "and since I have not yet had the pleasure of making your acquaintance she thought I should be familiar with you."

"Practical, I suppose," Adam replied, "but a bit of a risk. I had agreed to make the exchange with her, not you. I'd probably be smart to walk away right now, and then she'd have only herself to blame for not getting what she wanted." Adam offered the comment to buy some time for thought — it was interesting that Damory still looked at him as a potential problem, even though he was turning over the book. That suggested there really was something to be done, even if he didn't have the manuscript.

"Maybe so," Flambard said, "but then your friend would still be held captive and you would not be very happy either. I think we both know, as she knew, that the arrangement will go ahead as planned."

"As long as there are no more surprises," Adam replied. "But as long as you're satisfying your curiosity, maybe you'll satisfy mine as well." Louis Flambard was another strange fit in the Sunrise Foundation, and Adam was convinced that understanding how the group was motivated was an important factor.

"Possibly," said Flambard affably. "What is it that you want to know? I'm afraid there some things I can't be open about with you, you understand." He seemed very casual, almost flippant, in his mannerisms. Adam supposed it was an assumed persona for dealing with interviews of various kinds.

"I'd just like to know what a person like you — respected, admired, a success by any standard — is doing associating with a bunch of crackpots like the Sunrise Foundation," Adam declared firmly, "and why you're willing to risk everything you're trying to accomplish on this nonsense of Damory's."

"Nonsense?" asked Flambard with a slight smile. "I think you believe otherwise, if for no other reason than how difficult you have made it for us to get this book."

"Well, let's assume you're right," Adam allowed. "That only makes it harder for me to understand why someone dedicated to the causes you promote would have the friends you apparently do."

"What, do you think they have me in the dark, or something?" Flambard demanded. "If you're looking for someone to convert to your cause, I'm afraid I must disappoint you."

"You do seem to be avoiding telling me why that is," Adam said. "Maybe it's just that you never really believed all those charming words about saving the planet I heard the other night."

"You are determined to doubt my sincerity, Monsieur Godwinson. I assure you that I have always meant exactly what I said, but it is just that I have been saying it for a very long time now. I found myself very tired," Flambard explained, "of shouting warnings at people who are deaf by choice, and throwing a life preserver to people determined to drown themselves. We are going to kill this planet, soon it will be too late to prevent it and no one cares enough to do what is necessary to stop that happening."

"No one? I'm not sure your audience of a few nights ago would agree," Adam observed. Indeed it was hard to connect the warm, impassioned speaker from that evening to the flat cynicism Flambard was currently displaying, but perhaps it really had been a performance after all, or at least a re-enactment of things he had once believed.

"Poseurs and people making themselves feel better, primarily," Flambard declared derisively. "Not all of them, perhaps, to be fair, but not nearly enough are genuine. Anyway I decided I cannot stand by while we murder this world, not at any cost."

"I'm only judging from what I've read, of course," Adam said mildly, "but it doesn't sound like what you and your friends are trying to do will accomplish anything other than a world-wide disaster."

"Ah, possibly, but a disaster for who?" Flambard said. "For the civilization that has brought the planet to the brink of terrible things? The Earth has had cataclysms before, Monsieur Godwinson, and it has recovered. I do not pretend to know what the shape of things will be after the Eater of the Sun is released from the darkness, but I know there will be a shape for things to have, and whatever comes after cannot possibly be as short sighted, selfish, and blind as we are. Anything will be better."

"So people keep telling me," Adam said. "But you sound to me like another person who's given up, Mr. Flambard."

"It's strange," Flambard replied. "I feel very determined these days." He offered a tight little smile that had none of the warmth he showed to his audience.

"Sometimes we're most single-minded when we're being self-destructive," Adam observed. "Anyway, I'm not here to debate philosophy with you. I came to make an exchange."

"Yes, the book you have been stubbornly protecting for your friend," Flambard said with a little curl of his lip. "Don't you think you're giving up, yourself, by handing the book to us in this way?"

"I think," Adam answered firmly, "that I know what's important, and what I can afford to lose. Mr. Kale has suffered enough and I will not have him further injured if I can prevent it."

"Yes, you are doing what is necessary," Flambard smiled. "Just as I am, and just as we all are. Not so different after all. So, you give me the book, I will take a moment to verify it is the genuine article, and then I will tell you which room your friend is in. We go our separate ways and I don't expect we will see each other again."

"You might be surprised," said Adam, passing over the manuscript in a plastic bag. Flambard took it out and took a few minutes to scrutinize a selection of the pages. Adam wasn't sure, but it didn't seem as though he was reading the text. "Are you satisfied?" he asked finally.

"Yes, it seems most satisfactory," Flambard said agreeably. "I assume you know there will be consequences if Matilda should discover there is a problem after all." He paused a moment, and then scowled when he didn't receive a reply. "I'm sure we understand each other. Your friend is in room 10, here is the key." Flambard also passed over a plastic case-cutter knife. "You also may need this to release him from the bedframe. Good night, Monsieur Godwinson. It would be better not to get in our way again."

Adam waited while Flambard's car pulled away. He was risking a lot on his new understanding of the situation, but he had meant it when he said Bones had already suffered enough. There was no question that the exchange had been the right thing to do, but it was hard to ignore how confident Flambard and Damory were in their plans. It's a bit late to second guess now, Adam told himself, as he walked across the brickwork towards room No. 10.

Adam unlocked the door and discovered that Bones was secured to the bed using plastic zip ties. "Oh, Hi Father," he said, "nice you came by, why don't you come in?" Adam bent over him to cut through the ties and looked around the room, which seemed to be fairly standard budget motel fare.

"Are you doing ok, Mr. Kale?" he asked. Bones looked a little pale but had no obvious fresh injuries.

"Yeah, I'm good Father, I'm good," Bones assured him. "I just feel a little dumb I guess, the way they got me from the hospital."

"What exactly happened? The staff was a little confused about it all," Adam said.

"Well, a couple of guys came by and said I was being moved to a different room, on account of my recovery and all," Bones explained, a little ruefully. "They put me in a wheelchair because that's how they do things in hospitals most of the time — I remembered from when my mom was sick last year, you know?" Adam did remember hearing that Mrs. Kale had had hip replacement surgery the previous spring. He had visited her during her recovery afterwards, long enough ago now that Bones had still been dating his last girlfriend.

"Sounds pretty straightforward so far," Adam said. Once you were in a hospital, or really any medical setting, it was surprising how quickly you came to accept whatever requests and orders you were given. Something about the sterile environments and the implied medical consequences of every activity made you blithely accepting of whatever the next requirement happened to be.

"Yeah, well once they had me in the elevator they said they had Bella someplace and if I made any problems they'd do stuff to her, you know?" Bones went on, a slight note of concern in his voice now. "So I didn't say anything as they wheeled me right on out of there and into one of their vans. I been here basically ever since."

"Do they still have your girlfriend, Bones?" Adam asked softly. If Sunrise had another captive — another hostage, he supposed the correct term was — it would make taking any further actions against them extremely difficult. It was even possible there might be more demands, demands that would again be very difficult to turn down. And again also, there would be little point in contacting the police.

"That's the part I feel stupid about, Father, because I'm not sure they ever had her at all," Bones admitted. "Like they never put her on the phone or anything and didn't mention it again once I was in the van. I guess I should have made them prove it or something but I didn't think of it right then, you know?" Adam supposed it was an easy enough threat to make and that whoever had abducted Bones had probably been relying on their victim not wanting to take any risks. Fear and stress also did bad things to people's judgement, he knew.

"It's easy to think of all the right things to do," Adam said wryly, "until you actually find yourself in a difficult situation. Then it becomes very simple to make all sorts of mistakes. I wouldn't be too hard on yourself about it."

"Yeah, but maybe we could call Bella before we leave? Just to make sure?" Bones asked. He was clearly trying to sound calm but the underlying concern was evident. It must have been very difficult the past hours, held in the motel room and wondering whether his girlfriend was safe, or not.

"Of course. You can use my phone if you need to," Adam suggested.

"Kind of gonna have to — they cut the cord on the one in here. That dude is not getting his deposit back," Bones said with a grin. Fortunately he seemed to have come through this latest ordeal in reasonably good spirits, once again. Adam was determined to get him back under medical supervision, though, at least if a side trip to visit Bella could be avoided.

"I think we'll leave checking out to be his responsibility as well, if you don't mind. You make your call, but I think we should be going," Adam said. Flambard and Damory had probably chosen this particular motel for a reason, and he didn't like the idea that he was under observation here, or perhaps standing in a trap of some kind. Now that they had the book he couldn't think what else they might want with him, but he didn't think it was out of the realm of possibility that Damory might arrange something unpleasant out of spite.

"Can't argue with that, Father. But can I ask you something? Did you give them that book they wanted?" Bones inquired, with a concerned look at Adam.

"Yes, I did. They weren't very open to negotiating the price of your release," Adam explained.

"Well, I appreciate it, but isn't it pretty bad, them having the book and all?" Bones asked. "It's what they needed for their ... whatever it is they think they're going to do." It still wasn't precisely clear to any of them what Damory and the rest of the Sunrise Foundation were planning to do, but the hints from the documents Jane had found, and Warrington's writings, made it clear that whatever it was would be very nasty, and was potentially very dangerous.

"Even if it was pretty bad," Adam replied, "having you safe would be worth it. However, I don't think that book is nearly as important as they believe it to be." At least, he reflected inwardly, he hoped so. He had begun to formulate a strategy for, perhaps, undermining Damory's plans, but it all hinged on his new understanding of that book, and that understanding was built on the ramblings of a mentally disturbed homeless person and second-rate fiction from 65 years ago.

"Jeez Father," said Bones with exaggerated surprise. "It cost me a hundred bucks you know."

Chapter 33

Adam decided it was time to try to explain what he thought needed to be done, or at least could be done. Again, he felt it was important for Bones to be involved and so he suggested they gather at the hospital. He made the phone calls and immediately felt an odd sense of relief, perhaps that he was beginning to set things in motion rather than waiting for them to happen.

When they were all gathered at Bones' hospital room, Adam began to lay out his thinking, going over some key passages from *The Eater of the Sun* to fill in the background. "I've looked at what Warrington wrote several times, and the material that Jane found from the Sunrise Foundation," he explained. "I think it's clear that they're going to attempt some sort of ritual that will bring whatever it is Warrington describes here. I wouldn't give an idea like that any credit at all if not for our experience at the canal a few nights ago." The memory was still vibrant in its ability to unsettle.

"How will they do it?" Sophia asked. "The book by Warrington doesn't say."

"I honestly don't know," Adam admitted. "Perhaps Warrington didn't know either. Obviously they've found something that gives them access to special powers. Maybe whatever that is also told them how to accomplish their final goal."

"They needed that book I bought, though," Bones said. "Now they have it."

"There's certainly something about that book that is very important to them," Adam agreed. He had wrestled with the idea of laying out all of his theories now, but having so little to support them he had decided against it. Either they would be willing to help, or not, and if they were hesitant he was not really sure they were wrong to feel that way.

"So now if you're right, they have everything they need," Fred said flatly. "We're screwed."

"I do still think there's a chance, a strong one, to stop what Damory and her friends are going to try to do," Adam said. He knew it was all based on what would sound like rather wild theories, but he was sure he was right. Going back over his conversation with Alex, and some of Warrington's books made it all seem very clear.

"Ok, good," Sophia replied. "How can we do it?"

"Well, I have a plan for interrupting their ceremony, or whatever they'll be doing," Adam said, "and I'll explain it to you in a minute. But there's some information we need first."

"Yeah, like where to go and when to be there," Fred shot back darkly. He had been glum ever since Adam had been forced to give up the book, and seemed resigned to being unable to interfere in the Sunrise Foundation's plans. Adam supposed Alex, or Charles Warrington, would say he was infected. Adam was also hoping to provide him with some prospects for recovery.

"We probably do know where," Jane objected. "They have that land out in the sticks for something. That would be the perfect place to do some creepy ritual." An isolated, wilderness setting also fit the general script for the occasion, Adam thought, but he wasn't ready to share that part of his thinking yet.

"That was what I thought as well," he agreed. "There's no sign that they ever built a camp on it, and I'm sure they didn't buy it for no reason. We'll assume that's where they'll be."

"Ok, but when?" Fred demanded. "I know you think it's going to be soon, but that doesn't narrow things down too much. You want to go pitch a tent out there or something?"

"That was something I was actually hoping you might be able to help with, Mr. Wallace," Adam replied. Fred was good with computers, very good, and if Adam was right they would need some sort of computer analysis to get the answer they wanted. He honestly had no idea how difficult it would be, but Fred would.

"Me?" Fred answered. "You know the mind reading stuff from my act is just a trick, right?" He was looking increasingly uncomfortable. "I wouldn't even know where to start looking, Father."

"I think I do," Adam explained. "I think it's going to be connected to some sort of astronomical phenomenon, or a special alignment of stars, something along those lines."

"Is that in one of those books you've been reading?" Fred demanded. Adam was tempted to say that it was, but there was nothing in Warrington's writings about star configurations or astronomy, at least not directly. Again, it was part of the symbolism of the thing — the magic ritual cast in the right place, when the sky was in its correct alignment.

"Not precisely," Adam replied. "I admit this is an educated guess, but I think it's a good one. Many sorts of ritual observances have been tied to the stars and planets, all throughout history. I think we'll find there's an unusual alignment of some kind coming up in the near future."

"That's a little thin, Father," Jane said. He couldn't disagree, either, although he was confident that the Sunrise Foundation was operating against some kind of deadline. If it wasn't somehow connected to astronomical factors, he had no idea what it was, so he would investigate the lead he had. Sometimes that was the only way to proceed with a problem. Worrying about what might happen if the idea proved to be futile was a luxury that was it was best not to indulge in.

"It's an idea," Sophia replied. "If we can check, maybe that gives us an answer. If not, we know we need to think of something else."

"So, what did you need me to do?" Fred asked.

"You'll have to forgive my ignorance, Mr. Wallace," Adam said. "But there must be astronomical resources that can give us this kind of information. I'm afraid I wouldn't know where to begin looking, but maybe you can track something down." Fred chewed his bottom lip as he thought the idea over.

"Well," he replied finally, "there's going to be some kind of software for it, for sure. They basically don't do astronomy without computers, anymore. Main question is whether I can get access to anything in the time we have." He was chewing his lip again, which usually meant that he was thinking something over.

"Just do your best then, Freddie," Jane said. "If anyone's going to dig anything up, you will." Adam was thankful that she left off the needling that was usually part of any exchange between the pair, this time. They had been doing that since high school and there were various interpretations as to why. Bones had long been convinced that Jane and Fred were destined to end up together, since they 'clearly couldn't leave each other alone'. Whatever the reason, Adam was glad that she had simply chosen to be encouraging, this time.

"Anyway, all I ask is that you try," Adam added finally. If Fred didn't find anything useful, he supposed it was possible that Jane might be able to dig something up somehow, but it was clear that Damory and her people were also aware of Jane's investigations. Adam was worried about what steps might be taken if she proved to be too much of a problem for them.

It was also true that Sunrise would probably be working fairly hard to keep their schedule secret if they could, especially now that they knew they had opposition. Jane's task would be very difficult.

They separated then, to begin some of the preparations Adam had suggested. If he was right and time was short, it was best to begin as soon as possible, and if nothing else it kept everyone busy.

Later that evening, Adam's got a call from a very excited Fred Wallace. "I got it, I really think I did, Father," he said excitedly. The pessimism and gloom Fred had been in the grip of earlier seemed to be gone completely. Adam reflected that this had probably been a useful exercise just for that reason, even if the information Fred had come up with didn't turn out to be very useful.

"All right," Adam replied, "What did you find?"

"Well, in three days there's a full moon," Fred declared. Adam glanced over at his calendar and saw the little white circle that confirmed the fact.

"Good," he said, "but I think we must be looking for something a little more specific than that. They could just wait a month for another full moon." For the level of urgency that Adam now believed the Sunrise Foundation was displaying, it must be a much more stringent set of circumstances they needed for their ritual.

"Yeah, I know," Fred went on, "but this full moon comes along with a bunch of weird things where planets line up with constellations and stuff. I can give you the details if you want but the main thing is, it's weird." That was exactly the sort of thing Adam had hoped would end up being involved. Now, exactly how Fred had put it together wasn't yet clear, but if he knew Fred, not only would he be glad to explain later, but he would probably insist on demonstrating whatever software he had used to solve the problem or the database he had found his answer in. For a magician, Fred Wallace took a strange pleasure in showing how the trick was done.

"How weird are we talking, Mr. Wallace?" Adam asked.

"Well, the thing with the planets and the constellations won't happen again this way for another ten years," Fred replied. That was reasonably unusual, but not an impossible length of time to wait, especially for a group whose leadership were all reasonably young. Steven Smiles was the oldest, in his fifties, and even he wouldn't regard the upcoming configuration as a last chance.

"Better," Adam agreed. "Did you happen to find out when it will happen at the same time as full moon again?" Hopefully there was more, otherwise there was a fairly good chance that even if his plan worked, Damory and her people would simply be able to try again later.

"That's the good part," Fred answered with glee. "If you miss this, you have to wait 183 years."

"Ah," Adam said. "That sounds like the sort of deadline you might get very stressed out about." Not only would none of the Sunrise leadership be alive for their next opportunity, but it would also be extremely difficult to arrange for a group of successors to carry out the ritual either. There were not many traditions that were passed down for nearly two centuries without being distorted, deliberately changed, or just forgotten.

Fred's discovery was excellent news. The opportunity three days from now was, for all practical purposes, the only chance to attempt this particular ritual. If Adam's plan could be made to work, the problem was essentially solved. Adam reflected that this too fit the script of things — the secret rite that needed to be performed in a particular place or at a particular time usually couldn't be simply repeated later.

"So I guess we know when it's gonna be," Fred declared happily.

"Well, it's a very good guess at least," said Adam. "If their deadline is that close it would explain a great deal about how they've been doing things, and especially why they've chosen to take so many risks. Either they succeed and will never have to face the consequences of their actions, or they will have failed utterly and I expect they may not care very much what happens afterwards."

"Gives us a chance though, huh Father?" Fred suggested.

"It gives us a chance," Adam agreed. He had expected that there would be, must be, some kind of opportunity to intervene in the course of events, and now it certainly seemed as though he had been correct. At one time he supposed he would have offered a prayer of thanks, but now he didn't feel the need. Adam had suggested a possible avenue of investigation and Fred had found the answers. Nothing had been handed to them from on high. What that meant in a broader cosmological sense was something Adam wasn't done wrestling with, but there were still some gratitude to express.

"You've done very well, Mr. Wallace," Adam said. "Thanks for putting the time in for me. I wouldn't have had the slightest idea how to start finding all this out."

"Oh, it was no problem once I got started," Fred replied. "I'll show you how to do it next time you're over if you want. Anyway, so now we know where and when, I guess you better explain this plan of yours." Adam rubbed a hand over his forehead. What he had in mind was undeniably risky, but it was the best approach he could imagine. There wasn't much time to explore alternatives.

"Yes, I guess that's next," he agreed. "Let's all meet at the hospital, that way Bones can be part of the conversation too. I'll explain what I think we can do, and you can give me your ideas. We'll come up with something good."

"Sure thing, Father," Fred answered cheerily. "We usually do." After he hung up, Adam decided that Fred Wallace's infection seemed to have cleared up very nicely.

Chapter 34

They reassembled the following day to share results. Adam was feeling strangely optimistic after how quickly Fred had been able to find astronomical data that confirmed — possibly — one of his theories. With luck the rest of his ideas would also survive being put to the test. "Thanks to Jane's investigation, I believe we know where they're going to try to do their final task, whatever that turns out to be like," he began. "And now thanks to Fred, I think we also know when it will be." Fred briefly ran down his research into the upcoming astronomical confluence and the rarity of the event.

"Now that they have the book," Adam went on, "things certainly look difficult. However, I believe it will still be possible to stop them doing much damage."

"But we don't know what to do," Jane objected. "You could never read that old book, could you? So even if we're in the right place at the right time, we don't know what needs to happen." It was a sound criticism, Adam agreed. He had been assuming that the book held some crucial answer for quite a while, and perhaps it did.

"I've given that a lot of thought," he answered. "I still think it's possible to stop them, but what I have in mind will work much better if I have your help." Adam went through the best idea he had come up with to disrupt Matilda Damory's plans, with luck, decisively. Even to him the plan sounded fairly tenuous and several flaws were glaringly evident. "If you don't want anything to do with this, I don't blame you," he said. "I don't feel very good even asking for your help, and I wouldn't have except that I think this is very important." He paused and then admitted, "If I didn't think this was a fairly crucial thing to do, I wouldn't be getting involved myself, either."

"Of course I'll help, however I can," Sophia said. "But I'm not sure this is the best way."

"If you have better ideas," Adam replied, "I want to hear them. I've thought about this and come up with the best that I can, but I'm a little outside my usual areas of expertise." That got a little chuckle.

"Father, don't take this wrong, but why don't we just call the freaking cops?" Fred demanded. "I mean, yeah, let's make sure this doesn't happen, but why are we the ones to take care of it?"

"You want to call the police?" Bones asked. "Your word against Inspector Kolb, you let me know how that goes. Even if he's not actually around, whoever starts looking at it is going to find his name and put it right on the bottom of their list of priorities. You can forget it."

"Well, don't go to Ottawa cops then," Jane interjected. "Kolb can't be connected everywhere."

"So what, you gonna call the RCMP and tell 'em there's a crazy cult out in the woods ready to summon up some big ol' space alien?", Bones asked skeptically. "Anyone want to bet on what their response time would be like for that?"

"Don't be a jerk, Bones," Jane persisted. "We'd just tell them we saw a grow op, or heard about terrorists, or whatever would get them out there. Then they could just take care of it. Freddie's right."

Adam nodded slowly. "That really might work," he allowed. "If that's what you want to do, then I think you should. If that takes care of things, then so much the better." He smiled gently, and then went on. "I'm still going myself, though, and I can use the help of any of you who are willing to come with me. It may be that we'll get up there, find the Mounties all over the place, and all we'll have done is had a nice drive in the country. If they don't listen, though, or don't move quickly, then there may be no one else who is able to do anything about this. Bad things happen every day, and no one can stop all of them. On the other hand, when we can do something, I believe we should try, especially if there's no one else. Tomorrow night I think there's no-one else. I think we have to try."

"OK, so let's say we're going to do something ourselves," Jane said, breaking an uncomfortable silence. "What exactly do you imagine us doing?"

"I think Mr. Wallace and I will drive out to that campsite," Adam said, "We will insert ourselves into their plans and find a way to cause them to go awry." He had more specific ideas about precisely how that would work, but they weren't entirely in a form he felt ready to explain, just yet. Perhaps they could only be demonstrated.

"You don't seriously think you're going without me," asked Sophia, in a tone that clearly expected no contradiction. Adam found his throat was suddenly very tight.

"Dear Sophia," was all he could say, for a moment. Then he clasped her shoulders and smiled. "There is no one, no one in the world I would rather have beside me in bad times. You know that. But I need you to do something else for me, this time. Will you forgive me?"

It took a few minutes for him to explain the rest of his plan for interrupting Damory's ceremony. Adam had known that Sophia especially would not like being left out of the opening stages, but there was no one else available who could do her part of it. "Are we agreed? And is there time for our preparations?"

"Ok, Father," Sophia agreed finally. "We'll do it this way but if I'm not there you're going to need rescuing." Jane and Fred also nodded their agreement with the scheme he had devised. It wasn't airtight, far from it, but he couldn't think of another way of doing what needed to be done, and it did seem that time was of the essence, now. Still, from giving the book to Damory onwards, everything he had asked of them had been a risk of some kind, and yet they were going along with adding more to it.

Adam smiled again, warmed by their trust in him. "Of course," he said. "I'm counting on it."

He and Fred would drive up in Adam's car, but Sophia and Jane would need another vehicle for their part of things. "I always wanted to be part of a plan that had phases," Fred observed gravely. "This is awesome."

"Glad to oblige you, Mr. Wallace," Adam said. "Now, the

ladies have some preparations to make and you have some lessons to teach me. There isn't much time so we'll hope I'm a quick study."

"Well you know what they say about old dogs," replied Fred with a grin. "I'll do my best but you can't expect miracles in a couple of hours," he finished a little more seriously. Adam knew the timing of things was more than a little tight, but he was equally confident that Damory would act as soon as possible, now that she had the book in her hands.

"Last thing on my mind," he said. "We'll all do the best we can, and I trust that will be enough." He didn't add that what he was trusting was nothing more substantial than an untested set of suppositions created over the last few days, but there was nothing else to go on. It was either this, or do nothing, and in Adam's mind, anything would be better than to do that.

Bones had been listening to all the planning with obvious interest, but quietly. His doctors had called for bed rest for at least another day, and no serious physical exertion for at least a week beyond that. Still, it was clear from his expression that he had misgivings. Whether they were about the plan itself, or just the result of his friends taking some substantial risks, was hard to know. Adam supposed that if he had strong objections, he would say so, and also that Bones might be feeling unhappy at being left out.

"Did you want to come and see how it all works out?" asked Adam. "It'd be good to have you along, if you feel up to it." If he was right, there wouldn't be any need for Bones to do anything strenuous, and Adam believed the physical danger would be low. Or, he admitted to himself, at least no worse than it would be if Bones stayed here and Damory succeeded in bringing some kind of apocalyptic entity to the Ottawa valley.

"Nah, sir, nah," Bones said cheerfully. "I'll go blow one of them ram horns or something." Seeing a confused expression on Adam's face, he gave a gentle smile and went on, "I know you got this, Father."

"Thank you, Mr. Kale," said Adam. "That means a lot." Now, he mused, just to make sure that he really did have things under control. He was sure, though, that he knew what the answer to it all was, if only he could make it all come out right. They had a little more than two days to do the best they could.

Chapter 35

Upon thinking back, Adam had to admit that he hadn't specifically checked the tail light on his car in quite some time. And by 'quite some time', he meant that he couldn't remember the last time he had done it. That the tail lights came on when they were supposed to, the turn signals signaled turns, and that the bumper was still where it was supposed to be were all things he assumed to be true, or took on a kind of faith, until provided with contradictory evidence by a friend, a mechanic, or, at times, police officers. So it was possible that the tail light on his car had been out for quite some time.

However, Adam had also been driving around downtown Ottawa more than usual over the last few days, and no-one had said anything about the car. So he found it hard not to read some unfriendly purpose behind the police cruiser lights that appeared in his rear view mirror, at just this particular moment, and into the explanation from the earnest young officer that one of his brake lights was out. Was it possible that Sunrise had sent someone out to sabotage any attempt he might make to interfere?

He supposed it was possible, mulling things over as the officer did a circuit of the car, and wrote something in his notebook. Then again, if they were going to sabotage things, they could have chosen a more reliable means of doing so, and if they wanted him removed from the situation they probably could have done that more directly as well. Still, it was hard not to feel as though the situation was conspiring against him, as the officer returned to the driver's side window and stooped down to speak with him again.

"I'll need to see your license and registration," the officer said politely. At the same time, Adam abruptly realized that the policeman's face was indeed familiar, that his name was Tessier, and had been the more helpful of the officers who had responded to the confrontation with Hugh Thomas. As he retrieved the necessary documents, he tried to decide if this was further stroke of poor fortune, or perhaps finally one of good luck.

"Here you are," Adam said a little bleakly, passing the license and insurance papers to Tessier. He supposed he was about to find out, and there was probably not much to be done about it, either way. Even if he suddenly drove off, he doubted a pursuit would end very well, and almost certainly wouldn't end up with their arrival at the parcel of Sunrise land by this evening.

Tessier took a moment to look at the license and then confirmed Adam's worst imaginings. "Mr. Godwinson," he said with a new level of interest. "I think we have some questions for you."

"Is that right, Officer?" Adam found himself asking. "I can't imagine what for." In fact he could imagine fairly easily why things might have been arranged to have him stuck answering questions at a police station, but not what the excuse would be. Perhaps there had been a witness to the altercation at the hospital, after all?

"It's regarding that kid who was attacked near the canal a while back," Tessier explained. "Maybe you know something about that?" He looked at Adam a little searchingly, although Adam didn't hear much enthusiasm in his voice. This was a slight surprise but confirmed his suspicions about who was responsible for trying to have them sidetracked.

Adam tried stay positive. He had not yet been asked to get out of his car. "I wonder who thinks that," he said as lightly as possible. "Inspector Kolb, no doubt." Adam doubted it would be possible to charge him with anything relating to the attack on Bones, but it would definitely be possible to keep him sidetracked at a police station for hours. Sophia, Jane, and Fred could continue on their own, of course, but he knew they trusted him more than they trusted the actual plan. "I don't know if you'll remember, Officer Tessier, but we met not too long ago," he continued, although he wasn't really sure why. "Another incident, on Elgin Street."

Tessier seemed to think it over for a moment. "I do," he said eventually. "Junkie with a knife, and I guess you or your friend were the intended victim, eh?" Adam wondered how many incidents Tessier had responded to, since then, to make it difficult to remember the confrontation with Hugh Thomas. Probably the police coped with more things than most people imagined.

"Something like that," Adam agreed. "Did you hear what happened to that man? He was a friend of mine, you might remember that too." Partly he was genuinely hoping to get some fresh news about Hugh. However, Adam was also hoping to buy a little time to think of a way out of ending the evening at a police station, or in a jail cell.

Tessier took another long moment before responding. "Last I heard he's still in hospital," he answered. "Doctors aren't too sure what's wrong with him, I think." Adam nodded and waited for the 'please step out of the vehicle' he was certain was coming next. Instead there was another question. "Where are you off to this afternoon?"

"Oh, just a drive into the country," Adam said. "It looks like it will be a pleasant evening." Somehow he didn't think that explaining that they were off to crash a cult meeting was a very wise idea. In fact, he couldn't even be sure that Tessier wasn't one of Damory's many allies, possibly through Kolb.

"It's a pleasant evening to have you down to the station," Tessier replied severely. "Why don't you tell me what's going on with you, Mr. Godwinson, and then we'll see where we are from there." The tone of his voice made it very clear that this was not really a request. It was now Adam's turn to take a few moments to think things over before replying.

"I would truly be very happy to explain it all to you," he began, "but you must believe me when I say that there really isn't time. I know my word doesn't count for much against a detective-inspector, or whoever else it is that wants me brought in for questioning, but I do promise you that I have something very important that needs to be done, and it must be done tonight, and I'm afraid that if I don't take care of it, no one else will, and something very bad will happen." Again, he expected to be asked to step out of the car almost right away. He hadn't given the policeman much to go on and the two of them could hardly be said to know each other.

Tessier squinted up at the sky and tapped his fingers on the car door. "You're supposed to be a friend of that kid in the hospital, right?" Adam presumed he meant Bones.

"Yes, another old friend," he replied. "I did talk to the police at some length about the case already." Tessier didn't really seem to be listening to this last comment.

"Your friends are having a tough time lately," the policeman said flatly.

"They are," Adam agreed. "I'm doing all I can for them. It's not as much as I would like, I suppose, but I will always do what I can."

"Used to be a priest, I think they said," Tessier went on. He still gave no sign that he was paying much attention to Adam's replies. Perhaps he was buying time to think, himself.

"A long time ago, but yes," Adam answered. It was hard to know whether that would help him, or hurt him, given how the church was regarded these days.

"Well, I guess you might know about good and bad things then," the policeman mused. He drummed his fingers on the car door a little more. "I guess I'm going to have one of those times," Tessier went on, "where you don't make the connection between things until it's too late, you know? I probably won't realize you were the person Inspector Kolb wanted to talk to until after I look at my notes again, probably at the end of my shift."

"That..." Adam paused. "Is that the sort of thing that gets you in trouble?"

"Oh, these things happen," Tessier replied blithely. "Maybe their description wasn't so good, and maybe they didn't explain so well exactly why you needed to be pulled in so urgently. And maybe, once you're done with whatever it is you need to do today, you can present yourself to the station, all on your own, and answer those questions."

"Of course, yes," Adam agreed. If things went as planned tonight, he supposed those might be some very difficult questions indeed, but that was a problem that could be left for the future, because if things didn't go as planned, then answering questions at a police station might be the last thing he would be worried about, and interrogating a bookseller might be the last thing the police would be concerned with.

Tessier squinted up at the sky again. "Maybe a storm coming, Mr. Godwinson?" he asked casually.

"Might be," Adam allowed. "We'll see what happens, I guess."

"I guess we will. You drive safe, then," Tessier said. "Also get that tail light fixed. Cops all over these roads, you know."

Chapter 36

The property owned by the Sunrise Foundation turned out to be several hours north of the city, and on a side road that wound very close to the Quebec border. There was very little in the immediate area aside from a few gas stations which also offered live bait, and a boarded up motel. Despite the documents suggesting that it was the site of a summer camp, there was no sign to indicate it, or even that the chunk of land was owned by anyone in particular. Adam and Fred had to deduce its location by using the emergency numbers from adjacent properties to narrow things down. Even after doing this, all they could find in what seemed to be an unbroken swath of bush was a single laneway, wide enough for one car, barred by a barbed wire gate, with a weathered, plastic sign with DayGlo orange letters declaring 'No Trespassing' on a faded black background.

They drove along the little laneway at a very slow pace, scrutinizing the bush on either side, but saw nothing that gave any sign of where Damory and her group might be. If, indeed, they were really here, Adam thought. He would feel tremendously foolish if they were in the wrong place, but from Jane's investigation everything had seemed quite straightforward. It was easier to feel confident looking at a bunch of neatly typed documents than an overgrown path into the forest, though.

"You think they put up a sign or something, Father?" Fred asked eventually. "If it's like this all the way back we might be looking a while, otherwise."

"They must have made some kind of preparations," Adam said, trying to reassure himself as much as Fred. "I've no doubt they will have wanted to be well back from the road, though."

"I just don't want to be too late, you know?" Fred explained. It had undeniably been stressful, as they drove through the countryside, looking for the address Jane had uncovered. Several

244 | Evan May

times they had taken wrong turns, or had to backtrack, and all the time they didn't know if they might already be too late to prevent the Sunrise Foundation from accomplishing their task.

"I have a feeling we're going to be just in time," Adam replied, stopping the car. The feeling that there was a pattern to all of this was very strong, even down to the idea that he and Fred Wallace would not simply be too late to act against Matilda Damory and her followers. The laneway ended quite suddenly, at three cars that looked to have been brought out into the forest sometime in the 1980s and abandoned. None had tires, all were heavily rusty, and one had a healthy looking poplar growing out of the trunk. "I guess this is as far as we go."

"Sure," Fred agreed, stepping out into the weeds at the edge of the laneway. "But where do we go from here?" A light breeze stirred the bushes along the sides of the lane but it was otherwise very quiet, with just a few insects among the weeds and rusting vehicles.

"Just the two of you, Father?" called a familiar voice from the shadows of the forest. Matilda Damory stepped into view, with an amused look at Adam and Fred. "It's very gallant of you, I suppose, to leave the ladies at home, but what do you think just the pair of you can accomplish? Especially when I have so many friends." She made a beckoning motion towards the woods and a sizeable group of people, all wearing hooded robes, in a variety of colours, emerged from both sides of the laneway. Fred muttered a heartfelt profanity, while Adam concentrated on keeping his expression absolutely steady.

"Oh the ladies aren't at home," he assured Matilda. "Perhaps we're not as alone as we appear?" It was potentially a little foolish to offer the suggestion that Sophia and Jane were here somewhere — if the Sunrise people became too vigilant, Adam's plan probably stood very little chance of working. However, he was persuaded by the idea that Damory didn't truly have that many people working with her, and he knew that the more unsettled she became now, the better chance there was that things would go as he wanted them to later.

"You're hoping to worry me," Damory replied, "but even if you're not bluffing, and they're lurking around here somewhere,

I'm not the least bit concerned about anything they can do, now. You've missed your chance if you wanted to disrupt things, but still here you are." She smiled a crooked smile and walked over to him confidently, looking as in control here as she did on the set of one of her television programs, or as she would in a board room, Adam imagined.

"Here I stand," he said mildly. "I can do no other." In retrospect it made perfect sense that they would be keeping watch over what was apparently the only path into the midst of these woods. While it was a slight relief to at least know he was, in fact, in the right place after all, the feeling of having stepped into a trap was rather more disturbing.

"Somehow I knew you wouldn't be able to resist getting involved," Damory purred. "We gave you every chance to keep out of our business, Father, but here you are just in time for my ceremony, and I regret to tell you that the ceremony does require a sacrifice."

"Of course it does," Adam said dryly. He looked up at the sky, which was now darkly covered with swirling clouds. They had rolled in rather quickly, hadn't they? Was this somehow Damory's doing as well? Could she, or one of the other Sunrise people, really do such things? In any case, he reflected, the darkening sky and the roiling bank of clouds also fit with the pattern.

"As a contingency I could have used one of our devoted congregation," Matilda went on, "But as I said, I really did expect some poor fool or other would be along in time to volunteer. What did you hope to accomplish, Father? All my preparations are complete, since you put the book back in my hands." She drew out the leather-bound manuscript and ran her fingers along the spine. "You're too late to do any good now."

"But how long did I have the book for, Ms. Damory?" Adam asked calmly. "Maybe I had all the time with it I needed, and perhaps it was you that was too late, in getting it back." Matilda looked at him curiously for a few moments.

"There's nothing you can do now," she decided eventually. "Kolb, restrain these idiots and then bring them along. There's plenty to do before midnight." One of the cloaked figures pushed back their hood and revealed the face of the Ottawa detective, who also produced two pairs of handcuffs. He stepped forward and secured Adam and Fred's hands.

"I tried to have you kept busy back in the city," he said, sounding slightly apologetic. "You don't seem like bad folks but you should have gotten out of the way when you had the chance." Damory had stalked off along a path into the forest, and the rest of the group was beginning to file along after her. Kolb jerked his head in the same direction. "Let's go then, she's not really in the mood to fool around tonight."

"Yeah, nice serving and protecting there, detective," Fred shot back scornfully. "What's wrong with you, dude?"

"Listen kid," Kolb said, "Damory doesn't need you to be anything but alive to do her ceremony thing, so why don't you quiet down before this experience gets a lot more painful for you?" The threat was offered flatly, somehow a little more unsettling for not being invested with any particular venom or emotion.

"On the other hand, detective," Adam put in, "It isn't too late for you to change what is going to happen here tonight. What would happen if we just walked away right now?" Some things are worth the effort, even when you don't expect them to work.

"What would happen is Damory probably does what she's going to do anyway," Kolb declared, "except when she's finished she'll be wicked pissed at me. In other words, why don't we just move along, here?" He gave Adam a little push down the path, and they set out into the forest.

"Hey, Father," Fred asked quietly, "how did you know it was going to take until midnight for them to do this thing?" Above them, the sky made an unquiet noise and wind stirred the trees restlessly.

Adam smiled briefly. "When else would it be, Mr. Wallace?" he asked. It was remarkable how much of this was unfolding as expected, and he hoped that the pattern would continue. If it did, then he thought he knew just what to do, when the moment presented itself. Otherwise, he admitted, he and Fred Wallace would have to scramble just to stay alive.

Chapter 37

The path led through forest that was more brush than woods — this was land that had once been cleared and was now being reclaimed, colonized by raspberry bushes, goldenrod, and slender poplars and maples. In a tangle of vines and pine trees, Adam made out the shapes of several small buildings engaged in a slow implosion of decay. Perhaps there had once been a camp of some kind here, for hunters or loggers. The rusted skeleton of a mattress and a roll of what looked to be fencing lurked in the weeds on the other side of the path.

This was a place that had been given up on, at some point. Whoever had owned it, however many years ago now, had decided that keeping the buildings fixed up and the land clear was too much trouble, too expensive, too little reward. Even removing the refuse of their occupation wasn't possible or worth it. So they had left things to rust and fall down and be covered by weeds and decay. It was, Adam reflected, an appropriate place for Matilda Damory and the Sunrise Foundation to have chosen for these proceedings.

The path led on, past a heap of trash old enough to include rusting pop cans, and into deeper forest that smelled of damp and let a muffled quiet settle in around the file of figures making their careful way along the path that was now spotted with moss and moist pine needles. Adam noted that many of the cloaked people stumbled or slipped a little, from time to time. Clearly they were not particularly at home in the woods, not even that familiar with this place. Perhaps that would be an advantage, later, but he admitted that several things needed to go right before they got that far.

Finally, they came to another clearing, this one created by a gently rounded, low hump of stone rearing up out of the earth to create a wide gap in the trees, perhaps 20 yards across. The men and women in their cloaks stood in a clump near the edge of the clearing, watching silently as Matilda Damory used a bundle of long twigs to sweep the leaves and pine needles out of a ten-foot circle in the clearing's centre.

Spaced around the edge of her circle, at what looked to be roughly equal intervals, were little tokens or fetishes of some kind. There was a little pile of bills, of various denominations and currencies. A small UN flag, of the type that might be used to decorate a desk. A little plastic model of the Parliament Buildings, sold by the hundreds to tourists along Sparks Street. Next to that was a small set of scales that looked to be made of brass, and kept out of balance by a weight on one side. Beside that was a crucifix necklace, a menorah, and a book Adam thought was a Koran. Then finally, a portable television.

Adam took this in and then nodded in understanding. They were symbols — money, politics, religion, the law, the media. All the things Matilda Damory and the other leaders of Sunrise railed against, to varying degrees. All their justifications for what they were gathered in the woods to try and do tonight. It was a circle of rejection, a circle of despair, a circle of things given up on.

In the middle of the circle, someone had piled up a mound of rough stones, and on top they had laid two final ones, broad and flat. It was unmistakably meant to be an altar. On the altar was an old book, bound in fading brown leather, sitting closed on a square of white cloth. Next to it was a knife, gleaming brightly even in the sullen light of a cloudy afternoon, with a long, curved blade that might have been made of silver, and a smooth white handle that looked to have been carved from bone.

"Jeez," Fred Wallace observed, taking the scene in. "They really went all in for this evil cult business, huh Father?" Adam grinned and was glad Fred was staying reasonably calm. As long as he was making jokes, things weren't too bad.

"They have a script to follow," Adam said, "so certain things are unavoidable, I suppose." It was possible, he imagined, that he might give a little too much of his intentions away with comments like that, but he was somewhat hoping that Fred would understand where he was coming from as well. It was also true, he thought, that if things went according to plan it wouldn't matter whether Damory and her followers were expecting it, or not.

Matilda looked around the circle she had cleared and, evidently satisfied, laid her roughly-made broom down in front of the altar. She took out a piece of chalk and traced out the border of the circle, and then looked over towards Adam and Fred. "Ah good," she said, "bring our friends here, please."

Kolb gave Adam another little push in the back, towards Damory and the altar. "Come on, Mr. Wallace," Adam said quietly. "Let's see this through to the end." They walked over ground covered by moss and leaves, and then up the gentle curve of the rock, to the spot in the centre where Damory waited.

"Well, Father," she said. "We tried several times to have you help us instead of being a difficulty, and you were determined to decline. Now, all that determination is just going to end with you helping me anyway. I need one more thing to perform our ceremony tonight, can you guess what it is?"

"I'm sure I can," Adam replied dryly, "but I'm also sure you'll enjoy telling me, and your followers."

Matilda ran her fingers along the curve of the knife on the altar. "They know perfectly well already, Father," she said. "If you hadn't appeared, one of them would have had to volunteer to spill their blood to bring forth the exiled one, but now that won't be necessary."

"Volunteer? How optimistic," Adam said. "What were you going to do when no one did?" Possibly that idea would unsettle at least a few of the anonymous cloaked, hooded figures. Probably not — Damory and the other leaders of Sunrise had had months or years to cement their loyalty. The attempt cost nothing, though, and anything that might increase their uncertainty would help when the time came.

"Every person here is dedicated to our purpose," Damory insisted. "Each of us has been prepared to do anything to bring us to this moment. I have lived a life I detested for years to have my chance to cut the heart out of this world, and I made sure every person who works with me is just as dedicated." She turned to her group of followers, now. "Who can deny that we are right, when events conspire with us? Fate has brought us our sacrifice, exactly where and when it was required. Let that banish the last wisps of doubt from your minds, as we finish our task. Now, take your places."

The cloaked and hooded figured formed a semicircle, facing the altar, and knelt down. Kolb joined them. Damory walked over to the midpoint of the arc and knelt herself, facing the rest of them. Adam could hear her muttering soft words, some kind of prayer, or incantation, presumably. Another inevitable detail, the ceremonial words with uncertain meanings.

"It won't be long now," Adam said softly. "When things start to happen, just stick to the plan." Of course, he wasn't completely certain when things would start to happen, but as long as they did, he was confident that the plan would work. Much depended on Sophia and Jane, how much time they would have to do their part of the scheme, whether they would arrive in time, and whether they could remain undetected as they did so. It had been one thing for Adam and Fred to blunder in straight ahead and, in fact, Adam had more or less assumed they would end up getting caught. That shouldn't be a problem, as long as Sophia and Jane were able to complete their task, though.

"You're sure it's going to work?" Fred asked. "I mean, we're kind of in a bad spot here." He was trying to sound casual but the tightness in his voice was clear. Adam imagined it might be a strange sort of person who wouldn't be worried in a situation like this one, but it was important that Fred keep himself together nonetheless. He and Adam had their end of things to hold up as well.

"I wouldn't have put us in this position if I wasn't quite sure," Adam replied. He was, truly, as sure as he could be. The ideas that the plan was based on made logical sense, at least according to the worldview of an obscure fantasy writer and a mentally disturbed transient. Intuitively, Adam trusted what they had to say now, and so he trusted that his plan had a chance to succeed. Even if things didn't go exactly as he imagined, at least they were in a place and moment where it was possible to accomplish something.

"All right then," Fred nodded. "Can't have a good trick without building it up right, I guess." There was an element of performance to both sides of this, certainly.

"Later you can try that one with the spoon again," Adam suggested. He was, with an effort, keeping his tone light. In part this was to reassure Fred, but, he admitted, it was useful to him as well. Adam had once read, in a baseball memoir of all things, that the best way to become relaxed was to adopt the appearance of being relaxed — lean up against a wall, close your eyes, that sort of thing. He had discovered that this long-ago ball player had been right, and that the trick worked for more than one state of mind.

Keeping himself at ease became more difficult as Damory's prayers, or incantations, or whatever they were, gradually became louder and, to Adam's ear, more heartfelt, although he didn't understand the words or even recognize the language. Abruptly she broke off with a noise of annoyance and held up one pale hand for quiet.

Two figures emerged from the forest, not RCMP officers or anyone else likely to break up the proceedings, in Adam's estimation — these people were also wearing the long dark robes. In fact, Adam recognized one immediately by his build — the rotund frame was unlikely to be anyone other than Samuel Smiles. He didn't identify the other until he pushed back his hood; this was Louis Flambard. They stopped at the edge of the clearing and waited.

"You're late," said Damory eventually. "So I began without you." She stood up and looked at the pair with annoyance. Adam had assumed they had been here all along, although none of the other acolytes looked quite large enough to be Smiles, upon reflection. Still, here they were now, and hopefully their arrival did not mean bad news about Sophia, Jane, and their part in the plan.

"We did as you suggested," Flambard replied blandly, "and checked the roads on either edge of the property. I found no one." He smiled his media-friendly smile, and polished his glasses with a corner of his robes.

"Good, then," Damory said, "it would be better if we weren't interrupted again, but your presence is required for the ceremony, you know that." She beckoned towards the waiting group of her kneeling followers imperiously.

"Yes, of course," Flambard answered, "it is so difficult to find people to hold candles." Perhaps he rolled his eyes a little, but whether he was reacting to Damory's manner or to the ceremony itself was difficult to say. Was he less devoted to the cause than the others, and a potential chink in the Sunrise Foundation's edifice? If he was, it was also too late to take advantage of it, Adam admitted. He would have to trust in the plan as already laid out, for it was too late to change anything now.

Damory made an exasperated noise. "You've come so far, and yet you still don't seem to take things very seriously, Louis." She pushed a hand through her hair in a reflexive, irritated gesture.

"I am exactly serious enough to have come this far, Matilda," Flambard replied. "It's strange that you question my sincerity because I am a little behind the time, and because I do not take any great fascination in my part in this."

"Being late in this case could have been very serious for you," Damory said severely. "Once we free the exile, only the people directly involved in its release can expect any kind of mercy. The book was very clear on that."

"Ah, the precious book, yes," Flambard smiled. "So it has confirmed things, then?"

"The *Libri* had all those answers, had you bothered to study it as I asked you to, Louis," Damory said. "I have not needed confirmation of anything for a very long time, you should know that."

"As you wish, Matilda," Flambard replied. "Now, do tell me where I should stand so we can proceed." Damory pointed to one end of the semicircle of kneeling worshippers, and Flambard made his way there.

"You're very quiet, Samuel," Damory said. "No second thoughts, at such a late stage, I hope?" She was gentler, more solicitous, in her manner now, and even placed a friendly hand on his hip to politely guide the Reverend towards the group of followers.

"Indeed not," Smiles answered, taking up a position opposite Flambard. "I merely feel the gravity of the situation, the weight of the hour, now that it is upon us." He had left his hood in place, although whether this was for ceremonial reasons, or a desire for privacy, Adam could not have said.

"It will be the greatest moment the world has seen in far too long," Matilda declared, striding back to her place at the center of the semicircle. "I know you've all done many things to bring us to this point. We're here at last. It is a great achievement, and I am more than ready for the waiting to be finished."

She walked back over to the altar, and from behind it retrieved two long, red tapers, and lit them with a propane barbecue lighter. "Not too long now, Father," Damory said. "The hour is nearly here, then you and your friend will have your little part to play, and then the king will return."

"Pride goeth," Adam said softly. It wasn't much of a warning, and indeed he wasn't entirely sure what he might be warning her against, but he felt she deserved one. Probably the exact choice of words was less than ideal for the audience, but certain habits do run deep.

Matilda laughed merrily. "Oh dear," she said, "if a dusty old cliché is the best you have to offer, then you really are out of ideas. Watch as your world ends, Father." Damory turned and took one candle to Flambard, and one to Smiles. Finally, she knelt down at the center of the semicircle again and started muttering her soft words again.

Overhead the sky was darkening as evening turned into night, and most of it was covered by clouds. In the distance, there were grudging grumbles of thunder, but the air felt dry and the growing wind did not carry the smell of rain. Adam was strangely relieved not to hear anything like a whisper in it, either.

"Gang's all here, huh Father," Fred observed softly. Adam glanced over and his face was hard to read, now. He hoped Fred had some expectation that the plan would work, but at least he was here and willing to do his part.

"Well, at least they're all in one place," Adam said, "and all accounted for."

"You figure this is all of them?" Fred asked. Adam thought he knew what he was thinking of — if there were any of Damory's followers in reserve, perhaps maintaining a perimeter, then Sophia and Jane might run into a surprise.

"I hope so, Mr. Wallace," Adam replied, "and there can't be that many people wanting to sign up for the end of the world." A lot of what he had seen in how the Sunrise Foundation was doing things led him to believe they were a small enough group. Hopefully, they were precisely this small, that their manpower was limited enough to give him a chance to execute his plan.

Chapter 38

"Everything is ready now, Father," Matilda said, after a time. "Once your blood hits the stones the exile will return and it will all be over. Don't you have anything to say?" She spread her hands invitingly and waited.

"Why do you need me to say something?" Adam asked, raising his voice a little over the whipping gusts of wind. "Are you hoping to be talked out of this, even now? If you want to stop, just stop. It's all in your hands, Matilda."

"Yes, yes it is," she shot back. "Maybe I just wanted to hear one of the tired old arguments people like you make, one last time, so that I would know, one last time, how right I am. How right we all are! But no, fine, you've quit, you've given up, just like you accused me of doing."

"Touched a nerve with that, I see," Adam said. "That should tell you something. Anyway, who says I've given up?"

"What, haven't you?" Matilda demanded. "You walked in here like a sheep to the slaughterhouse, and that's after you handed over the book without even putting up a fight. What do you think you have left to do?"

Adam shrugged. "Stop this, just in time," he said. He nurtured a little flicker of hope that she might really be persuaded to abandon the whole grotesque project. He wasn't depending on it, and had planned for the alternative, but it would have made him feel much better about everything if Matilda Damory had reconsidered in the end.

"If you're not a quitter, you're a failure," she said with a laugh. "If you thought you'd appeal to my better nature, you weren't listening to me very well. I'm not the one who needed to be convinced to do the right thing, Father. This world is full of people who do the wrong thing every day and they get rich and they get famous and they get worshipped. It breaks my heart, and I'm going to be the one who's brave enough to stop it."

"Which of us are you trying to convince, Matilda?" Adam asked.

"That's enough of your bargain bin psychology, Father," Damory replied. "You're not going to sweet talk me like one of your idiot children, and a kind word and sympathetic face isn't going to get you out of this."

"I suppose it was never likely to," Adam admitted softly. Damory walked over to the altar, circled around Adam and Fred, and plucked the knife up from the altar. She took a few steps down towards the semicircle of her kneeling followers and held the blade up so it caught the modest light that penetrated the cloud cover. The wind died abruptly, as though somewhere, a switch had been thrown.

"Come! Come now, Sun Eater, return now, Exiled One," screamed Matilda Damory. "Let the blood of these cattle open your way back in to the light, and come to us! Come and tear this awful world to shreds, let it all burn! Aliquid Melius, Sun Eater — ANYTHING WILL BE BETTER!"

Then there was silence in the forest for a moment. Just a little noise of wind stirring the branches and the breathing of Damory and the people kneeling behind her. A heartbeat later, there was a clicking noise, and the clatter of steel on stone. And then the Astounding Alfred stood up by the altar, flexed his hands, and said, "Nah. I don't think so."

Fred grabbed up the book and held on tight with both hands. "Yeah, now you don't have your fucking book, your date isn't here yet, and once Adam finishes what is really a very elementary escape, you won't have your fucking sacrifices either. I was wrong, Father — this really was a great plan!" He was wriggling with excitement and glee as he stood beside Damory's altar, holding the book she presumably needed to finish her ritual.

Adam had hoped that Damory wouldn't have noticed Fred's work on his handcuffs, and he had kept her talking for as long as possible to give him as much time as possible to work. There wasn't much danger that the rest of the group would notice anything, hooded in the dim light, but Damory had been moving much closer, and so Adam hoped a little verbal fencing would keep her mind on him and off of Fred Wallace.

One of the things Adam had spent the last hours in Ottawa on had been trying to learn some simple escapes from Fred. He assumed that they might very well end up bound somehow, and it was important that at least one of them get free to disrupt things. Ideally it would be both of them, and so Fred had given him a crash course in escapology.

What he had learned was that if he was tied up with ropes by someone who knew what they were doing he was probably stuck. Getting out of well tied knots was not something he could learn in an afternoon, so if it had been ropes, the escape would have been entirely up to Fred. Instead they had concentrated on handcuffs, because, as Fred had encouraged him, they really weren't designed to hold people for extended periods of time, and not unsupervised time. They were meant to keep you under the control of (presumably) a police officer who was right there with you. If you left someone alone in a pair of cuffs, and especially if they had something to work with, they could get out relatively easily.

Adam had been able to undo one of Fred's practice sets a couple of times before they ran out of time and had to start out for the Sunrise Foundation's rural property. He really wasn't that confident in his ability to do it again, especially since Fred had explained there were lots of different kinds of handcuffs, some more vulnerable to attack than others. Fortunately, he was confident in Fred, knew that Kolb had made things easier on him by locking his hands in front of his body, and that Fred would, somehow, have one of those tools to work with.

Hearing the cuffs fall to the stone had been a relief, and there was also the satisfaction of knowing that he had been right about his friend. Adam's own struggles with his handcuffs had been — so far — far from satisfactory, but that hardly mattered now. The ceremony was disrupted. The rest of the plan should flow from there.

Inspector John Kolb watched the scene at the altar unfold and felt a little thrill of energy pass through the knot of Damory's followers. These people were about to panic, most of them would run and the entire plan was about to fall completely apart, not really because of the stupid little jerk and his magic tricks, but because of failure to pay attention to details. Damory had not thought about what might go wrong, but in John's experience things almost always went wrong. They were going wrong now; the first people were scrambling to their feet.

Kolb felt a sudden clarity of purpose that he hadn't felt in years. There was a time when he knew exactly what he wanted to do in life and what he wanted to achieve. He had felt that when he applied to the police academy and still felt it when he got his badge. John Kolb had wanted to help people out of bad situations, and basically had a long career of trying to do just that.

But almost immediately, he had realized things were more complicated than they were supposed to be. People didn't always look at you as on their side, or didn't look at themselves as on yours, anyway. A lot of times even when you were trying to do something for their benefit, they'd fight you every step of the way or at least be as unhelpful as possible. Over the years it had gotten worse. John had been called a pig by children not yet old enough to drive. Fuck the Police. Snitches get stitches.

After a while, when people kept treating him like the enemy, it was hard to see them as anything else, and that was when Matilda Damory's ideas started to make some sense. A society that was so twisted up that it was against its own laws was a sick animal that needed to be put down.

Now it was all very clear. Damory still had her fancy dagger but both of the 'sacrifices' were loose now, and John doubted she was really the knife-fighting type. On the other hand, he always had a Leatherman tool on him, and so he opened it up, stood and leapt up to that altar, waited for a moment, and then slit his own throat from ear to ear. He got to hear the spattering of blood on the stones before things started getting misty, and then he was on the ground. There was light from somewhere, but then it was all very dark.

Chapter 39

Matilda Damory's laughter was the first sound that broke the hush after Kolb's body hit the rock, and his little knife clattered on the rock. Fred Wallace, for once, had nothing to say, and Adam just stood and stared at the pool of blood spreading from the detective's neck. Whatever he had imagined happening tonight had not included this.

Then there was a dazzling flashing of noon-bright light, a deep hum like a million wasps, and a hole tore itself into the middle of the night. It expanded rapidly until it was several meters across, bounded by that flickering, blue-white light. Whatever the light touched turned to an ash-like powder in an instant, and not all of Damory's on-looking followers got clear. Louis Flambard never even had a chance to scream before the light ate him.

As they all stood and watched, the hole continued to expand, but more slowly now. On the other side, or in the middle of it, was nothing but darkness, and an intensity of blackness that stood out even in the shadowy night in the forest. It was a darkness in which nothing could be discerned at all. Adam immediately felt a slight, uncomfortable feeling, like a pressure on his senses, a vague indication from all of them that something was no longer quite right about his surroundings.

"It's like out of the movies," Fred Wallace observed in awe.

"Of course it is," Adam agreed. That made sense in more than one way, if what he understood from Warrington and Alex was right. The magic book, the gateway into darkness, the monster behind it. All of it fit into an all-too familiar pattern that was very tempting to go along with, to follow along to its conclusion.

"Guess the plan isn't going so good right now, hey, Father?" Fred asked. "Almost though, huh?" He was staring at the tear in the night and moved his feet to keep them out of the growing pool of blood.

"Show's not over quite yet, Mr. Wallace," Adam replied quietly. "Hang in a little longer."

"A little longer is all you have," Matilda Damory declared with delight. "It worked, exactly the way I knew it would, and now this awful world is going to die." Expectations, Adam thought, are very important here. Our idea of what something will be like colours our experience of what it is like. Our beliefs about the world change the way we perceive it, and therefore, how it is, for us. Our expectations of whether we are surrounded by threats, or by allies. Of whether the world should be saved, or whether it should be destroyed. Either you believe it or you don't, he told himself, and hoped that he truly did believe.

Chapter 40

Suddenly there was a series of flashes and bangs from the treeline, very loud and bright in the dark forest. There was a rushing of bodies from the woods as well, and just as suddenly, whatever purpose Matilda Damory had instilled in her followers seemed to vanish. They were abruptly ordinary people in the woods after dark, with a dead person on the ground and, it seemed, enemies close at hand. Their instincts seized them and they ran, trying to find the winding path back to the laneway, crashing into the underbrush in their haste to be gone from that place.

It was a fine display, not as colourful as the one that had enriched a long-ago church picnic, but Sophia Beaudry had been short on time and materials, and had done the best she could. Now she and Jane emerged from the woods making as much noise as possible, against the backdrop of the squibs and flash pots the two had been preparing for the past few minutes.

"I think my cavalry's here," Adam said with a smile. They hadn't worked out the timing of when Sophia and Jane were supposed to intervene precisely, but they had chosen an excellent moment as far as he could tell.

Damory was alone now; all of the others had disappeared into the forest. She stood with her knife as Jane and Sophia ran out of the darkness and the pyrotechnics the two young women had been preparing while Fred and Adam worked on escapes finished going off. The last of her acolytes had vanished into the woods, and finally even Matilda herself began to back away from the altar, the book, and the rapidly opening tear in the night. "They're too late," cried Matilda defiantly, "You're all too late!"

Sophia and Jane hurried up to the altar as their fireworks died off and a heavy silence settled back over the clearing and the woods. "You're wrong about that," Adam said. "And that was very well done, ladies — I think they thought there were a lot of you."

"We took too long, Father," said Sophia with a little edge of horror in her voice. "Didn't we?" She was staring at the widening gateway in the darkness, and didn't seem to have noticed Kolb's body at all, yet. Then again, Adam reflected, perhaps that was something more in line with her military training, whereas giant glowing doorways were definitely not the sort of thing anyone prepared themselves for.

"No, you're just in time," Adam reassured her. "Just in time." Just in time, he admitted to himself, to find out whether he was right, or if he was very, very wrong.

"We got here as fast as we could," Jane explained, "but we thought we should walk in from the road so no one would hear a car, and then it took a while to set up the stuff, and now that bitch has already done her thing, hasn't she?" Jane had also taken it upon herself to take hold of Matilda Damory, who stared now at the gate with rapt expectation.

"Jane," Adam said, "It's all right. You weren't too late — we're still here, all of us are fine, and there's still time to do something about all this. It's very rare, you see," he went on, "that it's really too late to do anything at all."

"But Father," Fred objected, "they already opened their gate thing there, and I don't think we have too much time here, you know?" Adam understood his concern perfectly. The feeling of wrongness in the air, the creeping feel of approaching danger, was growing with every moment. "What are we going to do?"

"We're going to do what we can," Adam said. "Sophia, keep an eye on the forest, just in case any of our friends do decide to come back, please." She moved quickly to a position where she had a good view of the path back through the woods, unobstructed by the gateway. Adam nodded, and picked up the strange old book and underhanded it into the shimmering rip in the night. The feeling of that crushing presence was getting stronger, and the rip was still getting larger. The book vanished into the disturbance without a sound. "There, that's one problem solved," he said.

"Father, I ... I know we couldn't read it, but how do we stop this without that book?" Fred demanded. Frost was forming on the undergrowth near the hole in things and the urge to run into the bush was getting harder and harder to ignore. Adam forced calm into his voice.

"We don't need the book," he said as clearly as possible. "We never did. Damory couldn't read it either, I'm sure of it." Adam had thought this was the answer since before he had made the trade, the book for Bones. Now, in the moment, he was absolutely positive. "She didn't even pick it up during that ceremony, you saw that, Fred," he went on. "She didn't even look at it. She didn't use it at all, and I'm sure that's because she didn't have any better idea of how to read it than I ever did."

Damory's face twisted in a disgusted expression but she still kept silent, watching the opening in things that she had done so much to orchestrate. "But everything they did to get it!" Jane objected. "Why would they do it if they didn't even need it?" This was the part Adam was hoping, very much, that he now understood correctly. His last conversation with Alex had seemed to make things so clear, but it was a little different now, in the woods at night, with a hole in the world in front of him.

"They needed it, because they thought they did. Their whole idea was that they couldn't do ... this ... without the book, and so they had to have it. Warrington understood though, and so did Alex," Adam said, shouting without noticing that he had raised his voice, "It's just part of the trick."

It was all a trick Damory and her followers had played on themselves — the need for a book in an unknown language, for a stone altar in the forest, and a ceremony done at midnight on a particular day. They were all symbols that only had as much importance as people gave to them — but if one gave a symbol enough importance, then it was tremendously powerful. So Damory had been desperate for the book, and the rest of it, because she was sincere in her belief that these things were necessary.

Adam slowly walked over, and laid his hand on the altar of stones Damory had built in the forest, surrounded by representations of the world she had given up on and stained with the blood of John Kolb's despair. "They needed it," Adam said firmly. "I don't."

The shimmering gate of energy went out like a match in a gust of wind. All at once it was very quiet in the woods. After a moment, the crickets and frogs and the rest of the forest life started calling to each other again, the strange disturbance in their nocturnal routines forgotten, or at least of lesser importance than calling for mates and protecting territory.

"Never let them tell you it can't be done," Adam said quietly, to himself. He thought perhaps Matilda Damory let out a little despairing moan, then, but he would never be sure, for in the next instant she lashed out with an elbow, catching Jane by surprise and in the side of the head, and was free to make her dash into the woods as well, everything forgotten except escape.

Sophia made a half-hearted lunge at catching her but Damory was gone, and then it was somehow much more important to see that Jane would be fine, perhaps an unpleasant bruise, but no serious injury.

"Uh, Father," Fred began, after a while. "That was, like, pretty cool, and all, and don't take this the wrong way, but what the heck is going on, man? How did you do that?"

"You never read the book," Jane put in, "so how could you do that?"

"It's what Warrington wrote about," Adam explained. "The book you can't read is all part of the trap of how they want you to think. They want everyone to believe that you're not smart enough or strong enough or fast enough to oppose these things. They want you do give up and look for somewhere to hide. It gets you thinking that you're a tiny little speck in the grip of implacable forces and that there's nothing to be done. But it's only true if you believe it."

"You're kidding me," Fred objected. "This whole thing was about the book, and the things you could do with it. We all saw that thing by the canal, and that gate or whatever it was."

"It was never about a struggle over a book with power," Adam insisted, trying to find a way to frame what he had, eventually, learned from Alex in a straightforward way. "The power is in the ideas; the struggle is being paralyzed and in a situation you can't win against there always being something worth doing. I knew, and I truly believed, that if Damory could open some kind of gate here in the woods just because she believed she could, there had to be a way to close it again. There had to be a way. Fortunately, I finally understood things right."

"So this whole thing was a fake, or what?" Fred demanded. "I mean, was it imaginary, or was something really going to come through there and start ripping things up?"

"Oh, I have no doubt there was something very unpleasant on the other side of that gateway," Adam replied. "But there are always bad things out there. Everyone knows that. The danger is letting ourselves think there's nothing we can do about them. There's always a way to respond, somehow, as long as we don't convince ourselves otherwise."

"Well, since you understand things so well," said Sophia with a little smile, "Maybe you can tell us what to do about Matilda Damory and all her little friends. They all ran away through the woods, and there aren't enough of us to catch them, even without the head start they have."

"What would we do with them anyway?" Jane wondered. "It's not like we can take them into the cops and get them arrested for demon worship, or whatever the hell you call it. What can we prove they did?"

"Bones could maybe get them for kidnapping or whatever," Fred suggested, "from when they scooped him from the hospital." That was a loose end, Adam considered, one that Damory had probably never expected to need to tie off. If things had gone according to her plan tonight, an abduction case would have been the last thing on most people's minds.

"How many of them do you think he actually saw," Sophia asked. "And I don't think we'll get Miss CEO Damory into a courtroom with just a story from a guy recovering from head trauma." Adam expected she was probably right. A clever lawyer, which Damory probably had in considerable supply, would probably rip holes in any testimony from Bones. At worst, she might have to claim that she had had no knowledge of Louis Flambard's actions — he had been the one actually at the motel, and who had made the exchange — and thus deflect culpability onto a man who was now vanished.

"There has to be something we can do," Jane insisted. "Letting them go is just — lame." Fred let out a short laugh and Sophia shook her head. "Well, it is!" Jane declared, with great dignity.

"I don't think we should do anything," Adam decided. "I think they'll have a very hard time explaining secret meetings in the forest and handcuffing people to stone altars in the middle of the night. Without the book, they won't be able to try again, and I think if we give them the opportunity they'll leave things quite alone." It was a risk, he imagined, but courtrooms were more the home turf of Matilda Damory and people like her; it seemed a bleak proposition to try challenging her there, without better ammunition than they currently had.

"Should we, you know, keep an eye on them, Father?" Jane asked. "I mean, just in case they have other crazy things they'd like to do in awful places?" Adam thought about it, and his first impulse was to go home and try to forget the Sunrise Foundation, the strange book Bones had found, and all the rest of it. He would help see Bones through his recovery, he would find a way to get involved in things outside of W.M. Howard, Bookseller, and he would not neglect his friends any longer.

Tempting though the idea was, he also knew that Matilda Damory had only been prevented from whatever harm she might have done to however many people the thing Charles Warrington had called the "Eater of the Sun" because he, Sophia, Jane, and Fred had done what they could about a problem they were in a position to help solve. Pretending an issue didn't exist, or that it wasn't his problem, or their problem, seemed to be part of the "infection" Alex had warned him about.

"It's probably a good idea," Adam admitted. "There might be another day, when we can get a more satisfactory resolution than this, eventually. There may be more evidence we can find, or people who will be willing to talk to us. It might mean taking up more of each other's time, though."

"I'll bring the food for the first night," said Sophia firmly, "but we are using your barbeque."

"Splendid," Adam agreed. "Shall we say Friday?"

Author s note

Throughout the book I have done my best to reproduce the real urban geography of Ottawa; for any errors I plead either narrative necessity or (more likely) my imperfect memory. Although there are several used book stores in and around the ByWard Market, W.M. Howard, Bookseller is not based directly on any of them.

Readers familiar with Parliament Hill in particular will have noticed that the shelter for the Canadian Parliamentary Cats was removed in 2013, after the bulk of the writing for *The King in Darkness* had been done. I liked the scene with the shelter enough (and have enough fond memories of it) to leave it in; I suppose this fixes the events in the story at a point in the not-too-distant past, and this is all right with me.

There is, to my knowledge, no St. Michael's Church in Ottawa. The real church of St. Michael's and All Angels is not intended to be the former parish of Adam Godwinson. It exists only in my imagination, and now perhaps your own.

Perhaps obviously, the Hand of God ministry is also an invention.

Acknowledgements

I would like to especially thank everyone who volunteered their time to read all or part of drafts of *The King in Darkness* and provided their comments and feedback. This was an incredible resource and every one of you helped make the final version a much better story.

I am also grateful to Dr. Rick McCendie for his thoughts on mental illness, which were very useful in writing the character of Alex Sloan. Any errors of fact here are entirely my own.

Thanks are due as well to my publishers and editors at Renaissance Press, who took a chance on a new author and helped bring the book to publication. I know I had a lot to learn when we started out and your guidance and patience was invaluable.

Journey of a Thousand Steps
by Madona Skaff-Koren
Mystery

Naya had the perfect life. Co-owner of a fast growing security software company, she ran marathons in her spare time. Suddenly everything changed when she developed multiple sclerosis, and now she can barely climb a flight of stairs. Hiding at home, her computer the only contact with the outside world, she reconnects with her childhood best friend.

But when her friend disappears and the police dismiss her concerns, Naya leaves the safety of her home to find her. She ignores her physical limitations to follow a convoluted trail from high tech suspects to drug dealers, all while becoming an irritant to the police.

http://renaissancebookpress.com/2015/05/25/journey-of-a-thousand-steps/

If you enjoyed this book, you should check out these similar Renaissance titles!

Family by Choice series by Caroline Frechette

Supernatural suspense

An action-packed, fast-paced series about superpowers, crime, survival, and responsibility towards others. Alex Winters is a young man involved in organized crime who also has the ability to manipulate fire. Through various confrontations which put him and his loved ones in danger, he learns that there is more to life than just survival.

All four volumes available now!

Here's what people are saying about Family by Choice:

"I loved this. If you like dark fiction, supernatural, and a good dose of action, then try out this series. You will not be disappointed." - *I Heart Reading book reviews*

"Alex is a great character. He's complicated, and has many different layers. The story was good, and the writing was spot on the entire time. I was drawn into this book from the first page, and enjoyed it very much."
Forever Book Lover reviews

"Caroline Fréchette is one of my favourite fantasy writers in the National Capital Region. (...) The story has a great pace and the strong writing makes them an easy read."
Alejandro Bustos, *Apartment 613*

"While I find this series to be a quick read, it is also an incredibly good read." - *Geeky Godmother reviews*

http://renaissancebookpress.com/2014/09/03/family-by-choice-series/